# The Sins of Séver[

Sax Rohmer

**Alpha Editions**

This edition published in 2023

ISBN : 9789357934763

Design and Setting By
**Alpha Editions**
www.alphaedis.com
Email - info@alphaedis.com

# Contents

# CHAPTER I

## TO INTRODUCE MR. JULIUS ROHSCHEIMER

"There's half a score of your ancestral halls," said Julius Rohscheimer, "that I could sell up to-morrow morning!"

Of the quartet that heard his words no two members seemed quite similarly impressed.

The pale face of Adeler, the great financier's confidential secretary, expressed no emotion whatever. Sir Richard Haredale flashed contempt from his grey eyes—only to veil his scorn of the man's vulgarity beneath a cloud of tobacco smoke. Tom Sheard, of the *Gleaner*, drew down a corner of his mouth and felt ashamed of the acquaintance. Denby, the music-hall comedian, softly whistled those bars of a popular ballad set to the words, "I stood in old Jerusalem."

"Come along to Park Lane with me," continued Rohscheimer, fixing his dull, prominent eyes upon Sheard, "and you'll see more English nobility than you'd find inside the House of Lords!"

"What's made him break out?" the comedian whispered, aside, to Adeler. For it was an open secret that this man, whose financial operations shook the thrones of monarchy, whose social fêtes were attended by the smartest people, was subject to outbursts of the kind which now saw him seated before a rapidly emptying magnum in a corner of the great restaurant. At such times he would frequent the promenades of music-halls, consorting with whom he found there, and would display the gross vulgarity of a Whitechapel pawnbroker or tenth-rate variety agent.

"'S-sh!" replied the secretary. "A big coup! It is always so with him. Mr. Rohscheimer is overwrought. I shall induce him to take a holiday."

"Trip up the Jordan?" suggested Denby, with cheery rudeness.

The secretary's drooping eyelids flickered significantly, but no other indication of resentment displayed itself upon that impassive face.

"A good Jew is proud of his race—and with reason!" he said quietly. "There are Jews and Jews."

He turned, deferentially, to his employer—that great man having solicited his attention with the words, "Hark to him, Adeler!"

"I did not quite catch Mr. Sheard's remark," said Adeler.

"I merely invited Mr. Rohscheimer to observe the scene upon his right," explained Sheard.

The others turned their eyes in that direction. Through a screen of palm leaves the rose-shaded table lights, sparkling silver, and snowy covers of the supper room were visible. Here a high-light gleamed upon a bare shoulder; there, a stalwart male back showed, blocked out in bold black upon the bright canvas. Waiters flitted noiselessly about. The drone of that vocal orchestra filled the place: the masculine conversation, the brass and wood-wind—the sweeter tones of women, the violins; their laughter, tremolo passages.

"I'm observing it," growled Rohscheimer. "Nobody in particular there."

"There is comfort, luxury, there," said Sheard.

The financier stared, uncomprehensively.

"Now look out yonder," continued the other.

It was a different prospect whereto he directed their eyes.

The diminuendo of the Embankment lamps, the steely glitter of the waters beyond, the looming bulk of the bridge, the silhouette shape of the On monolith; these things lay below them, dimly to be seen from the brilliant room. Within was warmth, light, and gladness; without, a cold place of shadows, limned in the grey of discontent and the black of want and desolation.

"Every seat there," continued Sheard, as the company gazed vaguely from the window, "has its burden of hopelessness and misery. Ranks of homeless wretches form up in the arch yonder, awaiting the arrival of the Salvation Army officials. Where, in the whole world, can misery in bulk be found thus side by side with all that wealth can procure?"

There was a brief silence. Sheard was on his hobbyhorse, and there were few there disposed to follow him. The views of the *Gleaner* are not everybody's money.

"What sort of gas are you handing us out?" asked Rohscheimer. "Those lazy scamps don't deserve any comfort; they never worked to get it! The people here are moneyed people."

"Just so!" interrupted Sheard, taking up the challenge with true *Gleaner* ardour. "Moneyed people! That's the whole distinction in two words!"

"Well, then—what about it?"

"This—that if every guest now in the hotel would write a cheque for an amount representing 1 per cent. of his weekly income, every man, woman, and child under the arch yonder would be provided with board and lodging for the next six months!"

"Why do it?" demanded Rohscheimer, not unreasonably. "Why feed 'em up on idleness?"

"Their idleness may be compulsory," replied Sheard. "Few would employ a starving man while a well-nourished one was available."

"Cut the Socialist twaddle!" directed the other coarsely. "It gets on my nerves! You and your cheques! Who'd you make 'em payable to? Editor of the *Gleaner*."

"I would suggest," said Sir Richard Haredale, smiling, "to Séverac Bablon."

"To who?" inquired Rohscheimer, with greater interest than grammar.

"Séverac Bablon," said Sheard, informatively, "the man who gave a hundred dollars to each of the hands discharged from the Runek Mill, somewhere in Ontario. That's whom you mean, isn't it, Haredale?"

"Yes," assented the latter. "I was reading about it to-day."

"We had it in this morning," continued Sheard. "Two thousand men."

"Eh?" grunted Rohscheimer hoarsely.

"Two thousand men," repeated Sheard. "Each of them received notes to the value of a hundred dollars on the morning after the mill closed down, and a card, 'With the compliments of Séverac Bablon.'"

"Forty thousand pounds!" shouted the millionaire. "I don't believe it!"

"It's confirmed by Reuter to-night."

"Then the man's a madman!" pronounced Rohscheimer conclusively.

"Pity he doesn't have a cut at London!" came Denby's voice.

"Is it?" growled the previous speaker. "Don't you believe it! A maniac like that would mean ruination for business if he was allowed to get away with it!"

"Ah, well!" yawned Sheard, standing up and glancing at his watch, "you may be right. Anyway, I've got a report to put in. I'm off!"

"Me, too!" said the financier thickly. "Come on, Haredale. We're overdue at Park Lane! It's time we were on view in Park Lane, Adeler!"

The tide of our narrative setting in that direction, it will be well if we, too, look in at the Rohscheimer establishment. We shall find ourselves in brilliant company.

Julius's harshest critics were forced to concede that the house in Park Lane was a focus of all smart society. Yet smart society felt oddly ill at ease in the salon of Mrs. Julius Rohscheimer. Nobody knew whether the man to whom he might be talking at the moment were endeavouring to arrange a mortgage with Rohscheimer; whether the man's wife had fallen in arrears with her interest—to the imminent peril of the family necklace; or whether the man had simply dropped in because others of his set did so, and because, being invited, he chanced to have nothing better to do.

These things did not add to the gaiety of the entertainments, but of their brilliancy there could be no possible doubt.

Jewish society was well represented, and neither at Streeter's nor elsewhere could a finer display of diamonds be viewed than upon one of Mrs. Rohscheimer's nights. The lady had enjoyed some reputation as a hostess before the demise of her first husband had led her to seek consolation in the arms (and in the cheque-book) of the financier. So the house in Park Lane was visited by the smartest people—to the mutual satisfaction of host and hostess.

"Where's the Dook?" inquired the former, peering over a gilded balustrade at the throng below. They had entered, unseen, by a private stair.

"I understand," replied Haredale, "that the Duke is unfortunately indisposed."

"Never turns up!" growled Rohscheimer.

"Never likely to!" was Haredale's mental comment; but, his situation being a delicate one, he diplomatically replied, "We have certainly been unfortunate in that respect."

Haredale—one of the best-known men in town—worked as few men work to bring the right people to the house in Park Lane (and to save his commission). This arrangement led Mr. Rohscheimer to rejoice exceedingly over his growing social circle, and made Haredale so ashamed of himself that, so he declared to an intimate friend, he had not looked in a mirror for nine months, but relied implicitly upon the good taste of his man.

"Come up and give me your opinion of the new waistcoats," said Rohscheimer. "I don't fancy my luck in 'em, personally."

Following the financier to his dressing-room, Haredale, as a smart maid stood aside to let them pass, felt the girl's hand slip a note into his own. Glancing at it, behind Rohscheimer's back, he read: "Keep him away as much as ever you can."

"She has spotted him!" he muttered; and, in his sympathy with the difficulties of poor Mrs. Rohscheimer's position, he forgot, temporarily, the difficulties of his own.

"By the way," said Rohscheimer, "did you bring along that late edition with the details of the Runek Mill business?"

"Yes," said Haredale, producing it from his overcoat pocket.

"Just read it out, will you?" continued the other, "while I have a rub down."

Haredale nodded, and, lighting a cigarette, sank into a deep arm-chair and read the following paragraph:

"A FAIRY GODMOTHER IN ONTARIO

"(*From our Toronto Correspondent*)

"The identity of the philanthropist who indemnified the ex-employees of the Runek Mill still remains a mystery. Beyond the fact that his name, real or assumed, is Séverac Bablon, nothing whatever is known regarding him. The business was recently acquired by J. J. Oppner, who will be remembered for his late gigantic operation on Wall Street, and the whole of the working staff received immediate notice to quit. No reason is assigned for this wholesale dismissal. But each of the 2,000 men thus suddenly thrown out of employment received at his home, in a plain envelope, stamped with the Three Rivers postmark, the sum of one hundred dollars, and a typed slip bearing the name, 'Séverac Bablon.' Mr. Oppner had been approached, but is very reticent upon the subject. There is a rumour circulating here to the effect that he himself is the donor. But I have been unable to obtain confirmation of this."

"It wouldn't be Oppner," spluttered Rohscheimer, appearing, towel in hand. "He's not such a fool! Sounds like one of these 'Yellow' fables to me."

Haredale shrugged his shoulders, dropping the paper on the rug.

"A man at once wealthy and generous is an improbable, but not an impossible, being," he said.

Rohscheimer stared, dully. There were times when he suspected Haredale of being studiously rude to him. He preserved a gloomy silence throughout the rest of the period occupied by his toilet, and in silence descended to the ballroom.

The throng was considerable, and the warmth oppressive at what time Mrs. Rohscheimer's ball was in full swing. Scarcely anyone was dancing, but the walls were well lined, and the crush about the doors suggestive of a cup tie.

"Who's that tall chap with the white hair?" inquired Rohscheimer from the palmy corner to which Haredale discreetly had conveyed him.

"That is the Comte de Noeue," replied his informant; "a distinguished member of the French diplomatic corps."

"We're getting on!" chuckled the millionaire. "He's a good man to have, isn't he Haredale?"

"Highly respectable!" said the latter dryly.

"We don't seem to get the dooks, and so on?"

"The older nobility is highly conservative!" explained Haredale evasively. "But Mrs. Rohscheimer is a recognised leader of the smart set."

Rohscheimer swayed his massive head in bear-like discontent.

"I don't get the hang of this smart set business," he complained. "Aren't the dooks and earls and so on in the smart set?"

"Not strictly so!" answered Haredale, helping himself to brandy-and-soda.

This social conundrum was too much for the millionaire, and he lapsed into heavy silence, to be presently broken with the remark:

"All the Johnnies holding the wall up are alike, Haredale! It's funny I don't know any of 'em! You see them in the sixpenny monthlies, with the girl they're going to marry in the opposite column. Give me their names, will you—starting with the one this end?"

Haredale, intending, good-humouredly, to comply, glanced around the spacious room—only to realise that he, too, was unacquainted with the possibly distinguished company of muralites.

"I rather fancy," he said, "a lot of the people you mean are Discoveries—of Mrs. Rohscheimer's, you know—writers and painters and so forth."

"No, no!" complained the host. "I know all that lot—and they all know me! I mean the nice-looking fellows round the wall! I haven't been introduced, Haredale. They've come in since this waltz started."

Haredale looked again, and his slightly bored expression gave place to one of curiosity.

---

# CHAPTER II

## "THIRTY MEN WHO WERE ALL ALIKE"

The room was so inconveniently crowded that dancing was a mere farce, only kept up by the loyal support of Mrs. Rohscheimer's compatriots. The bulk of the company crowded around in intermingling groups, to the accompaniment of ceaseless shuffling and murmuring which all but drowned the strains of the celebrated orchestra. But lining the wall around was a rank of immaculately groomed gentlemen who seemed to assume a closer formation as Haredale, from behind the palms, observed them.

In two particulars this rank excited his curiosity.

The individuals comprising it were, as Rohscheimer had pointed out, remarkably alike, being all of a conventional Army type; and they were unobtrusively entering, one behind the other, and methodically taking up their places around the room!

Even as he watched, the last man entered, and the big double doors were closed behind him!

"What's this, Haredale?" came a hoarse whisper from Rohscheimer. "Where are these Johnnies comin' from? Does Mrs. R. know they're here?"

"Couldn't say," was the reply. "But it would be a simple matter for a number of impostors to gain access to the house whilst dancing was in progress, provided they came in small parties and looked the part."

"Impostors!" growled Rohscheimer uneasily. "Don't you think they've been invited, then?"

"Well, who shut those doors?" muttered Haredale, leaning across the little table the better to observe what was going forward.

"You don't mean——" began Rohscheimer, and broke off, as the orchestra dashed through the coda of the waltz and ceased.

For stark amazement froze the words upon his tongue.

Coincident with the last pair of dancers performing their final gyration and the hum of voices assuming a louder tone, each of the men standing around the walls produced a brace of revolvers and covered the particular group nearest to him!

The conversational hum rose to a momentary roar, and ceased abruptly. The horns of taxi-cabs passing below could be plainly heard, and the drone and rattle of motor-buses. Men who had done good work in other emergencies looked down the gleaming barrels, back to the crowds of women—and had no inspiration, but merely wondered. Nobody moved. Nobody fainted.

"Held up!" came, in pronounced Kansas, from somewhere amongst the crush.

"Quick!" whispered Haredale. "We're overlooked! Through the conservatory, and——"

"Pardon me!"

Rohscheimer and Haredale turned, together, and each found himself looking directly into the little ring of a revolver's muzzle. A tall, slim figure in faultless evening dress stood behind them, half in the shadows. This mysterious stranger had jet black hair, and wore a black silk half-mask.

The melodramatic absurdity of the thing came home strongly to Haredale. But its harsh reality was equally obvious.

"Perhaps," continued the masked speaker, in a low, refined voice, and with a faint, elusive accent, "you will oblige me, Mr. Rohscheimer, by stepping forward so that your guests can see you? Sir Richard Haredale—may I trouble you?"

Rohscheimer, his heavy features slightly pale, rose unsteadily. Haredale, after a rapid glance about him, rose also, with tightened lips; and the trio moved forward into full view of the assembled company.

"The gentlemen surrounding you," said the man in the mask, slightly raising his voice, "are all sworn to the Cause which I represent. You would, perhaps, term them anarchists!"

An audible shudder passed through the assemblage.

"They are desperate men," he continued, "indifferent to death, and would, without compunction, shoot down everyone present—if I merely raised my hand! Each of them is a social pariah, with a price upon his head. Let no man think this is a jest! Any movement made without my permission will be instantly fatal."

*Dzing!* went the bell of a bus below. *Grr-r-r!* went the motor in re-starting. *OO-oo! OO-oo!* came from the horn of a taxi-cab. And around the wall stood the silent rank with the raised revolvers.

"I shall call upon those gentlemen whom I consider most philanthropic," resumed the musical voice, "to subscribe to my Cause! Mr. Rohscheimer, your host, will head the list with a diamond stud, valued at one thousand guineas, and two rings, representing, together, three thousand pounds! Place them on that pedestal, Mr. Rohscheimer!"

"I won't do it!" cried the financier, in rising cadence. "I defy you! I——"

"Cut it!" snapped Haredale roughly. "Don't be such a cad as to expose women——" He had caught sight of a pretty, pale face in the throng, that made the idea of these mysterious robbers opening fire doubly, trebly horrible. "It goes against the grain, but hand them over. We can do nothing—yet!"

"Thank you, Sir Richard!" said the masked spokesman, and waved aside the hand with which Haredale proffered his own signet ring. "I have not called upon you, sir! Mr. Hohsmann, your daughters would feel affronted did you not give them an opportunity of appearing upon the subscription list! The necklace and the aigrette will do! I shall post, of course, a formal receipt to Hamilton Place!"

And so the incredible comedy proceeded—until thousands of pounds' worth of jewellery lay upon the pedestal at the foot of a bronze statuette of Pandora!

"The list is closed!" called the spokesman. "Doors!"

Open came the doors at his command, and revealed to those who could see outside, a double rank of evening-dress bandits.

"The company," he resumed, "will pass out in single file to the white drawing-room. Mr. Rohscheimer—will you lead the way?"

In sullen submission out went Rohscheimer, and after him his guests—or, rather, his wife's guests—until that whole brilliant company was packed into the small white room. Someone had thoughtfully closed the shutters of the windows giving on Park Lane, and securely screwed them; so that, when the last straggler had entered, and the door was shut, they were in a trap!

"Listen, everybody!" came Haredale's voice. "Keep cool! You fellows by the door—get your shoulders to it!"

At his words, the men standing nearest to the door turned to execute these instructions, and were confronted by the following type-written notice pinned upon the white panels:—

"A detailed subscription list will appear in the leading papers to-morrow, and it will doubtless relieve and gratify subscribers to learn that *the revolvers were not loaded!*"

There was little delay after that. Within sixty seconds the door was open; within three minutes the wires were humming with the astounding news.

Tom Sheard, his work completed, was about to leave the *Gleaner* office, when—

"Sheard!" shouted the news editor from an upper landing. "Amazing business at Rohscheimer's in Park Lane! Robbery! Brigands! Terrific! Off you go! Taxi!"

And off went Sheard without delay.

He entered Park Lane, to find that part of the thoroughfare adjacent to the financier's house packed with vehicles of all sorts and sizes. Women in full dress, pressmen, policemen, loafers, were pouring out and rushing in to Mr. Rohscheimer's residence! Never before was such a scene witnessed at that hour of the night in Park Lane.

As he passed under the awning, pressing his way towards the steps, he encountered an excited young gentleman who wore a closed opera hat, but was evidently ignorant of his interesting appearance. This young gentleman he chanced to know, and having rectified the irregularity in his toilet, from him he secured some splendid copy.

"You see, I just dropped in to take a look round, and as I strolled up a mob of jokers jumped out of a cab just in front of me, and we all crawled in together, sort of thing. I happened to notice a footman going upstairs and two of the jokers I spoke about behind him. They were laughing, and so forth, and he was just on the first landing, when they nabbed him from behind—positive fact!—and threw the chap down on his face! I'm thinking it's a poor kind of joke when the other two fellows jolly well nobble *me*! Before I know what's up, I'm pushed into an anteroom or somewhere, and I hear these chaps banging the front door and running upstairs! I should have sung out like steam, only they'd handcuffed me wrong way round and tied a beastly cork arrangement in my mouth!

"Just before I burst a blood-vessel it occurred to me that I might as well keep quiet; so I sat on the floor listening; but I didn't hear anything for what seemed like an hour! Then there was a mob of fellows came downstairs—and the door opened. They seemed to slip out in twos and threes from what I could gather, and by the time they'd nearly all gone a perfect pandemonium broke out, upstairs and down!

"The servants—who'd all been locked in the cellar—got out first. Then Haredale came bounding downstairs, and, luckily for me, heard me kicking at the door. Then everybody was rushing about! Rohscheimer was bawling in the telephone! Some other chap was rushing for a doctor—for Adeler, who got knocked on the head in the library. Now here's the wretched police arresting everybody who looks as though he'd been in the Army! That's all the beastly description anyone can give! They suspected Dick Langley the minute they saw him, because he's got a military appearance! And I shouldn't be surprised to hear that they'd arrested every fellow in the Guards' Club!

"Here's the thing, though: they've all got clean away! With about forty thousand pounds' worth of jewellery! It's a preposterous sort of thing, isn't it?"

Sheard agreed that it was the most preposterous sort of thing imaginable; and, leaving his excited acquaintance, he set out to seek further particulars. But very few were forthcoming.

As to the manner in which the clique had obtained admission, that called for little explanation. They had simply presented themselves, armed with invitations, singly and in small parties, whilst dancing was in progress, and in a house open to such mixed society had been admitted without arousing suspicion. There was little that was obscure or inexplicable in the coup; it was an amazing display of *force majeure*, an act of stark audacity. It pointed to the existence in London of a hitherto unsuspected genius. Such was Sheard's opinion.

From an American guest, who had kept perfectly cool during the "hold-up," and had quietly taken stock of the robbers, he learnt that, exclusive of the spokesman, they numbered exactly thirty; were much of a similar build, being well-set-up men of military bearing; and, most extraordinary circumstance, were facially all alike!

"Gee! but it's a fact!" declared his informant. "They all had moderate fair hair, worn short and parted left-centre, neat blonde moustaches, and fresh complexions, and the whole thirty were like as beans!"

Two other interesting facts Sheard elicited from Adeler, who wore a white bandage about his damaged skull. The whole of the guests victimised were compatriots of their host.

"It is from those who are of my nation that they have taken all their booty," he said, smiling. "This daring robber has evidently strong racial prejudices! Then, each of the victims had received, during the past month threatening letters demanding money for various charities. These letters did not emanate from the institutions named, but were anonymous appeals. The point seems worth notice."

And so, armed with the usual police assurance that several sensational arrests might be expected in the morning, Sheard departed with this enthralling copy hot for the machines that had been stopped to take it.

When, thoroughly tired, he again quitted the *Gleaner* office, it was to direct his weary footsteps towards the Embankment and the all-night car that should bear him home.

Crossing Tallis Street, he became aware of a confused murmur proceeding from somewhere ahead, and as he approached nearer to the river this took definite form and proclaimed itself a chaotic chorus of human voices.

As he came out on to the Embankment an extraordinary scene presented itself.

Directly in his path stood a ragged object—a piece of social flotsam—a unit of London's misery. This poor filthy fellow was singing at the top of his voice, a music-hall song upon that fertile topic, "the girls," was dancing wildly around a dilapidated hat which stood upon the pavement at his feet, and was throwing sovereigns into this same hat from an apparently inexhaustible store in his coat pocket!

Seeing Sheard standing watching him, he changed his tune and burst into an extempore lyric, "*The quids! The quids! The golden quids—the quids!*" and so on, until, filled with a sudden hot suspicion, he snatched up his hat, with its jingling contents, hugged it to his breast, and ran like the wind!

Following him with his eyes as he made off towards Waterloo Bridge, the bewildered pressman all but came to the conclusion that he was the victim of a weird hallucination.

For the night was filled with the songs, the shouts, the curses, the screams, of a ragged army of wretches who threw up gold in the air—who juggled with gold—who played pitch-and-toss with gold—who ran with great handfuls of gold clutched to their bosoms—who pursued one another for gold—who fought to defend the gold they had gained—who wept for the gold they had lost.

One poor old woman knelt at the kerb, counting bright sovereigns into neat little piles, and perfectly indifferent to the advice of a kindly policeman, who, though evidently half dazed with the wonders of the night, urged her to get along to a safer place.

Two dilapidated tramps, one of whom wore a battered straw hat, whilst his friend held an ancient green parasol over his bare head, appeared arm-in-arm, displaying much elegance of deportment, and, hailing a passing cab, gave the address, "Savoy," with great aplomb.

Fights were plentiful, and the available police were kept busy arresting the combatants. Two officers passed Sheard, escorting a lean, ragged individual whose pockets jingled as he walked, and who spoke of the displeasure with which this unseemly arrest would fill "his people."

Presently a bewildered Salvation Army official appeared. Sheard promptly buttonholed him.

"Don't ask me, sir!" he said, in response to the obvious question. "Heaven only knows what it *is* about! But I can tell you this much: no less than forty thousand pounds has been given away on the Embankment to-night! And in gold! Such an incredible example of ill-considered generosity I've never heard of! More harm has been done to our work to-night than we can hope to rectify in a twelvemonth!

"Of course, it will do good in a few, a very few, cases. But, on the whole, it will do, I may say, incalculable harm. How was it distributed? In little paper bags, like those used by the banks. It sent half the poor fellows crazy! Just imagine—a broken-down wretch who'd lived on the verge of starvation for, maybe, years, suddenly has a bag of sovereigns put into his hand! Good heavens! what madness!"

"Who did the distributing?"

"That's the curious part of it! The bags were distributed by a number of men wearing the dark overcoats and uniform caps of the Salvation Army! That's how they managed to get through with the business without arousing the curiosity of the police. I don't know how many of them there were, but I should imagine twenty or thirty. They were through with it and gone before we woke up to what they had done!"

Sheard thanked him for his information, stood a moment, irresolute; and turned back once more to the *Gleaner* office.

---

Thus, then, did a strange personality announce his coming and flood the British press with adjectives.

The sensation created, on the following day, by the news of the Park Lane robbery was no greater than that occasioned by the news of the extraordinary Embankment affair.

"What do we deduce," demanded a talkative and obtrusively clever person in a late City train, "from the circumstance that all thirty of the Park Lane brigands were alike?"

"Obviously," replied a quiet voice, "that it was a 'make-up.' Thirty identical wigs, thirty identical moustaches, and the same grease-paint!"

A singularly handsome man was the speaker. He was dark, masterful, and had notably piercing eyes. The clever person became silent.

"Being all made up as a very common type of man-about-town," continued this striking-looking stranger, "they would pass unnoticed anywhere. If the police are looking for thirty blonde men of similar appearance they are childishly wasting their time. They are wasting their time in any event—as the future will show."

Everyone in the carriage was listening now, and a man in a corner asked: "Do you think there is any connection between the Park Lane and Embankment affairs, sir?"

"Think!" smiled the other, rising as the train slowed into Ludgate Hill. "You evidently have not seen this."

He handed his questioner an early edition of an evening paper, and with a terse "Good morning," left the carriage.

Glaringly displayed on the front page was the following:

WHO IS HE?

"We received early this morning the following advertisement, prepaid in cash, and insert it here by reason of the great interest which we feel sure it will possess for our readers:

"'ON BEHALF of the Poor Ones of the Embankment, I thank the following philanthropists for their generous donations:'

*(Here followed a list of those guests of Mrs. Rohscheimer's who had been victimised upon the previous night, headed with the name of Julius Rohscheimer himself; and beside each name appeared an amount representing the value of the article, or articles, appropriated.)*

"'They may rest assured that not one halfpenny has been deducted for working expenses. In fact, when the donations come to be realised the Operative may be the loser. But no matter. "Expend your money in pious uses, either voluntarily or by constraint."

"'(Signed) SÉVERAC BABLON.'"

The paper was passed around in silence.

"That fellow seemed to know a lot about it!" said someone.

None of the men replied; but each looked at the other strangely—and wondered.

# CHAPTER III

## MIDNIGHT—AND THE MAN

The next two days were busy ones for Sheard, who, from a variety of causes—the chief being his intimacy with the little circle which, whether it would or not, gathered around Mr. Julius Rohscheimer—found himself involved in the mystery of Séverac Bablon. He had interviewed this man and that, endeavouring to obtain some coherent story of the great "hold up," but with little success. Everything was a mysterious maze, and Scotland Yard was without any clue that might lead to the solution. All the Fleet Street crime specialists had advanced theories, and now, on the night of the third day after the audacious robbery, Sheard was contributing his theory to the Sunday newspaper for which he worked.

The subject of his article was the identity of Séverac Bablon, whom Sheard was endeavouring to prove to be not an individual, but a society; a society, so he argued, formed for the immolation of Capital upon the altars of Demos.

The course of reasoning that he had taken up proved more elusive than he had anticipated.

His bundle of notes lay before him on the table. The news of the latest outrage, the burning of the great Runek Mills in Ontario, had served to convince him that his solution was the right one; yet he could make no headway, and the labours of the last day or so had left him tired and drowsy.

He left his table and sank into an arm-chair by the study fire, knocking out his briar on a coal and carefully refilling and lighting that invaluable collaborator. With his data presently arranged in better mental order, he returned to the table and covered page after page with facile reasoning. Then the drowsiness which he could not altogether shake off crept upon him again, and staring at the words "Such societies have existed in fiction, now we have one existing in fact," he dropped into a doze—as the clock in the hall struck one.

When he awoke, with his chin on his breast, it was to observe, firstly, that the MS. no longer lay on the pad, and, secondly, on looking up, that a stranger sat in the arm-chair, opposite, reading it!

"Who——" began Sheard, starting to his feet.

Whereupon the stranger raised a white, protesting hand.

"Give me but one moment's grace, Mr. Sheard," he said quietly, "and I will at once apologise and explain!"

"What do you mean?" rapped the journalist. "How dare you enter my house in this way, and——" He broke off from sheer lack of words, for this calm, scrupulously dressed intruder was something outside the zone of things comprehensible.

In person he was slender, but of his height it was impossible to judge accurately whilst he remained seated. He was perfectly attired in evening-dress, and wore a heavy, fur-lined coat. A silk hat, by an eminent hatter, stood upon Sheard's writing-table, a pair of gloves beside it. A gold-mounted ebony walking-stick was propped against the fireplace. But the notable and unusual characteristic of the man was his face. Its beauty was literally amazing. Sheard, who had studied black-and-white, told himself that here was an ideal head—that of Apollo himself.

And this extraordinary man, with his absolutely flawless features composed, and his large, luminous eyes half closed, lounged in Sheard's study at half-past one in the early morning and toyed with an unfinished manuscript—like some old and privileged friend who had dropped in for a chat.

"Look here!" said the outraged pressman, stepping around the table as the calm effrontery of the thing burst fully upon him. "Get out! *Now!*"

"Mr. Sheard," said the other, "if I apologise frankly and fully for my intrusion, will you permit me to give my reasons for it?"

Sheard again found himself inarticulate. He was angrily conscious of a vague disquiet. The visitor's suave courtesy under circumstances so utterly unusual disarmed him, as it must have disarmed any average man similarly situated. For a moment his left fist clenched, his mind swung in the balance, irresolute. The other turned back a loose page and quietly resumed his perusal of the manuscript.

That decided Sheard's attitude, and he laughed.

Whereat the stranger again raised the protestant hand.

"We shall awake Mrs. Sheard!" he said solicitously. "And now, as I see you have decided to give me a hearing, let me begin by offering you my sincere apology for entering your house uninvited."

Sheard, his mind filled with a sense of phantasy, dropped into a chair opposite the visitor, reached into the cabinet at his elbow, and proffered a box of Turkish cigarettes.

"Your methods place you beyond the reach of ordinary castigation," he said. "I don't know your name and I don't know your business; but I honestly admire your stark impudence!"

"Very well," replied the other in his quiet, melodious voice, with its faint, elusive accent. "A compliment is intended, and I thank you! And now, I see you are wondering how I obtained admittance. Yet it is so simple. Your front door is not bolted, and Mrs. Sheard, but a few days since, had the misfortune to lose a key. You recollect? I found that key! Is it enough?"

"Quite enough!" said Sheard grimly. "But why go to the trouble? What do you want?"

"I want to insure that one, at least, of the influential dailies shall not persistently misrepresent my actions!"

"Then who——" began Sheard, and got no farther; for the stranger handed him a card—

SÉVERAC BABLON

"You see," continued the man already notorious in two continents, "your paper, here, is inaccurate in several important particulars! Your premises are incorrect, and your inferences consequently wrong!"

Sheard stared at him, silent, astounded.

"I have been described in the Press of England and America as an incendiary, because I burned the Runek Mills; as a maniac, because I compensated men cruelly thrown out of employment; as a thief, because I took from the rich in Park Lane and gave to the poor on the Embankment. I say that this is unjust!"

His eyes gleamed into a sudden blaze. The delicate, white hand that held Sheard's manuscript gripped it so harshly that the paper was crushed into a ball. That Séverac Bablon was mad seemed an unavoidable conclusion; that he was forceful, dominant, a power to be counted with, was a truth legible in every line of his fine features, in every vibrant tone of his voice, in the fire of his eyes. The air of the study seemed charged with his electric passion.

Then, in an instant, he regained his former calm. Rising to his feet, he threw off the heavy coat he wore and stood, a tall, handsome figure, with his hands spread out, interrogatively.

"Do I look such a man?" he demanded.

Despite the theatrical savour of the thing, Sheard could not but feel the real sincerity of his appeal; and, as he stared, wondering, at the fine brow, the widely-opened eyes, the keen nostrils and delicate yet indomitable mouth and chin, he was forced to admit that here was no mere up-to-date cracksman, but something else, something more. "Is he mad?" flashed again through his mind.

"No!" smiled Séverac Bablon, dropping back into the chair; "I am as sane as you yourself!"

"Have I questioned it?"

"With your eyes and the left corner of your mouth, yes!" Sheard was silent.

"I shall not weary you with a detailed exculpation of my acts," continued his visitor; "but you have a list on your table, no doubt, of the people whom I forced to assist the Embankment poor?"

Sheard nodded.

"Mention but one whose name has ever before been associated with charity; I mean the charity that has no relation to advertisement! You are silent! You say"—glancing over the unfinished article—"that 'this was a capricious burlesque of true philanthropy.' I reply that it served its purpose—of proclaiming my arrival in London and of clearly demonstrating the purpose of my coming! You ask who are my accomplices! I answer—they are as the sands of the desert! You seek to learn who I am. Seek, rather, to learn *what* I am!"

"Why have you selected me for this—honour?"

"I overheard some remarks of yours, contrasting a restaurant supper-room with the Embankment which appealed to me! But, to come to the point, do you believe me to be a rogue?"

Sheard smiled a trifle uneasily.

"You are doubtful," the other continued. "It has entered your mind that a proper course would be to ring up Scotland Yard! Instead, come with me! I will show you how little you know of me and of what I can do. I will show you that no door is closed to me! Why do you hesitate? You shall be home again, safe, within two hours. I pledge my word!"

Possessing the true journalistic soul, Sheard was sorely tempted; for to the passion of the copy-hunter such an invitation could not fail in its appeal. With only a momentary hesitation, he stood up.

"I'll come!" he said.

A smart landaulette stood waiting outside the house; and, without a word to the chauffeur, Séverac Bablon opened the door and entered after Sheard.

The motor immediately started, and the car moved off silently. The blinds were drawn.

"You will have to trust yourself implicitly in my hands," said Sheard's extraordinary companion. "In a moment I shall ask you to fasten your handkerchief about your eyes and to give me your word that you are securely blindfolded!"

"Is it necessary?"

"Quite! Are you nervous?"

"No!"—shortly.

There was a brief interval of silence, during which the car, as well as it was possible to judge, whirled through the deserted streets at a furious speed.

"Will you oblige me?" came the musical voice.

The journalist took out his pocket-handkerchief, and making it into a bandage, tied it firmly about his head.

"Are you ready?" asked Séverac Bablon.

"Yes."

A click told of a raised blind.

"Can you see?"

"Not a thing!"

"Then take my hand and follow quickly. Do not speak; do not stumble!"

Cautiously feeling his way, Sheard, one hand clasping that of his guide, stepped out into the keen night air, and was assisted by some third person—probably the chauffeur—on to the roof of the car!

"Be silent!" from Séverac Bablon. "Fear nothing! Step forward as your feet will be directed and trust implicitly to me!"

As a man in a dream Sheard stood there—on the roof of a motor-car, in a London street—and waited. There came dimly to his ears, and from no great distance, the sound of late traffic along what he judged to be a main road. But immediately about him quiet reigned. They were evidently in some deserted back-water of a great thoroughfare. A faint scuffling sound arose, followed by that of someone lightly dropping upon a stone pavement.

Then an arm was slipped about him and he was directed, in a whisper, to step forward. He found his foot upon what he thought to be a flat railing.

His ankle was grasped from below and the voice of Séverac Bablon came, "On to my shoulders—so!"

Still with the supporting arm about him, he stepped gingerly forward—and stood upon the shoulders of the man below.

"Stand quite rigidly!" said Séverac Bablon.

He obeyed; and was lifted, lightly as a feather, and deposited upon the ground! It was such a feat as he had seen professional athletes perform, and he marvelled at the physical strength of his companion.

A keen zest for this extravagant adventure seized him. He thought that it must be good to be a burglar. Then, as he heard the motor re-started and the car move off, a sudden qualm of disquiet came; for it was tantamount to burning one's boats.

"Take my hand!" he heard; and was led to the head of a flight of steps. Cautiously he felt his way down, in the wake of his guide.

A key was turned in a well-oiled lock, and he was guided inside a building. There was a faint, crypt-like smell—vaguely familiar.

"Quick!" said the soft voice—"remove your boots and leave them here!"

Sheard obeyed, and holding the guiding hand tightly in his own, traversed a stone-paved corridor. Doors were unlocked and re-locked. A flight of steps was negotiated in phantom silence; for his companion's footsteps, like his own, were noiseless. Another door was unlocked.

"Now!" came the whispered words: "Remove the handkerchief!"

Rapidly enough, Sheard obeyed, and, burning with curiosity, looked about him.

"Good heavens!" he muttered.

A supernatural fear of his mysterious cicerone momentarily possessed him. For he thought that he stood in a lofty pagan temple!

High above his head a watery moonbeam filtered through a window, and spilled its light about the base of a gigantic stone pillar. Towering shapes, as of statues of gods, loomed, awesomely, in the gloom. Behind the pillar dimly he could discern a painted procession of deities upon the wall. Glancing over his shoulder, he saw that the tall figure of Séverac Bablon was at his elbow.

"Where do you stand?" questioned his low voice.

And, like an inspiration, the truth burst in upon Sheard's mind.

"The British Museum!" he whispered hoarsely.

"Correct!" was the answer; "the treasure-house of your modern Babylon! Wait, now, until I return; and, if you have no relish for arrest as a burglar, do not move—do not breathe!"

With that, he was gone, into the dense shadows about; and Henry Thomas Sheard, of the *Gleaner*, found himself, at, approximately, a quarter-past two in the morning, standing in an apartment of the British Museum, with no better explanation to offer, in the event of detection, than that he had come there in the company of Séverac Bablon.

He thought of the many printing-presses busy, even then, with the deductions of Fleet Street theorists, regarding this man of mystery. All of their conclusions must necessarily be wrong, since their premises were certainly so. For which of them who had assured his readers that Séverac Bablon was a common cracksman (on a large scale) would not have reconsidered his opinion had he learned that the common cracksman held private keys of the national treasure-house?

His eyes growing more accustomed to the darkness, Sheard began to see more clearly the objects about him. A seated figure of the Pharaoh Seti I. surveyed him with a scorn but thinly veiled; beyond, two towering Assyrian bulls showed gigantic in the semi-light. He could discern, now, the whole length of the lofty hall—a carven avenue; and, as his gaze wandered along that dim vista, he detected a black shape emerging from the blacker shadows beyond the bulls.

It was Séverac Bablon. In an instant he stood beside him, and Sheard saw that he carried a bag.

"Follow me—quickly!" he said. "Not a second to spare!"

But too fully alive to their peril, Sheard slipped away in the wake of this greatly daring man. The horror of his position was strong upon him now.

"This way!"

Blindly he stumbled forward, upstairs, around a sharp corner, and then a door was unlocked and re-locked behind them. "Egyptian Room!" came a quick whisper. "In here!"

A white beam cut the blackness, temporarily dazzling him, and Sheard saw that his companion was directing the light of an electric torch into a wall-cabinet—which he held open. It contained mummy cases, and, without quite knowing how he got there, Sheard found himself crouching behind one. Séverac Bablon vanished.

Darkness followed, and to his ears stole the sound of distant voices.

The voices grew louder.

Behind him, upon the back of the cabinet, danced a sudden disc of light, and, within it, a moving shadow! Someone was searching the room!

Muffled and indistinct the voices sounded through the glass and the mummy-case; but that the searchers were standing within a foot of his hiding-place Sheard was painfully certain. He shrank behind the sarcophagus lid like a tortoise within its shell, fearful lest a hand, an arm, a patch of clothing should protrude.

---

# CHAPTER IV

## THE HEAD OF CÆSAR

The voices died away. A door banged somewhere.

Then Sheard all but cried out; for a hand was laid upon his arm.

"*Ssh!*" came Séverac Bablon's voice from the next mummy-case; and a creak told of the cabinet door swinging open. "This way!"

Sheard followed immediately, and was guided along the whole length of the room. A door was unlocked and re-locked behind them. Downstairs they passed, and along a narrow corridor lined with cases, as he could dimly see. Through another door they went, and came upon stone steps.

"Your boots!" said his companion, and put them into his hands.

Rapidly enough he fastened them. A faint creak was followed by a draught of cool air; and, being gently pushed forward, Sheard found himself outside the Museum and somewhere in the rear of the building. The place lay in deep shadow.

"*Sss! Sss!*" came in his ear. "Quiet!"

Whilst he all but held his breath, a policeman tramped past slowly outside the railings. As the sound of his solid tread died away, Séverac Bablon raised something to his lips and blew a long-sustained, minor note—shrill, eerie.

A motor-car appeared, as if by magic, stopped before them, and was backed right on to the pavement. The chauffeur, mounting on the roof, threw a short rope ladder across the railings.

"Up!" Sheard was directed, and, nothing loath, climbed over.

He was joined immediately by his companion in this night's bizarre adventures; and, almost before he realised that they were safe, he found himself seated once more in the swiftly moving car.

"What's the meaning of it?" he demanded rapidly.

"Fear nothing!" was the reply. "You have my word!"

"But to what are you committing me?"

"To nothing that shall lie very heavily upon your conscience! You have seen, to-night, something of my opportunities. With the treasures of the nation thus at my mercy, am I a common cracksman? If I were, should I not ere this have removed the portable gems of the collection? I say to you again, that no door is closed to me; yet never have I sought to enrich myself. But why should these things lie idle, when they are such all-powerful instruments?"

"I don't follow you."

"To-morrow all will be clear!"

"Why did you blindfold me?"

"Should you have followed had you seen where I led? I wish to number you among my friends. You are not of my people, and I can claim no fealty of you; but I desire your friendship. Can I count upon it?"

The light of a street-lamp flashed momentarily into the car, striking a dull, venomous green spark from a curious ring which Séverac Bablon wore. In some strange fashion it startled Sheard, but, in the ensuing darkness, he sought out the handsome face of his companion and found the big, luminous eyes fixed upon him. Something about the man—his daring, perhaps, his enthusiasm, his utterly mysterious purpose—appealed, suddenly, all but irresistibly.

Sheard held out his hand. And withdrew it again.

"To-morrow——" he began.

"To-morrow you will have no choice!"

"How so? You have placed yourself in my hands. I can now, if I desire, publish your description!—report all that you have told me—all that I have seen!"

"You will not do so! You will be my friend, my defender in the Press. Of what you have seen to-night you will say nothing!"

"Why?"

"No matter! It will be so!"

A silence fell between them that endured until the car pulled up before Sheard's gate.

With ironic courtesy, he invited Séverac Bablon to enter and partake of some refreshment after the night's excitement. With a grace that made the journalist slightly ashamed of his irony, that incomprehensible man accepted.

Leaving him in the same arm-chair which he had occupied when first he set eyes upon him, Sheard went to the dining-room and returned with a siphon, a decanter, and glasses. He found Séverac Bablon glancing through an edition of Brugsch's "Egypt Under the Pharaohs." He replaced the book on the shelf as Sheard entered.

"These Egyptologists," he said, "they amuse me! Dissolve them all in a giant test-tube, and the keenest analysis must fail to detect one single grain of imagination!"

His words aroused Sheard's curiosity, but the lateness of the hour precluded the possibility of any discussion upon the subject.

When, shortly, Séverac Bablon made his departure, he paused at the gate and proffered his hand, which Sheard took without hesitation.

"Good-night—or, rather, good-morning!" he said smilingly. "We shall meet again very soon!"

The other, too tired to wonder what his words might portend, returned to the house, and, lingering only to scrawl a note that he was not to be awakened at the usual time, hastened to bed. As he laid his weary head upon the pillow the cold grey of dawn was stealing in at the windows and brushing out the depths of night's blacker shadows.

It was noon when Sheard awoke—to find his wife gently shaking him.

He sat up with a start.

"What is it, dear?"

"A messenger boy. Will you sign for the letter?"

But half awake, he took the pencil and signed. Then, sleepily, he tore open the envelope and read as follows.

"DEAR MR. SHEARD,—

"You were tired last night, so I did not further weary you with a discourse upon Egyptology; moreover, I had a matter of urgency to attend to; but you may remember I hinted that the initiated look beyond Brugsch.

"I should be indebted if you could possibly arrange to call upon Sir Leopold Jesson in Hamilton Place at half-past four. You will find him at home. It is important that you take a friend with you. In your Press capacity, desire him to show you his celebrated collection of pottery. Seize the opportunity to ask him for a subscription (not less than £10,000) towards the re-opening of the closed ward of Sladen Hospital. He will decline. Offer to accept, instead, the mahogany case which he has in his smaller Etruscan urn. When you have secured this, decide to accept a cheque also. Arrange to be alone in your study at 12.40 to-night.

"By the way, although Brugsch's book is elementary, there is something more behind it. Look into the matter.—S.B."

This singular communication served fully to arouse Sheard, and, refreshed by his bath, he sat down to a late breakfast. Propping the letter against the coffee-pot, he read and re-read every line of the small, neat, and oddly square writing.

The more he reflected upon it the more puzzled he grew. It was a link with the fantastic happenings of the night, and, as such, not wholly welcome.

Why Séverac Bablon desired him to inspect the famous Jesson collection he could not imagine; and that part of his instructions: "Decide to accept a cheque," seemed to presume somewhat generously upon Sheard's persuasive eloquence. The re-opening of the closed ward was a good and worthy object, and the sum of ten, or even twenty thousand pounds, one which Sir Leopold Jesson well could afford. But he did not remember to have heard that the salving of derelict hospitals was one of Sir Leopold's hobbies.

Moreover, he considered the whole thing a piece of presumption upon the part of his extraordinary acquaintance. Why should he run about London at the behest of Séverac Bablon?

"Eleven-thirty results!" came the sing-song of a newsboy. And Sheard slipped his hand in his pocket for a coin. As he did so, the boy paused directly outside the house.

"Robbery at the British Museum! Eleven-thirty!"

His heart gave a sudden leap, and he cast a covert glance towards his wife. She was deep in a new novel.

Without a word, Sheard went to the door, and walking down to the gate, bought a paper. The late news was very brief.

BRITISH MUSEUM MYSTERY

"An incredibly mysterious burglary was carried out last night at the British Museum. By some means at present unexplained the Head of Cæsar has been removed from its pedestal and stolen, and the world-famous Hamilton Vase (valued at £30,000) is also missing. The burglar has left no trace behind him, but as we go to press the police report an important clue."

Sheard returned to the house.

Seated in his study with the newspaper and Séverac Bablon's letter before him, he strove to arrange his ideas in order, to settle upon a plan of action—to understand.

That the "important clue" would lead to the apprehension of the real culprit he did not believe for a moment. Séverac Bablon, unless Sheard were greatly mistaken, stood beyond the reach of the police measures. But what was the meaning of this crass misuse of his mysterious power? How could it be reconciled with his assurances of the previous night? Finally, what was the meaning of his letter?

He wished him to interview Sir Leopold Jesson, for some obscure reason. So much was evident. But by what right did he impose that task upon him? Sheard was nonplussed, and had all but decided not to go, when the closing lines of the letter again caught his eye. "Although Brugsch's book is elementary, there is something more behind it———"

A sudden idea came into his head, an unpleasant idea, and with it, a memory.

His visitor of the night before had brought a mysterious bag (which Sheard first had observed in his hand as they fled from the Museum) into the house with him. It was evidently heavy; but to questions regarding it he had shaken his head, smilingly replying that he would know in good time why it called for such special attention. He remembered, too, that the midnight caller carried it when he departed, for he had rested it upon the gravel path whilst bidding him good-night.

Frowning uneasily, he stepped to the bookcase.

It was a very deep one, occupying a recess. With nervous haste he removed "Egypt Under the Pharaohs," and his painful suspicion became a certainty.

Why, he had asked himself, should he run about London at the behest of Séverac Bablon? And here was the answer.

Placed between the books and the wall at the back, and seeming to frown upon him through the gap, was the stolen Head of Cæsar!

Sheard hastily replaced the volume, and with fingers that were none too steady filled and lighted his pipe.

His reflections brought him little solace. He was in the toils. The intervening hours with their divers happenings passed all but unnoticed. That day had space for but one event, and its coming overshadowed all others. The hour came, then, all too soon, and punctually at four-thirty Sheard presented himself in Hamilton Place.

Sir Leopold Jesson's collection of china and pottery is one of the three finest in Europe, and Sheard, under happier auspices, would have enjoyed examining it. Ralph Crofter, the popular black-and-white artist who accompanied him, was lost in admiration of the pure lines and exquisite colouring of the old Chinese ware in particular.

"This piece would be hard to replace, Sir Leopold?" he said, resting his hand upon a magnificent jar of delicate rose tint, that seemed to blush in the soft light.

The owner nodded complacently. He was a small man, sparely built, and had contracted, during forty years' labour in the money market, a pronounced stoop. His neat moustache was wonderfully black, blacker than Nature had designed it, and the entire absence of hair upon his high, gleaming crown enabled the craniologist to detect, without difficulty, Sir Leopold's abnormal aptitude for finance.

"Two thousand would not buy it, sir!" he answered.

Crofton whistled softly and then passed along the room.

"This is very beautiful!" he said suddenly, and bent over a small vase with figures in relief. "The design and sculpture are amazingly fine!"

"That piece," replied Sir Leopold, clearing his throat, "is almost unique. There is only one other example known—the Hamilton Vase!"

"The stolen one?"

"Yes. They are of the same period, and both from the Barberini Palace."

"Of course you have read the latest particulars of that extraordinary affair? What do you make of it?"

Jesson shrugged his shoulders.

"The vase is known to every connoisseur in Europe," he said. "No one dare buy it—though," he added smiling, "many would like to!"

Sheard coughed uneasily. He had a task to perform.

"Your collection represents a huge fortune, Sir Leopold," he said.

"Say four hundred thousand pounds!" answered the collector comfortably.

"A large sum. Think of the thousands whom that amount would make happy!"

Having broken the ice, Sheard found his enforced task not altogether distasteful. It seemed wrong to him, unjust, and in strict disaccordance with the views of the *Gleaner*, that these thousands should be locked up for one man's pleasure, while starvation levied its toll upon the many. Moreover, he nurtured a temperamental distaste for the whole Semitic race—a Western resentment of that insidious Eastern power.

Crofter looked surprised, and clearly thought his friend's remark in rather bad taste. Sir Leopold faced round abruptly, and a hard look crept into his small bright eyes.

"Mr. Sheard," he said harshly. "I began life as a pauper. What I have, I have worked for."

"You have enjoyed excellent health."

"I admit it."

"Had you, in those days of early poverty, been smitten down with sickness, of what use to you would your admittedly fine commercial capacity have been? You would then, only too gladly, have availed yourself of such an institution as the Sladen Hospital, for instance."

Sir Leopold started.

"What have you to do with the Sladen Hospital?"

"Nothing. It has accomplished great work in the past."

"Do you know anything of *this*?"

Jesson's manner became truculent. He pulled some papers from his pocket, and selecting a plain correspondence card, handed it to Sheard.

The card bore no address, being headed simply: "Final appeal." It read:

"Your cheque toward the re-opening of the Out-Patient's Wing of Sladen Hospital has not been forwarded."

Sheard failed to recognise the writing, and handed the card back, shaking his head.

"Oh!" said Jesson suspiciously; "because I've had three of these anonymous applications—and they don't come from the hospital authorities."

"Why not comply?" asked Sheard. "Let me announce in the *Gleaner* that you have generously subscribed ten thousand pounds."

"*What!*" rapped Sir Leopold. "Do you take me for a fool?" He glared angrily. "Before we go any farther, sir—is this touting business the real object of your visit?"

The pressman flushed. His conduct, he knew well, was irreconcilable with good form; but Jesson's tone had become grossly offensive. Something about the man repelled Sheard's naturally generous instincts, and no shade of compunction remained. A score of times, during the past quarter of an hour, he had all but determined to throw up this unsavoury affair and to let Séverac Bablon do with him as he would. Now, he stifled all scruples and was glad that the task had been required of him. He would shirk no more, but would go through with the part allotted him in this strange comedy, lead him where it might.

"Yes, and no!" he answered evasively. "Really I have come to ask you for something—the mahogany case which is in your smaller Etruscan urn!"

Jesson stared; first at Sheard, and then, significantly, at Crofter.

"I begin to suspect that you have lunched unwisely!" he sneered.

Sheard repressed a hot retort, and Crofter, to cover the embarrassment which he felt at this seeming contretemps, hummed softly and instituted a painstaking search for the vessel referred to. He experienced little difficulty in finding it, for it was one of two huge urns standing upon ebony pedestals.

"The smaller, you say?" he called with affected cheeriness.

Sheard nodded. It was a crucial moment. Did the pot contain anything? If not, he had made a fool of himself. And if it did, in what way could its contents assist him in his campaign of extortion?

The artist, standing on tiptoe, reached into the urn—and produced a mahogany case, such as is used for packing silver ware.

"What's that?" rapped Jesson excitedly. "I know nothing of it!"

"You might open it, Crofter!" directed Sheard with enforced calm.

Crofter did so—and revealed, in a nest of black velvet, a small piece of exquisite pottery.

A passage hitherto obscure in Séverac Bablon's letter instantly explained itself in Sheard's mind. "I did not further weary you with a discourse upon Egyptology; moreover, *I had a matter of urgency to attend to!*"

Sir Leopold Jesson took one step forward, and then, with staring eyes, and face unusually pale, turned on the journalist.

"The Hamilton Vase! You villain!"

"Sir Leopold!" cried Sheard with sudden asperity, "be good enough to moderate your language! If you can offer any explanation of how this vase, stolen only last night from the national collection, comes to be concealed in your house, I shall be interested to hear it!"

Jesson looked at Crofter, who still held the case in his hands; the artist's face expressed nothing but blank amazement. He looked at Sheard, who met his eyes calmly.

"There is roguery here!" he said. "I don't know if there are two of you——"

"Sir Leopold Jesson!" cried Crofter angrily, "you have said more than enough! Your hobby has become a mania, sir! How you obtained possession of the vase I do not know, nor do I know how my friend has traced the theft to you; least of all how this scandal is to be hushed up. But have the decency to admit facts! There is no defence, absolutely!"

"What do you want?" said Jesson tersely. "This is a cunning trap—and I've fallen right into it!"

"You have!" said Crofter grimly. "I must congratulate my friend on a very smart piece of detective work!"

"What do you want?" repeated Jesson, moistening his dry lips.

His quick mind had been at work since the stolen vase was discovered in his possession, and although he knew himself the victim of an amazing plot, he also recognised that rebellion was out of the question. As Crofter had said, there was no defence.

"Suppose," suggested Sheard, "you authorise the announcement in the *Gleaner* to which I have already referred? I, for my part, will undertake to return the vase to the proper authorities and to keep your name out of the matter entirely. Would you agree to keep silent, Crofter?"

"Can you manage what you propose?"

"I can!" answered Sheard, confidently.

"All right!" said Crofter slowly. "It's connivance, but in a good cause!"

"I shall make the cheque payable to the hospital!" said Jesson, significantly.

Sheard stared for a moment, then, as the insinuation came home to his mind: "How dare you!" he cried hotly. "Do you take us for thieves?"

"I hardly know what to take you for," replied the other. "Your proceedings are unique."

# CHAPTER V

## A MYSTIC HAND

"It amounts," said J. J. Oppner, the lord of Wall Street, "to a panic. No man of money is safe. I ain't boilin' over with confidence in Scotland Yard, and I've got some Agency boys here in London with me."

"A panic, eh?" grunted Baron Hague, Teutonically. "So you vear this Bablon, eh?"

"A bit we do," drawled Oppner, "and then some. After that a whole lot, and we're well scared. He held me up at my Canadian mills for a pile; but I've got wise to him, and if he crowds me again he's a full-blown genius."

Mrs. Rohscheimer's dinner party murmured sympathetically.

"Of course you have heard, Baron," said the hostess, "that in his outrage here—here, in Park Lane!—he was assisted by no fewer than thirty accomplices?"

"Dirty aggomblices, eh? Dirty?"

"Dirty's the word!" growled Mr. Oppner.

"The wonder is," said Sir Richard Haredale, "that a rogue with so many assistants has not been betrayed."

To those present at the Rohscheimer board this subject, indeed, was one of quite extraordinary interest, in view of the fact that it was only a few days since the affair of the dramatic ball. Sixteen diners there were, and in order to appreciate the electric atmosphere which prevailed in the airy salon, let us survey the board. Reading from left to right, as in the case of society wedding groups, the diners were:

Mrs. Julius Rohscheimer.[1]
Baron Hague.[1]
Miss Zoe Oppner.[1]
Sir Richard Haredale.
Mrs. Maurice Hohsmann.[1]
Mr. J. J. Oppner.[1]
Mrs. Wellington Lacey.
Mr. Sheard (Press).Miss Salome
Hohsmann.[1]Sir Leopold Jesson.[1]
Lady Vignoles.[1]

Mr. Julius Rohscheimer.[1]
Lady Mary Evershed.Lord
Vignoles.Miss Charlotte Hohsmann.[1]
Mr. Antony Elschild.[1]

[1] Representatives of capital.

"I understand that the man holds private keys to the British Museum!" cried Mrs. Hohsmann.

"Nobody would be surprised to hear," came the thick voice of Julius Rohscheimer, "that he'd got a private subway between his bedroom and the Bank of England!"

Extravagant though this may appear, it would not indeed, at this time, have surprised the world at large to learn *anything*—however amazing in an ordinary man—respecting Séverac Bablon. The real facts of his most recent exploit were known only to a select few; but it was universal property how, at about half-past eleven one morning shortly after the theft from the British Museum, and whilst all London, together with a great part of the Empire, was discussing the incredibly mysterious robbery, a cab drove up to the main entrance of that institution, containing a District Messenger and a large box.

The box was consigned to the trustees of the Museum, and the boy, being questioned, described the consigner as "a very old gentleman, with long, white hair."

It contained, carefully and scientifically packed, the Hamilton Vase and the Head of Cæsar!

Furthermore, it contained the following note:

"GENTLEMEN,—

"I beg to return, per messenger, the Head of Cæsar and the Hamilton Vase. My reason for taking the liberty of borrowing them was that I desired to convince a wealthy friend that a rare curio is a powerful instrument for good, and that to allow of great wealth lying idle when thousands sicken and die in poverty is a misuse of a power conferred by Heaven.

"I trust that you will forgive my having unavoidably occasioned you so much anxiety.

"SÉVERAC BABLON."

The contents of the note were made public with the appearance of the 3.30 editions; nor was there a news-sheet of them all that failed to reprint, from the *Gleaner*, a paragraph announcing that Sir Leopold Jesson had made the magnificent donation of £10,000 to the Sladen Hospital. But the link that bound these items together was invisible to the eyes of the world. Two persons at Rohscheimer's table, however, were aware of all the facts; and although Sheard often glanced at Jesson, he studiously avoided meeting his eyes.

Séverac Bablon's activities had not failed to react upon the temperature of the Stock Exchange. Loudly it was whispered that influential and highly-placed persons were concerned with him. No capitalist felt safe. No man trusted his staff, his solicitor, his broker. It was felt that minions of Séverac Bablon were everywhere; that Séverac Bablon was omnipresent.

"You've gone pretty deep into the case, Sheard," said Rohscheimer. "What do you know about these cards he sends to people he's goin' to rob?"

Sheard cleared his throat somewhat nervously. All eyes sought him.

"The authorities have established the fact," he replied, "that all those whom Séverac Bablon has victimised have received—due warning."

Sir Leopold Jesson was watching him covertly.

"What do you mean by 'due warning'?" he snapped.

"They have been requested, anonymously," Sheard explained, "to subscribe to some worthy object. When they have failed voluntarily to comply they have been *compelled*, forcibly, to do so!"

Julius Rohscheimer began to turn purple. He spluttered furiously, ere gaining command of speech.

"Is this a free country?" came in a hoarse roar. "If a man ain't out buildin' hospitals for beggars does he have to be held up——"

He caught Mrs. Rohscheimer's glance, laden with entreaty.

"Good Lord!" he concluded, weakly. "Isn't it funny!"

Baron Hague was understood to growl that he should no longer feel safe until back to Berlin he had gone.

"I am told," said Mr. Antony Elschild, "that a new Séverac Bablon outrage is anticipated by the authorities."

That loosed the flood-gates. A dozen voices were asking at once: "Have *you* received a card?"

It seemed that this was a matter which had lain at the back of each mind; that each had feared to broach; that each, now, was glad to discuss. An extraordinary and ominous circumstance, then, was now brought to light.

A note had been received by each of the capitalists present, stating that £1,000,000 was urgently needed by the British Government for the establishment of an aerial fleet. That was all. But the notes all bore a certain seal.

"How many of us"—Julius Rohscheimer's coarse voice rose above them all—"have got these notes?"

A moment's silence, wherein it became evident that five of the gentlemen present had received such communications. Mrs. Hohsmann stated that her husband had been the recipient of a note also.

"With Hohsmann," resumed Rohscheimer, "six of us."

"It appears to me," the soft voice was Antony Elschild's, "that no time should be lost in ascertaining how many of these notes have been sent——"

"Why?" asked Rohscheimer.

"Because, from what we know of Séverac Bablon, it is evident that he intends to raise this sum, or a great part of it, for this highly patriotic purpose, amongst our particular set. One is naturally anxious to learn the amount of one's share in the responsibility!"

Baron Hague inquired, in stentorian but complicated English, whether *he* was to be expected to contribute towards the establishment of a British aerial fleet.

"You have British interests, Baron!" said Sheard, smiling.

"What about me?" said Mr. Oppner.

Replied his beautiful daughter, laughing:

"You've got Canadian interests, Pa!"

So the impending outrage—for all present felt that these notes presaged an outrage—was treated lightly enough, and the question, serious though it was felt to be, might well have given place to topics less exciting, when a buzz of conversation arose at the lower end of the table.

"Exactly the same," came Miss Salome Hohsmann's voice, "as the one father received!"

She was observed to be passing something to her neighbour—Mr. Sheard. He examined it curiously, and passed it on to Mrs. Lacey. Thus, from hand to hand it performed a circuit of the table and came to Julius Rohscheimer.

"That's one of 'em!" He threw it down upon the cloth—a small, square correspondence card. It bore the words:

"£1,000,000 is required by His Majesty's Government, immediately, in order to found an aerial service commensurate with Great Britain's urgent requirements. A fund for the purpose (under the patronage of the Marquess of Evershed and the Lord Mayor) has been opened by the *Gleaner.*"

At the foot was a seal, designed in the form of two triangles crossed.

"Whose is this?" continued Rohscheimer, and turned the card over.

He read what was neatly type-written upon the other side, and his gross, empurpled face was seen to change, to assume a patchy greyness.

The superscription was:

"To Baron Hague, Sir Leopold Jesson, Messrs. Julius Rohscheimer, John Jacob Oppner, and Antony Elschild.

*"Second Notice"*

He clutched the arms of his chair, and stood up. A dead silence had fallen.

"Where"—Rohscheimer moistened his lips—"did this come from?"

A moment more of silence, then:

"Sir Leopold passed it to me," came Salome Hohsmann's frightened voice.

Rohscheimer stared at Jesson. Jesson turned and stared at Miss Hohsmann.

"You are mistaken," he replied slowly. "I have not had the card in my hand!"

Miss Hohsmann's fine, dark eyes grew round in wonder.

"But, Sir Leopold!" she cried. "I *took* it from your hand!"

Jesson's face was a study in perplexity.

"I can only say," contributed Sheard, who sat upon the other side of the girl, "that I saw Miss Hohsmann looking at the card and I asked to be allowed to examine it. I then passed it on to Mrs. Lacey. I may add"—smiling—"that it does not emanate from the *Gleaner* office, and is in no way official!"

"Mrs. Lacey passed it along to me," came Oppner's parched voice.

"But," Sir Leopold's incisive tones cut in upon the bewildering conversation, "Miss Hohsmann is in error in supposing that she received the card from me. I have not handled it—neither, I believe, has Lady Vignoles?" He turned to the latter.

She shook her head.

"No, sir," she said transatlantically, "I saw Mr. Rohscheimer take it from Mary" (Lady Mary Evershed).

"I mean to say, Sheila"—Lord Vignoles leant forward in his chair and looked along to his wife—"I mean to say, *I* had it from Miss Charlotte Hohsmann, on my left."

Rohscheimer's protruding eyes looked from face to face. Wonder was written upon every one.

"Where the——" Mrs. Rohscheimer coughed.

The great financier sat down. Let us conclude his sentence for him:

*Where had the ominous "second notice" come from?*

Amid a thrilling silence, the guests sought, each in his or her own fashion, for the solution to this truly amazing conundrum. The order may be seen from a glance at the foregoing list of guests. It has only to be remembered that they were seated around a large oval table and their relative positions become apparent.

"It appears to me," said Sir Leopold Jesson, "that the mystery has its root here. Miss Hohsmann is under the impression that I handed the card to her. I did not do so. Miss Hohsmann, as well as myself, has been victimised by this common enemy, so that"—he smiled dryly—"we cannot suspect her, and you cannot suspect me, of complicity. Was there any servant in the room at the time?"

A brief inquiry served to show that there had been no servant on that side of the room at the time.

"Did you pick it up from the table, dear," cried Mrs. Hohsmann, "or actually take it from—someone's hand?"

Amid a tense silence the girl replied:

"From—someone's hand!"

# CHAPTER VI

## THE SHADOW OF SÉVERAC BABLON

The mystery of personality is one which eludes research along the most scientific lines. It is a species of animal magnetism as yet unclassified. Personality is not confined to the individual: it clings to his picture, his garments, his writing; it has the persistency of a civet perfume.

From this slip of cardboard lying upon Rohscheimer's famous oval table emanated rays—unseen, but cogent. The magnetic words "Séverac Bablon" seemed to glow upon the walls, as of old those other words had glowed upon a Babylonian wall.

There were those present to whom the line "Who steals my purse steals trash" appealed, as the silliest ever written. And it was at the purses of these that the blow would be struck—*id est*, at the most vital and fonder part of their beings.

"That card"—Julius Rohscheimer moistened his lips—"can't have dropped from the ceiling!"

But he looked upward as he spoke; and it was evident that he credited Séverac Bablon with the powers of an Indian fakir.

"It would appear," said Antony Elschild, "that a phantom hand appeared in our midst!"

The incident was eerie; a thousand times more so in that it was associated with Séverac Bablon. Rohscheimer gave orders that the outer door was on no account to be opened, until the house had been thoroughly searched. He himself headed the search party—whilst Mrs. Rohscheimer remained with the guests.

All search proving futile, Rohscheimer returned and learnt that a new discovery had been made. He was met outside the dining-room door by Baron Hague.

"Rohscheimer!" cried the latter, "my name on that card, it is underlined in red ink!"

Rohscheimer's rejoinder was dramatic.

"The diamonds!" he whispered.

Indeed, this latest discovery was significant. Baron Hague had brought with him, for Rohscheimer's examination, a packet of rough diamonds. Rohscheimer had established his fortunes in South Africa; and, be it whispered, there were points of contact between his own early history and the history of the packet of diamonds which Hague carried to-night. In both records there were I.D.B. chapters.

The two men stared at each other—and sometimes glanced into the shadows of the corridor.

"He must be in league with the devil," continued Rohscheimer, "if he has got to know about those stones! But it certainly looks as though——"

"Where can I hide them from *him*—from this man who I hear cannot be kept out of anywhere?"

"Hague," said Rohscheimer, shakily, "you'd be safer at your hotel than here. He's held people up in my house once before!"

As may be divined, Rohscheimer's chiefest fear was that *his* name, *his* house, should be associated with another mysterious outrage. He knew Baron Hague to have about his person stones worth a small fortune, and he was all anxiety—first, to save them from Séverac Bablon, the common enemy; second, if Baron Hague *must* be robbed, to arrange that he be robbed somewhere else!

"I have not ordered my gar until twelve o'clock," said the Baron.

"Mine can be got ready in——"

"I won't wait! Gall me a gab!"

That proposal fell into line with Rohscheimer's personal views, and he wasted not a moment in making the necessary arrangements.

The library door opening, and Adeler, his private secretary, appearing, with a book under his arm, Mr. Rohscheimer called to him:

"Adeler!"

Adeler approached, deferentially. His pale, intellectual face was quite expressionless.

"If you're goin' downstairs, Adeler, tell someone to call a cab for the Baron: Heard nothing suspicious while you've been in the library, have you?"

"Nothing," said Adeler—bowed, and departed.

The two plutocrats rejoined the guests. Sir Leopold Jesson was standing in a corner engaged in an evidently interesting conversation with Salome Hohsmann.

"You positively saw the hand?"

"Positively!" the girl assured him. "It just slipped the card into mine as Mr. Sheard leaned over and asked me if my diamond aigrette had been traced—the one that was stolen from me here, in this house, by Séverac Bablon."

Sheard was standing near.

"I saw you take the card, Miss Hohsmann!" he said; "though I was unable to see from whose hand you took it. Sir Leopold sat on your left, however, and there was no one else near at the time."

Sir Leopold Jesson stared hard at Sheard. Sheard stared back aggressively. There was that between them that cried out for open conflict. Yet open conflict was impossible!

"Now then, you two!" Rohscheimer's coarse voice broke in, "what's the good o' fightin' about it?"

But the atmosphere of uneasiness prevailed throughout the gilded salon. Mrs. Rohscheimer, clever hostess though admittedly she was, found herself hard put to it to keep up the spirits of her guests—or those of her guests whose names had appeared upon the mysterious "second notice."

Lady Mary Evershed and Sir Richard Haredale sat under a drooping palm behind a charming statuette representing Pandora in the familiar attitude with the casket.

"It was through that door, yonder," said Haredale, pointing, "that the masked man came."

"Yes," assented the girl. "I was over there—by the double doors."

"You were," replied Haredale; "I saw you first of all, when I looked up!"

A short silence fell, then:

"Do you know," said Lady Mary, "I cannot sympathise with any of the people who lost their property. They were all of them people who never gave a penny away in their lives! In fact, Mr. Rohscheimer's particular set are all dreadfully mean! When you come to think of it, isn't it funny how everybody visits here?"

When he came to think of it, Haredale did not find it amusing in the slightest degree. Julius Rohscheimer was an octopus whose tentacles were fastened upon the heart of society. Haredale was so closely in the coils that, short of handing in his papers, he had no alternative but to appear as Rohscheimer's social *alter ego*. Lord and Lady Vignoles were regular visitors to the house in Park Lane; and although the Marquess of Evershed did not actually visit there, he countenanced the appearance of his daughter, chaperoned by Mrs. Wellington Lacey, at the millionaire's palace. Moreover, Haredale knew why!

What a wondrous power is gold!

Haredale was watching the fleeting expressions which crossed Lady Mary's beautiful face as, with a little puzzled frown, she glanced about the room.

Baron Hague came to make his *adieux*. He was a man badly frightened. When finally he departed, Julius Rohscheimer conducted him downstairs.

"Take care of yourself, Hague," he said with anxiety. "First thing in the morning I should put the parcel in safe deposit till it's wanted."

The Baron assured him that he should follow his advice.

Outside, in Park Lane, a taxi-cab was waiting, and Adeler held the door open. Baron Hague made no acknowledgment of the attention, ignoring the secretary as completely as he would have ignored a loafer who had opened the door for him.

Adeler seemed to expect no thanks, but turned and walked up the steps to the house again.

"Good-bye, Hague!" called Rohscheimer. "Don't forget what I told you about the one with the brown stain!"

The cab drove off.

A cloud of apprehension had settled upon the house, it seemed. Several others of the party determined, upon one pretence or another, to return home earlier than they had anticipated doing. From this Julius Rohscheimer did nothing to discourage them.

A family party was the next to leave, then, consisting of Lord and Lady Vignoles, Mr. J. J. Oppner and Zoe. Mrs. Hohsmann and the Misses Hohsmann followed very shortly. Mrs. Wellington Lacey, with Lady Mary Evershed, departed next, Sir Richard Haredale escorting them.

"Half a minute, though, Haredale!" called the host.

Haredale, in the hall-way, turned.

"I suppose," continued Rohscheimer, half closing his eyes from the bottom upward—"you haven't got any sort of idea how the card trick was done, Haredale? Do you think I ought to let the police know?"

"I haven't the slightest idea," was the reply. "In regard to the police, I should most certainly ring them up at once. Good night."

Haredale escaped, well aware that Rohscheimer was seeking some excuse to detain him. Even at the risk of offending that weighty financier he was not going to be deprived of the drive, short though it was, with Mary Evershed, with the possibility of a delightful little intimate chat at the end of it.

"I endorse what Haredale says," came Sheard's voice.

Rohscheimer turned. A footman was assisting the popular Fleet Street man into his overcoat. Mr. Antony Elschild, already equipped, was lighting a cigarette and evidently waiting for Sheard.

"What's the name of the man who has the Séverac Bablon case in hand?" asked the host.

"Chief Inspector Sheffield."

"Right-oh!" said Rohscheimer. "I'll give him a ring."

Upstairs Sir Leopold Jesson was waiting for a quiet talk with Rohscheimer.

"Come into the library," said the latter. "Adeler's finished, so there's no one to interrupt us."

The pair entered the luxuriously appointed library, with its rows of morocco-bound, unopened works. Jesson stood before the fire looking down at Rohscheimer, who had spread himself inelegantly in a deep arm-chair, and lay back puffing at the stump of a cigar.

"I distrust Sheard!" snapped Jesson suddenly.

"Eh," grunted the other. "Pull yourself together! It ain't likely that a man who gets his livin', you might say, by keepin' in with the right people" (he glanced down at his diamond studs) "is goin' to be mixed up with a brigand like Bablon!"

"I'm not so sure!" persisted Jesson. "My position is a peculiar one; but I'll go so far as to say that I don't trust him, and I won't go a step farther. I don't expect you," he added, "to quote my opinion to anybody."

"I shan't," said Rohscheimer. "It's too damn silly! What would he have to gain? He ain't one of us."

"I'll say no more!" declared Jesson. "But keep your eyes open!"

"I'll do that!" Rohscheimer assured him. "I suppose you haven't any idea who worked the card trick?"

"As to that—yes! I *have* an idea—but I can only repeat that I'll say no more."

"I hope Hague is all right," growled Rohscheimer. "He's got some good rough stuff on him to-night. Brought it over to show me. I didn't like that red line under his name. Looked as if he was sort of number one on the list!"

"That's how it struck me. By the way, what became of the card?"

"Don't know," was the reply. "Push that bell. I want a whisky and soda."

Jesson pressed the bell, and Rohscheimer, tossing the stump into the grate, dipped two fat fingers into his waistcoat pocket in quest of a new cigar. It was his custom to carry two or three stuck therein.

"Hallo!"

Jesson turned to him—and saw that he held a card in his hand.

"Have you got the card?"

"Yes," said Rohscheimer, and turned it over.

Whereupon his face changed colour, and became an unclean grey.

"What's the matter?" cried Jesson.

His hand shaking slightly, Rohscheimer passed him the card. Jesson peered at it anxiously.

The message which it bore was the same as that borne by the mysterious card which had caused such a panic at the dinner table, but, upon the other side, only one name appeared.

It was that of Julius Rohscheimer, and it was heavily underlined in red!

---

# CHAPTER VII

## THE RING

As the cab containing Baron Hague drove off along Park Lane, the Baron heaved a sigh of relief. This incomprehensible Séverac Bablon who had descended like a simoon upon London was a perturbing presence—a breath of hot fear that parched the mind! And the house in Park Lane, too, recently had been made the scene of a unique outrage by this most singular robber to afford any sense of security.

The Baron was glad to be away from that house, and, as the cab turned the corner by the Park, was glad to be away from Park Lane. A man with several thousand pounds' worth of diamonds upon him may be excused a certain nervousness.

Baron Hague was not intimately acquainted with London; but it seemed to him, now, that the taxi-driver was pursuing an unfamiliar route. Had he made some error? Perhaps that fool Adeler had directed him wrongly.

The Baron took up the speaking-tube.

"Hi!" he called. "Hi, you! Is it the Hotel Astoria you take me?"

No notice did the man vouchsafe; looking neither to right nor to left, but driving straight ahead. Baron Hague snorted with anger. Again he raised the tube.

A cloud of something seemed to strike him in the face.

He dropped the tube, and reached out towards a window. Vaguely he wondered to find it immovable. The lights of the thoroughfare—the sound of the traffic, were fading away, farther, farther, to a remote distance. He clutched at the cushions—slipping—slipping——

His next impression was of a cell-like room, the floor composed of blocks of red granite, the walls smoothly plastered. An unglazed window made a black patch in one wall; and upon a big table covered with books and papers stood a queer-looking lamp. It was apparently silver, and in the form of a clutching hand. Within the hand rested a globe of light, above which was attached a coloured shade. The table was black with great age, and a carven chair, equally antique, stood by it upon a coarse fibre mat. The place was the abode of an anchorite, save for a rich Damascene curtain draped before a recess at one end.

The Baron found himself to be in a heavily cushioned chair, gazing across at this table—whereat was seated a very dark and singularly handsome man who wore a garment like an Arab's robe.

This stranger had his large, luminous eyes set fixedly upon the Baron's face.

"I am dreaming!"

Baron Hague stood up, unsteadily, raising his hand to his head.

There was a faint perfume in the air of the room; and now Hague saw that the man who sat so attentively watching him was smoking a yellow-wrapped cigarette. His brain grew clearer. Memory began to return; and he knew that he was not dreaming. Frantically he thrust his hand into the inside breast pocket.

"Do not trouble yourself, Baron," the speaker's voice was low and musical; "the packet of diamonds lies here!"

And as he spoke the man at the table held up the missing packet.

Hague started forward, fists clenched.

"You have robbed me! Gott! you shall be sorry for this! Who the devil are you, eh?"

"Sit down, Baron," was the reply. "I am Séverac Bablon!"

Baron Hague paused, in the centre of the room, staring, with a sort of madness, at this notorious free-booter—this suave, devilishly handsome enemy of Capital.

Then he turned and leapt to the door. It was locked. He faced about. Séverac Bablon smoked.

"Sit down, Baron," he reiterated.

The head of the great Berlin banking house looked about for a weapon. None offered. The big, carven, chair was too heavy to wield. With his fingers twitching, he approached again, closer to the table.

Séverac Bablon stood up, keeping his magnetic gaze upon the Baron—seeming to pierce to his brain.

"For the last time—sit down, Baron!"

The words were spoken quietly enough, and yet they seemed to clamour upon the hearer's brain—to strike upon his consciousness as though it were a gong. Again Hague paused, pulled up short by the force of those strange eyes. He weighed his chances.

From all that he had heard and read of Séverac Bablon, his accomplices were innumerable. Where this cell might be situate he could form no idea, nor by whom or what surrounded. Séverac Bablon apparently was unarmed (save that his glance was a sword to stay almost any man); therefore he had others near to guard him. Baron Hague decided that to resort to personal violence at that juncture would be the height of unwisdom.

He sat down.

"Now," said Séverac Bablon, in turn resuming his seat, "let us consider this matter of the million pounds!"

"I will not——" began Hague.

Séverac Bablon checked him, with a gesture.

"You will not contribute to a fund designed to aid in the defence of England? That is unjust. You reap large profits from England, Baron. To mention but one instance—you must draw quite twenty thousand pounds per annum from the firm of Romilis and Imer, Hatton Garden!"

Baron Hague stared in angry bewilderment.

"I have nothing to do with Romilis and Imer!"

"No? Then you can have no objection to my placing in the proper hands particulars—which, you will find, have been abstracted from your notebook—of the manner in which this parcel of diamonds reached Hatton Garden! I have the letter from your agent in Cape Town, addressed to the firm, and I have one signed 'Geo. Imer,' addressed to *you*! Finally, I am a telephone subscriber, and De Beers' number is Bank 5740! Shall I ring up the London office in the morning and draw their attention to this parcel, and to the interesting correspondence bearing upon it?"

Baron Hague's large features grew suddenly pinched in appearance. He leant forward, his hands resting upon his knees. Rôles were reversed. The great banker found himself seeking for a defence—one that might satisfy the rogue for whom the police of Europe were seeking!

"Why do you make a victim of *me*?" he gasped. "Antony Elschild is——"

"Mr. Antony Elschild is a member of one of the greatest Jewish families in Europe, you would say? And his interests are wholly British? He has recognised that, Baron. I have his cheque for fifty thousand pounds!"

"For *how much*?"

"For fifty thousand pounds! Should you care to see it? I am forwarding it immediately to the *Gleaner*. Mr. Elschild is my friend. He it was who proposed that this fund be started by the great capitalists so as to stimulate smaller subscribers. His name is never absent from such lists, Baron."

The Baron gulped.

"In Berlin—they would say I was mad!"

"And what will they say in Berlin if I call up De Beers in the morning? Which reputation is preferable, Baron?"

Hague sat staring, fascinated, at the man in the long robe, who smoked yellow cigarettes and filled the air with their peculiar fumes. It seemed to him, suddenly, that he had taken leave of his senses, and that this cell—this pungent perfume—this man with the soul-searching eyes, the incisive voice—all were tricks of his senses.

What had he preserved the secret of his connection with the Hatton Garden firm for all these long years—each year determining to quit whilst safe, but each year lured on by the prospect of vaster gain—only to lay it at the feet of this Séverac Bablon, who would ruin him?

Faintly, sounds of occasional traffic penetrated. From a place of half-shadows beyond the table, Séverac Bablon's luminous eyes watched. Save for those distant sounds which told of a thoroughfare near by, silence lay like a fog upon the place, and upon the mind of Baron Hague.

It grew intolerable, this stillness; it bred fear. Who was Séverac Bablon? What was the secret of his power?

Hague looked up.

"Gott im Himmel!" he said hoarsely. "Who are you? Why do you persecute those who are Jewish?"

Séverac Bablon stretched his hand over the great carved table, holding it, motionless, beneath the lamp. From the bezel of the solitary ring which he wore gleamed iridescent lights, venomous as those within the eye of a serpent.

A device, which seemed to be formed of lines of fire within the stone, glowed, redly, through the greenness. The ring was old—incalculably old— as anyone could see at a glance. And, in some occult fashion, it *spoke* to Baron Hague; spoke to that which was within him—stirred up the Jewish blood and set it leaping madly through his veins.

Back to his mind came certain words of a rabbi, long since gone to his fathers; before his eyes glittered words which he had had impressed upon his mind more recently than in those half-forgotten childish days.

And now, he feared. Slowly, he rose from the big cushioned chair. He feared the man whom all the world knew as Séverac Bablon, and his fear, for once, was something that did not arise from his purse. It was something which arose from the green stone—and from the one who possessed it—who dared to wear it. Hague backed yet farther from the table, squarely, whereupon, beneath the globular lamp, lay the long white hand.

"*Gott!*" he muttered. "I am going mad! You cannot be—you——"

"I am *he!*"

Baron Hague's knees began to tremble.

"It is impossible!"

"Israel Hagar," continued the other sternly. "Those before you changed your ancient name to Hague; but to me you are Israel Hagar! You doubt, because you dare not believe. But there is that within your soul—that which you inherit from forefathers who obeyed the great King, from forefathers who toiled for Pharaoh—there is that within your soul which tells you *who I am!*"

The Baron could scarcely stand.

"Ach, no!" he groaned. "What do you want? I will do anything—anything; but let me go!"

"I want you," continued Séverac Bablon, "since you deny the ring, to draw aside yonder curtain and look upon what it conceals!"

But Hague drew back yet further.

"Ach, no!" he said, huskily. "I deny nothing! I dare not!"

"By which I know that you have recognised in whose presence you stand, Israel Hagar! Knowing yourself at heart to be a robber, a liar, a hypocrite, you dare not, being also a Jew, raise that veil!"

Baron Hague offered no defence; made no reply.

"You are found guilty, Israel Hagar," resumed the merciless voice, "of dragging through the mire of greed—through the sloughs of lust of gold—a name once honoured among nations. It is such as you that have earned for the Jewish people a repute it ill deserves. Save for such as Mr. Antony Elschild, you and your like must have blotted out for ever all that is glorious in the Jewish name. Despite all, you have succeeded in staining it—and darkly. I have a mission. It is to erase that stain. Therefore, when the list appears of those who wish to preserve intact the British Empire, your name shall figure amongst the rest!"

Hague groaned.

"It will be explained, for the benefit of the curious, and to the glory of the Jews, that in some measure of recognition of those vast profits reaped from British ventures, you are desirous of showing your interest in British welfare!"

"It will be my ruin in Berlin!"

"I should regret to think so. Had you, in the whole of your career, during the entire period that you have been swelling your money-bags with British money, devoted one guinea—one paltry guinea—to any charitable purpose here, I had spared you the risk. As matters stand, I shall require your cheque for an amount equal to that subscribed by Mr. Elschild."

"*Fifty thousand pounds!*" gasped Hague.

"Exactly! Pen and ink are on the table. Your cheque book I have left in your pocket!"

"I won't——"

Hague met the eyes of the incomprehensible man who watched him from beyond the table; he saw the gleam of the ring, as Séverac Bablon placed a pen within reach.

"You—must be—mad!"

"You will decidedly be mad, Baron, if you refuse, for I assure you, upon my word of honour, I shall lay those papers before those whom they will interest in the morning!"

"And—if—I give you such a——"

"Immediately your cheque is cleared I will return the papers."

"And—the diamonds?"

"I shall consider my course in regard to the diamonds."

"This—is robbery!"

"And your mode of obtaining the diamonds, Baron—what should you term that?"

"You mean to ruin me!"

"Be good enough either to draw the cheque, payable to the editor of the *Gleaner*—who will act in this matter, since I cannot appear—or to decline definitely to do so."

"It will ruin me."

"To decline? I admit that!"

Very shakily, having taken his cheque book from his pocket, Baron Hague drew and signed a cheque for the fabulous, the atrocious sum of £50,000.

A heavy smell—overpowering—crept to his nostrils as he bent forward over the table. He mentally ascribed it to the yellow cigarettes.

He laid down the pen with trembling fingers. That same sense of increasing distances which had heralded the stupor in the cab was coming upon him again. The cell-like room seemed to be receding. Séverac Bablon's voice reached him from a remote distance:

"In future, Israel Hagar, seek to make—better use of your—opportunities."

---

"Wake up, sir! Hadn't you better be getting home?"

Baron Hague strove to stand. What had happened? Where was he?

"Hold up, sir! Here's a cab waiting! What address, sir?"

The Baron rubbed his eyes and looked dazedly about him. He was half supported by a police constable.

"Officer! Where am I, eh?"

"*I* found you sitting on the step of the Burlington Arcade, sir! Where you'd been before that isn't for me to say! Come on, jump in!"

Hague found himself bundled into the cab.

"Hotel—Astoria!" he mumbled, and his head fell forward on his breast again.

---

# CHAPTER VIII

## IN THE DRESSING-ROOM

The house was very quiet.

Julius Rohscheimer stood quite motionless in his dressing-room listening for a sound which he expected to hear, but which he also feared to hear. The household in Park Lane slept now. Park Lane is never quite still at any hour of the night, and now as Rohscheimer listened, all but holding his breath, a hundred sounds conflicted in the highway below. But none of these interested him.

He had been in his room for more than half an hour; had long since dismissed his man; and had sat down, arrayed in brilliant pyjamas (quite a new line from Paris, recommended by Haredale, a sartorial expert with a keen sense of humour), for a cigarette and a mental review of the situation.

Having shown himself active in other directions, Séverac Bablon had evidently turned his eyes once more toward Park Lane. Julius Rohscheimer mentally likened himself and his set to those early martyrs who, defenceless, were subjected to the attacks of armed gladiators. No precautions, it seemed, prevailed against this enemy of Capital. Police protection was utterly useless. Thus far, not a solitary arrest had been made. So, now, in his own palatial house, but with a strip of cardboard lying before him bearing his name, underlined in red, Rohscheimer anticipated mysterious outrage at any moment—and knew, instinctively, that he would be unable to defend himself against it.

Again came that vague stirring; and it seemed to come, not from beyond the walls, but from somewhere close at hand—from——

Rohscheimer turned, stealthily, in his chair. The cigarette dropped from between his nerveless fingers, and lay smouldering upon the Persian carpet.

His bulging eyes grew more and more prominent, and his adipose jaw dropped. And he sat, quivering fatly, his gaze upon the doors of the big wardrobe which occupied the space between the windows. Distinctly he remembered that these doors had been closed. But now they were open.

Palsied with fear of what might be within, he sat, watched, and grew pale.

The doors were opening slowly!

No move he made toward defence. He was a man inert from panic.

Something gleamed out of the dark gap—a revolver barrel. Two fingers pushed a card into view. Upon it, in red letters, were the words:

*"Do not move!"*

The warning was, at once, needless and disregarded. Rohscheimer shook the chair with his tremblings.

A smaller card was tossed across on to the table.

The fat hand which the financier extended toward the card shook grotesquely; the diamonds which adorned it sparkled and twinkled starrily. Before his eyes a red mist seemed to dance; but, through it, Rohscheimer made out the following:

"There is a cheque-book in your coat pocket, and your coat hangs beside me in the wardrobe. I will throw the book across to you. You will make out a cheque for £100,000, payable to the editor of the *Gleaner*, and also write a note explaining that this is your contribution towards the fund for the founding, by patriotic Britons, of a suitable air fleet."

Rohscheimer, out of the corner of his eye, was watching the gleaming barrel, which pointed straightly at his head. From the dark gap between the wardrobe doors sped a second projectile, and fell before him on the table.

It was his cheque-book. Mechanically he opened it. Within was stuck another card. Upon it, in the same evidently disguised handwriting, appeared:

"A fountain pen lies on the table before you. Do not hesitate to follow instructions—or I shall shoot you. All arrangements are made for my escape. Throw the cheque and the note behind you and do not dare to look around again until you have my permission. If you do so once, I may only warn you; if you do so twice, I shall kill you."

Perfect silence ruled. Even the traffic in Park Lane outside seemed momentarily to have ceased. From the wardrobe behind Julius Rohscheimer came no sound. He took up the pen; made out and signed the preposterous cheque.

To the ruling but silent intelligence concealed behind those double doors he had no thought of appeal. He dared not even address himself to that invisible being. Such idea was as far from his mind as it must have been of old from the mind of him who listened to a Sybilline oracle delivered from the mystic tripod.

Sufficiently he controlled his twitching fingers to write a note, as follows— (what awful irony!):

"To the Editor of the *Gleaner*,

"SIR,—I enclose a cheque for £100,000" (as he wrote these dreadful words, Rohscheimer almost contemplated rebellion; but the silence—the fearful silence—and the thought of the one who watched him proved too potent for his elusive courage. He wrote on). "I desire you to place it at the disposal of the Government for purposes of ariel" (Rohscheimer was no scholar) "defence. I hope others will follow suit." (He *did*. It was horrible to be immolated thus, a solitary but giant sacrifice, upon the altar of this priest of iconoclasm)—"I am, sir, yours, etc.

"JULIUS ROHSCHEIMER."

Cheque and note he folded together, and stretching his hand behind him, threw them in the direction of the haunted wardrobe. His fear that, even now, he might be assassinated, grew to such dimensions that he came near to swooning. But upon no rearward glance did he venture.

Several heavy vehicles passed along the Lane. Rohscheimer listened intently, but gathered no sound from amid those others that gave clue to the enemy's movements.

Clutching at the table-edge he sat, and tasted of violent death, by anticipation.

The traffic sounds subsided again. A new stillness was born. Within the great house nothing moved. But still Julius Rohscheimer shook and quivered. Only his mind was clearing; and already he was at work upon a scheme to save his money.

One hundred thousand pounds. Heavens above! It was ruination!

A faint creak.

"Do not dare to look around again until you have my permission," read the card before his eyes. "If you do so once I *may* only warn you; if you do so twice, I shall kill you."

One hundred thousand pounds! He could have cried. But, after all, he was a rich man—a very rich man; not so rich as Oppner, nor even so rich as Hague; but a comfortably wealthy man. Life was very good in his eyes. There were those little convivial evenings—those week-end motoring trips. He would take no chances. Life was worth more than one hundred thousand pounds.

He did not glance around.

So, the minutes passed. They passed, for the most part, in ghostly silence, sometimes broken by the hum of the traffic below, by the horn of a cab or car. Nothing from within the house broke that nerve-racking stillness.

If only there had been a mirror, so placed that by moving his eyes only he could have obtained a glimpse of the wardrobe. But there was no mirror so placed.

Faintly to his ears came the striking of a clock. He listened intently, but could not determine if it struck the quarter, half, three-quarters, or hour. Certainly, from the decrease of traffic in Park Lane, it must be getting very late, he knew.

His limbs began to ache. Cautiously he changed the position of his slippered feet. The clock in the hall began to strike. And Rohscheimer's heart seemed to stand still.

It struck the half-hour. So it was half-past one! He had been sitting there for an hour—an agonised hour!

What could the Unseen be waiting for?

Gradually his heart-beats grew normal again, and his keen mind got to work once more upon the scheme for frustrating the audacious plan of this robber who robbed from incredible motives.

An air fleet! What rot! What did he care about air fleets? One hundred thousand pounds! But if he presented himself at the *Gleaner* office as soon as it opened that morning, and explained, before the editor (curse him!) had had time to deal with his correspondence, that by an oversight (late night; the editor, as a man of the world, would understand) he had been thinking of a hundred and had written a hundred thousand, and also had written too many noughts after the amount of his subscription to the *Gleaner* fund, what then? The editor could not possibly object to returning him his cheque and accepting one for a thousand. A thousand was bad enough; but a hundred thousand!

He was growing stiff again.

Two o'clock!

Beneath his eyes lay the card which read:

"If you do so once, I *may* only warn you——"

A sudden burst of courage came to Julius Rohscheimer. Anything, he now determined, was preferable to this suspense.

He began to turn his head.

It was a ruse, he saw it all; a ruse to keep him there, silent, prisoned, whilst his cheque, his precious cheque, was placed in the hands of the *Gleaner* people.

Around he turned—and around. The corner of the wardrobe came within his field of vision. Still farther he moved. The doors, now, were visible.

And the gleaming barrel pointed truly at his head!

"No; no!" he whispered tremulously, huskily. "Ah, God! no! Spare me! I swear—I swear—I will not look again. I won't move. I'll make no sound."

He dropped his head into his hands—quaking; the lamp, the table, were swimming about him; he had never passed through ten such seconds of dread as those which followed his spell of temerity.

Yet he lived—and knew himself spared. Not for *five* hundred thousand pounds would he have looked again.

The minutes wore on—became hours. It seemed to Julius Rohscheimer that all London slept now; all London save one unhappy man in Park Lane.

Three o'clock, four o'clock, five o'clock struck. His head fell forward. He aroused himself with a jerk. Again his head fell forward. And this time he did not arouse himself; he slept.

---

"Mr. Rohscheimer! Mr. Rohscheimer!"

There were voices about him. He could distinguish that of his wife. Adeler was shaking him. Was that Haredale at the door?

Shakily, he got upon his feet.

"Why, Mr. Rohscheimer!" exclaimed Adeler, in blank wonderment, "have you not been to bed?"

"What time?" muttered Rohscheimer, "what time——"

Sir Richard Haredale, who evidently thought that the financier had had one of his "heavy nights," smiled discreetly.

"Pull yourself together, Rohscheimer!" he said. "Just put your head under the tap and jump into a dressing-gown. The green one with golden dragons is the most unique. You'll have to hold an informal reception here in your dressing-room. We can't keep the Marquess waiting."

"The Marquess?" groaned Rohscheimer, clutching at his head. "The Marquess?"

It had been his social dream for years to behold a real live Marquess beneath that roof. He had gone so far as to offer Haredale five hundred pounds down if he could bring one to dinner. But Haredale's best achievement to date had been Lord Vignoles.

Rohscheimer's mind was a furious chaos. Had the horrors of the night been no more than a dream, after all?

Sheard, of the *Gleaner*, pressed forward and grasped both his hands. Rohscheimer became ghastly pale.

"Mr. Rohscheimer," said the pressman, "England is proud of you! On such occasions as this, all formality—*all* formality—is swept away. A great man is great anywhere—at any time, any place, in any garb! I have Mrs. Rohscheimer's permission, and therefore am honoured to introduce to this apartment the Premier, the Most Honourable the Marquess of Evershed!"

Trembling wildly, fighting down a desire to laugh, to scream, Rohscheimer stood and looked toward the door.

The Marquess entered.

He wore the familiar grey frock-coat, with the red rose in his buttonhole, as made famous by *Punch*. His massive head he carried very high, looking downward through the pebbles of the gold-rimmed pince-nez.

"No apologies, Mr. Rohscheimer!" he began, hand raised forensically. "Positively I will listen to no apologies! This entire absence of formality—showing that you had not anticipated my visit—delights me, confirms me in my estimation of your character. For it reveals you as a man actuated by the purest motive which can stir the human heart. I refer to love of country—patriotism."

He paused, characteristically thrusting two fingers into his watch-pocket. Sheard wrote furiously. Julius Rohscheimer fought for air.

"The implied compliment, Mr. Rohscheimer," continued the Premier, "to myself, is deeply appreciated. I am, of course, aware that the idea of this fund was suggested to its promoters by my speech at Portsmouth regarding England's danger. The promptitude of the *Gleaner* newspaper in opening a subscription list is only less admirable than your own in making so munificent a donation.

"My policy during my present term of office, as you are aware, Mr. Rohscheimer, has been different, wholly different, from that of my immediate predecessor. I have placed the necessity of Britain's ruling, not only the seas, but the air, in the forefront of my programme——"

"Hear, hear!" murmured Sheard.

"And this substantial support from such men as yourself is very gratifying to me. I cannot recall any incident in recent years which has afforded me such keen pleasure. It is such confirmation of one's hopes that he acts for the welfare of his fellow-countrymen which purifies and exalts political life. And in another particular where my policy has differed from that of my friends opposite—I refer to my *encouragement* of foreign immigration—I have been nobly confirmed.

"Baron Hague, in recognition of the commercial support and protection which our British hospitality has accorded to him, contributes fifty thousand pounds to the further safeguarding of our national, though most catholic, interests. At an early hour this morning, Mr. Rohscheimer, I was aroused by a special messenger from the *Gleaner* newspaper, who brought me this glorious news of your noble, your magnificent, response to my—to our—appeal. Casting ceremony to the winds, I hastened hither. Mr. Rohscheimer—your hand!"

At that, Rohscheimer was surrounded.

"Socially," Haredale murmured in his ear, "you are made!"

"Financially," groaned Rohscheimer, "I'm broke!"

Mrs. Rohscheimer, in elegant *décolletée*, appeared among the excited throng. She was anxious for a sight of her husband, whom she was convinced had gone mad. Sheard thrust his way to the financier's side.

"Is there anything you would care to say for our next edition?" he enquired, a notebook in his hand. "We're having a full-page photograph, and——"

Crash! Crackle! Crackle! Crackle! A blinding light leapt up.

"My God! What's that?"

"All right," said Sheard. "Only our photographer doing a flash. If there's anything you'd like to say, hurry up, because I'm off to interview Baron Hague."

"Say that I believe I've gone mad!" groaned the financier, clutching his hair, "and that I'm damn sure Hague has!"

Sheard laughed, treating the words as a witticism, and hurried away. Mrs. Rohscheimer approached and bent over her husband.

"Have you pains in your head, dear?" she inquired anxiously.

"No!" snapped Rohscheimer. "I've got a pain in my pocket! I'm a ruined man! I'll be the laughing-stock of the whole money market!"

Adeler reappeared.

"Adeler," said Rohscheimer, "get the rest of the people out of the house! And, Adeler"—he glanced about him—"what did you do with those cards that were on the table, here?"

Adeler stared.

"Cards, Mr. Rohscheimer? I saw none."

"Who came in here first this morning? Who woke me up?"

"I."

Rohscheimer studied the pale, intellectual face of his secretary with uneasy curiosity.

"And there were no cards on the table—no cheque-book?"

"No."

"Sure you were first in?"

"I am not sure, but I think so. I found you fast asleep, at any rate."

"Why do you ask, dear?" said Mrs. Rohscheimer in growing anxiety.

"Just for a lark!" snapped her husband sourly. "I want to make Adeler laugh!"

Haredale, who, failing Rohscheimer or Mrs. Rohscheimer, did the honours of the house in Park Lane, returned from having conducted the Marquess to his car. He carried a first edition copy of the *Gleaner*.

"They've managed to get it in, even in this one," he said. "When did you send the cheque—early last evening?"

"Don't talk about it!" implored Rohscheimer.

"Why?" inquired Haredale curiously. "You must have seen your way to something big before you spent so much money. It was a great idea! You're certain of a knighthood, if not something bigger. But I wonder you kept it dark from me."

"Ah!" said Rohscheimer. "Do you?"

"Very much. It's a situation that calls for very delicate handling. Hitherto, because of certain mortgages, the Marquess has not prohibited his daughter visiting here, with the Oppners or Vignoles; but you've forced him, now, to recognise you *in propria persona*. He cannot very well withhold a title; but you'll have to release the mortgage gracefully."

"I'll do it gracefully," was the reply. "I'm gettin' plenty of practice at chuckin' fortunes away, and smilin'!"

His attitude puzzled Haredale, who glanced interrogatively at Mrs. Rohscheimer. She shook her head in worried perplexity.

"Go and get dressed, dear," said Rohscheimer, with much irritation. "I'm not ill; I've only turned patriotic."

Mrs. Rohscheimer departing, Haredale lingered.

"Leave me alone a bit, Haredale," begged the financier. "I want to get used to bein' a bloomin' hero! Send Lawson up in half an hour—and you come too, if you wouldn't mind."

Haredale left the room.

As the door closed, Rohscheimer turned and looked fully at the wardrobe.

From the gap pointed a gleaming tube!

*"Ah!"*

He dropped back in his chair. Nothing moved. The activity of the household stirred reassuringly about him. He stood up, crossed to the wardrobe, and threw wide its doors.

In the pocket of a hanging coat was thrust a nickelled rod from a patent trousers-stretcher, so that it pointed out into the room.

Rohscheimer stared—and stared—and stared.

"My God!" he whispered. "He slipped out directly he got the cheque, and I sat here all night——"

# CHAPTER IX

## ES-SINDIBAD OF CADOGAN GARDENS

Upon the night following the ill-omened banquet in Park Lane was held a second dinner party, in Cadogan Gardens. Like veritable gourmets, we must be present.

It is close upon the dining hour.

"Zoe is late!" said Lady Vignoles.

"I think not, dear," her husband corrected her, consulting his celebrated chronometer. "They have one minute in which to demonstrate the efficiency of American methods!"

"Thank you—Greenwich!" smiled her vivacious ladyship, whose husband's love of punctuality was the only trace of character which six months of marital intimacy had enabled her to discover in him.

"You know," said Lord Vignoles to Zimmermann, the famous *littérateur* of the Ghetto, "she is proud of Yankee smartness. Only natural." And his light blue eyes followed his wife's pretty figure as she flitted hospitably amongst her guests. Admiration beamed through his monocle.

"Lady Vignoles is a staunch American," agreed the novelist. "I gather that your opinion of that nation differs from hers?"

"Well, you know," explained his host, "I don't seriously contend—that is, when Sheila is about—I don't contend that their methods aren't smart. But it seems to me that their smartness is all—just—well, d'you see what I mean? Look at these Pinkerton fellows!"

"Those who you were telling me called upon you this morning?"

"Yes. They came over with Oppner to look for this Séverac Bablon."

"What is your contention?"

"Well," said Vignoles, rather flustered at being thus pinned to the point, "I mean to say—they haven't caught him!"

"Neither has Scotland Yard!"

"No, by Jove, you're right! Scotland Yard hasn't!"

"Do you think it likely that Scotland Yard will?" asked the other.

But Lord Vignoles, having caught his wife's eye, was performing a humorous grimace, and, watch in hand, delivering a pantomimic indictment of American unpunctuality. At which moment Miss Oppner was announced, and Lady Vignoles made a pretty *moue* of triumph.

Zoe Oppner entered the room, regally carrying her small head crowned with the slightly frizzy mop of chestnut hair, conscious of her fine eyes, her perfect features, and her pretty shoulders, happy in her slim young beauty, and withal wholly unaffected. Therein lay her greatest charm. A beautiful woman, fully aware of her loveliness, she was too sensible to be vain of a gift of the gods—to pride herself upon a heavenly accident.

"Why, Zoe!" said Lady Vignoles, "what's become of uncle?"

"Pa couldn't get," announced Zoe composedly; "so I came along without him. Told me to apologise, but didn't explain. I've promised to rejoin him early, so I shall have to quit directly after dinner. The car is coming for me."

Lord Vignoles looked amused.

"*Les affaires!*" he said resignedly. "These Americans!"

Dinner was announced.

The usual air of slightly annoyed surprise crept over the faces of the company at the announcement, so that to the uninitiate it would have seemed that no one was hungry. However, they accepted the inevitable.

Then Vignoles made a discovery.

"I say, Sheila," he exclaimed, "where is your American efficiency? We're thirteen!"

His wife made a rapid mental calculation and flushed slightly.

"Anybody might do it!" she pouted; "and it's uncle's fault, anyway!"

"Why!" exclaimed Zoe Oppner, "you're surely not going to make a fuss over a silly thing like that!"

"A lot of people don't like it," declared Lady Vignoles hurriedly. "I shouldn't mind, of course, if it happened at somebody else's house."

Zimmermann strolled up to the group.

"I gather that we number thirteen?" he said.

"That is so," replied Vignoles; "but," dropping his voice, "I don't think anyone else has noticed it yet."

"A romantic idea occurs to me!" smiled the novelist. "I submit it in all deference——"

"Oh, go on, Mr. Zimmermann!" cried Zoe, with sparkling eyes.

"Why not, upon the precedent of our ancient Arabian friend, Es-Sindibad of the Sea, summon to the feast some chance wayfarer?"

"Oh, I say!" protested the host mildly. "Do you mean to go outside in Cadogan Gardens and stop anybody that comes along?"

"Well," said Zimmermann, "it should, strictly, be some pious person who tarries there to extol Allah! But if we waited for such a traveller I fear the soup would be spoiled! You are a gentleman short, I think? So make it, simply, the first gentleman."

"But he might be a tramp or a taxi-driver, or worse!" protested Vignoles.

"That is true," agreed the other. "So let us determine upon a criterion of respectability. Shall we say the first man, provided he be agreeable, who wears a dress-suit?"

"That's just grand!" cried Zoe Oppner enthusiastically. "It's too cute for anything! Oh, Jerry, let's! Make him do it, Sheila!"

Jerry, otherwise Lord Vignoles, clearly regarded the projected Oriental experiment with no friendly eye.

"I mean to say——"

"That's settled, Zoe!" said the pretty hostess calmly. "Never mind him! Alexander!"

The footman addressed came forward.

"You will step out on the front porch, Alexander, and say to the first gentleman who passes, if he's in evening dress: 'Lady Vignoles requests the pleasure of your company at dinner.' If he says he doesn't know me, reply that I am quite aware of that! Do you understand?"

Alexander was shocked.

"I mean to say, Sheila——" began his lordship.

"Did you hear me, Alexander?"

"I've got to stand out in Cadogan Gardens, my lady——"

"Shall I repeat it again, slowly?"

"I heard you, my lady."

"Very well. Show the gentleman into the library. You have only five minutes."

With an appealing look towards Lord Vignoles, who, having ostentatiously removed and burnished his eyeglass, seemed to experience some difficulty in replacing it, Alexander departed.

"*I* claim him!" cried Zoe, as the footman disappeared. "Whoever he is or whatever he's like, he shall take me in to dinner!"

"What I mean to say is," blurted Vignoles, "that it would be all right at a country-house party at Christmas, say——"

"It's going to be all right here, dear!" interrupted his wife, affectionately squeezing his arm. "Why, think of the possibilities! New York would just go crazy on the idea!"

A silence fell between them as, with Zoe Oppner and the Zimmermanns, they made their way to the library. Only a few minutes elapsed, to their surprise, ere Alexander reappeared. Martyr-like, he had performed his painful duty, and a beatific consciousness of his martyrdom was writ large upon him. In an absolutely toneless voice he announced:

"Detective-Inspector Pepys!"

"Here! I mean to say—we can't have a policeman——" began Vignoles, but his wife's little hand was laid upon his lips.

Zoe Oppner, with brimming eyes, made a brave attempt, and then fled to a distant settee, striving with her handkerchief to stifle her laughter.

The guest entered.

From her remote corner Zoe Oppner peeped at him, and her laughter ceased. Lady Vignoles looked pleased; her husband seemed surprised. Zimmermann watched the stranger with a curious expression in his eyes.

Detective-Inspector Pepys was a tall man of military bearing, bronzed, and wearing a slight beard, trimmed to a point. He was perfectly composed, and came forward with an easy smile upon his handsome face. His clothes fitted him faultlessly. Even Lord Vignoles (a sartorial connoisseur) had to concede that his dress-suit was a success. He looked a wealthy Colonial gentleman.

"This pleasure is the greater in being unexpected, Lady Vignoles!" he said. "I gather I am thus favoured that I may take the place of an absentee. Shall I hazard a guess? Your party numbered thirteen?"

His infectious smile, easy acceptance of a bizarre situation, and evident good breeding, bridged a rather difficult interval. Lord Vignoles had had an idea that detective-inspectors were just ordinary plain-clothes policemen, and had determined, a second before, to assert himself, give the man half-a-sovereign, and put an end to this ridiculous extravaganza. Now he changed his mind. Detective-Inspector Pepys was a revelation.

Vignoles (to his own surprise) offered his hand.

"It is very good of you," he said, rather awkwardly. "You are sure you have no other dinner engagement, Inspector?"

"None," replied the latter. "I am, strictly speaking, engaged upon official duty; but bodily nutriment is allowed—even by Scotland Yard!"

"You don't mind my presenting you to—the other guests—in your—ah—unofficial capacity—as plain Mr. Pepys? They might—think there was something wrong!"

He felt vaguely confused, as though he were insulting the visitor by his request, and with the detective's disconcerting eyes fixed upon his face was more than half ashamed of himself.

"Not in the least, Lord Vignoles. I should have suggested it had you not done so."

The host was resentfully conscious of a subtle sense of inward gratitude for this concession. Of the easy assumption of equality by the detective he experienced no resentment whatever. The circumstances possibly warranted it, and, in any event, it was assumed so quietly and naturally that he accepted it as a matter of course.

Since Lord Vignoles' marriage with an American heiress the atmosphere of his establishments had grown very transatlantic; so much so, indeed, that someone had dubbed the house in Cadogan Gardens "The Millionaires' Meeting House," and another wit (unknown) had referred to his place in Norfolk as "The Week-end Synagogue." Furthermore, Lady Vignoles had a weakness for "odd people," for which reason the presence of a guest hitherto socially unknown occasioned no comment.

Mr. Pepys having brought in Zoe Oppner, everyone assumed the late arrival to be one of Lady Vignoles' odd people, and everyone was pleasantly surprised to find him such a charming companion.

Zoe Oppner, for her part, became so utterly absorbed in his conversation that her cousin grew seriously alarmed. Zoe was notoriously eccentric, and, her cousin did not doubt, even capable of forming an attachment for a policeman.

In fact, Lady Vignoles, who was wearing the historic Lyrpa Diamond—her father's wedding-present—was so concerned that she had entirely lost track of the general conversation, which, from the great gem, had drifted automatically into criminology.

Zimmermann was citing the famous case of the Kimberley mail robbery in '83.

"That was a big haul," he said. "Twelve thousand pounds' worth of rough diamonds!"

"Fifteen!" corrected Bernard Megger, director of a world-famed mining syndicate.

"Oh, was it fifteen?" continued Zimmermann. "No doubt you are correct. Were you in Africa in '83?"

"No," replied Megger; "I was in 'Frisco till the autumn of '85, but I remember the affair. Three men were captured—one dead. The fourth—Isaac Jacobsen—got away, and with the booty!"

"Never traced, I believe!" asked the novelist.

"Never," confirmed Megger; "neither the man nor the diamonds."

"It was a big thing, certainly," came Vignoles' voice; "but this Séverac Bablon has beaten all records in that line!"

The remark afforded his wife an opportunity, for which she had sought, to break off the too confidential *tête-à-tête* between Zoe and the detective.

"Zoe," she said, "surely Mr. Pepys can tell us something about this mysterious Séverac Bablon?"

"Oh, yes!" replied Zoe. "He has been telling me! He knows quite a lot about him!"

Now, the dinner-table topic all over London was the mystery of Séverac Bablon, and Lady Vignoles' party was not exceptional in this respect. It had already been several times referred to, and at Miss Oppner's words all eyes were directed towards the handsome stranger, who bore this scrutiny with such smiling composure.

"I cannot go into particulars, Lady Vignoles," he said; "but, as you are aware, I have a kind of official connection with the matter!"

This was beautifully mysterious, and everyone became intensely interested.

"Of such facts as have come to light you all know as much as I, but there is a certain theory which seems to have occurred to no one." He paused impressively, throwing a glance around the table. "What is the notable point in regard to the victims of Séverac Bablon?"

"They are Jews—or of Jewish extraction," said Zoe Oppner promptly. "Pa has noticed that! He's taken considerable interest since his mills were burned in Ontario!"

"And what is the conclusion?"

"That he hates Jews!" snapped Bernard Megger hotly. "That he has a deadly hatred of all the race!"

"You think so?" said Pepys softly, and turned his eyes upon the gross, empurpled face of the speaker. "It has not occurred to you that he might himself be a Jew?"

That theory was so new to them that it was received in silent astonishment. Lady Vignoles, though her mother was Irish, had a marked leaning towards her father's people, and, as was usually the case, that ancient race was fairly represented at her dinner-table. Lord Vignoles, on the contrary, was not fond of his wife's Semitic friends—in fact, was ashamed of them; and he accordingly felt the present conversation to be drifting in an unpleasant direction.

"Consider," resumed Pepys, before the host could think of any suitable remark, "that this man wields an enormous and far-reaching influence. No door is locked to him! From out of nowhere he can summon up numbers of willing servants, who obey him blindly, and return—whence they came!

"He would seem, then, to be served by high and low, and—a notable point—no one of his servants has yet betrayed him! His wealth clearly is enormous. He invites the rich to give—as *he* gives—and if they decline he takes! For what purpose? That he may relieve the poor! No friend of the needy yet has suffered at the hands of Séverac Bablon."

"I believe that's a fact!" agreed Zoe Oppner. "He's my own parent, but Pa's real mean, I'll allow!"

Her words were greeted with laughter; but everyone was anxious to hear more from this man who spoke so confidently upon the topic of the hour.

"You may say," he continued, "that he is no more than a glorified Claude Duval, but might he not be one who sought to purge the Jewish name of the taint of greed—who forced those responsible for fostering that taint to disburse—who hated those mean of soul and loved those worthy of their ancient line? It is thus he would war! And the price of defeat would be—a felon's cell! Whom would he be—this man at enmity with all who have brought shame upon the Jewish race? Whom could he be, save a monarch with eight millions of subjects—a royal Jew? I say that such a man exists, and that Séverac Bablon, if not that man himself, is his chosen emissary!"

More and more rapidly he had spoken, in tones growing momentarily louder and more masterful. He burned with the enthusiasm of the specialist. Now, as he ceased, a long sigh arose from his listeners, who had hung breathless upon his words, and one lady whispered to her neighbour, "Is he something to do with the Secret Service?"

"Mr. Bernard Megger is wanted on the telephone!"

"How annoying!" ejaculated Lady Vignoles at this sudden interruption.

"Oh, I have said my say," laughed Pepys. "It is a pet theory of mine, that's all! I am alone in my belief, however, save for a writer in the *Gleaner*, who seems to share it."

---

# CHAPTER X

## KIMBERLEY

Dessert was being placed upon the table when Bernard Megger went out to the telephone, and a fairly general conversation upon the all-absorbing topic had sprung up when he returned—pale, flabby—a stricken man!

"Vignoles!" he said hoarsely. "A word with you."

The host, who did not care for the society of Mr. Megger, rose in some surprise and stepped aside with his wife's guest.

"I am a ruined man!" said Megger. "My chambers have been entered and my safe rifled!"

"But——" began Vignoles, in bewilderment.

"You do not understand!" snapped the other, "and I cannot explain. It is Séverac Bablon who has robbed me!"

"Séverac Bablon?"

"Yes! I must be off at once and learn exactly what has happened. I shall call at Scotland Yard——"

"*Ssh!*" whispered Vignoles. "There is no need for that! The man speaking to Miss Oppner there is Detective-Inspector Pepys!"

"Detective-Inspector Pepys! But what——"

"Never mind now, Megger; he is—that's the point. I'll bring him into the billiard-room. No doubt he can arrange to accompany you."

Too perturbed in mind to wonder greatly at the presence of a police officer at Lord Vignoles' dinner-table, Bernard Megger strode hurriedly into the billiard-room, his obese body quivering with his suppressed emotions, and was almost immediately joined by his host, accompanied by Pepys. The latter began at once:

"I understand that your chambers have been burgled by Séverac Bablon? By a curious instance of what literary critics term the long arm of coincidence I am in charge of the Séverac Bablon case—I and Inspector Sheffield."

"Before we go any further," said Megger rudely, "I don't share your tomfool ideas about the rogue!"

"No?" replied Pepys blandly. "Well, never mind. You must not suppose that, because of them, I am any less anxious to apprehend my man. Tell me, when was the burglary committed?"

"While Simons, my servant, was out on an errand. He returned to find the safe open—and empty. He immediately rang me up here."

"I believe you have already communicated with Scotland Yard in regard to Séverac Bablon?"

"Yes, I have. He has threatened me."

"In what form?"

"He endeavoured to extort money."

"By what means?"

Bernard Megger frowned, angrily. His flabby cheeks were twitching significantly.

"The point is," he said sharply, "that he has rifled my safe."

"Did it contain valuables?"

"Certainly."

"Diamonds?"

"It contained valuable papers."

"Where is the safe situated?"

"It is concealed, I thought securely, at the back of a bookcase. No one else holds a key. No one—not even my man—knows of its location. *Curse* Séverac Bablon! How, in Heaven's name, has he discovered it? I thought it secure from the fiend himself!"

Detective-Inspector Pepys scratched his chin thoughtfully, and Bernard Megger seemed to experience some difficulty in meeting the disconcerting gaze of his eyes.

"Possibly," said the inspector slowly, "an examination of your chambers may afford a clue. With your permission, Lord Vignoles, we will start at once."

"Certainly," said Vignoles. "I fear I have no car in readiness, so someone shall call a cab."

He moved to the bell.

"What's that, Jerry?" came a musical American voice. "Someone want a lift?"

The three men looked towards the door and saw there Zoe Oppner, a bewitching picture in her motor-furs.

"I was coming to say good-night," she explained. "I'm off to pick up Pa. But I've got time to run as far as Brighton and back, say. Nearly half an hour anyway!"

"You will not be called upon to create that amazing record, Zoe," responded Lord Vignoles. "Inspector Pepys and Mr. Megger are merely proceeding to Victoria Street."

"Is it something exciting?" asked Zoe, her bright eyes glancing from one to another of the three.

"Very!" replied the inspector. "A robbery at Mr. Megger's chambers!"

"Come right along!" said Zoe. "I'm glad I didn't miss this!" And the odd trio departed forthwith.

"Can I come in?" she asked, with characteristic disregard of the conventional, as her luxuriously appointed car pulled up in Victoria Street.

"I should greatly prefer that you did not, Miss Oppner!" said Pepys quietly.

"That's unkind! Why mayn't I?"

"I have a reason, believe me. If you will carry out your original plan and go on to join Mr. Oppner, it will be better."

She met the gaze of his earnest eyes frankly.

"All right!" she agreed. "But will you come to the hotel to-morrow, Inspector, and tell me all about it?"

"If you will inform no one of the appointment and arrange to be alone— yes, at eleven o'clock!"

Zoe's big eyes opened widely.

"You are mysterious!" she said; "but I shall expect you at eleven o'clock!"

"I shall be punctual!"

With that he turned and passed quickly through the door behind Bernard Megger. Up the stairs he ran and reached the first floor in time to see the other entering his chambers.

"Simons!" cried Megger, loudly.

But there was no reply.

"He must have gone at once to Scotland Yard," said Pepys. "Where is the safe?"

Megger switched on the light and unlocked a door on his immediate left. It gave access to a study. In the dim glow of the green shaded lamps the place looked quiet and reposeful. Everything was neatly arranged, as befits the sanctum of a business man. Nothing seemed out of place.

"There are no signs of burglars here!" said Pepys, in a surprised manner.

"Simons may have reclosed the safe door," replied Megger.

His voice trembled slightly.

Wheeling a chair across the thick carpet, he placed it by a tall, unglazed bookcase and mounted upon the seat.

"The safe is not open," he muttered excitedly.

And the man watching him saw that his puffy hand shook like a leaf in the breeze.

Removing a small oil-painting from the wall adjoining, he tore at his collar and produced a key attached to a thin chain about his neck. This he inserted in the cunning lock which the picture served to conceal. The next moment a hoarse cry escaped him.

"It hasn't been opened at all!" he shouted.

Snatching at the cord of a hanging lamp, he wildly hurled books about the floor and directed the light into a cavity that now had revealed itself. The other observed him keenly.

"Are you certain *nothing* is gone?" he asked.

Megger plunged his hand inside and threw out several boxes and some bundles of legal-looking documents. Leaning yet farther forward, he touched a hidden spring that operated with a sharp *click*.

"*That* hasn't gone, Inspector!" he cried triumphantly, and held out a large envelope, sealed in several places.

His eyes were feverish. His features worked.

"You are wrong, Isaac Jacobsen!" rapped Pepys, and snatched the packet in a flash. "It has!"

The man on the chair lurched. Every speck of colour fled from his naturally florid face, leaving it a dull, neutral grey. He threw out one hand to steady himself, and with the other plunged to his hip.

"Both up!" ordered Pepys crisply.

And Mr. Bernard Megger found himself looking down a revolver barrel that pointed accurately between his twitching eyebrows, nor wavered one hair's breadth!

Unsteadily he raised his arms—staring, with dilated pupils, at this master of consummate craft.

"It is by such acts of fatuity as your careful preservation of these proofs of identity," came in ironic tones, "that all rogues are bowled out, Jacobsen! I will admit that you had them well hidden. It was good of you to find them. I had despaired of doing so myself!" With that the speaker backed towards the open door.

"Inspector Pepys!" gasped Bernard Megger, swallowing between the words, "I shall remember you!"

"You will be wasting grey matter!" replied the man addressed, and was gone.

Megger, dropping heavily into the chair, saw that the departing visitor had thrown a slip of pasteboard upon the carpet.

As the key turned in the lock, and the dim footsteps sounded upon the stair, he lurched unsteadily to his feet, and, stooping, picked up the card.

Simons, his man, returned half an hour later, having been detained in his favourite saloon by a chance acquaintance who had conceived a delirious passion for his society. He found his master locked in the study—with the key on the wrong side—and, furthermore, in the grip of apoplexy, with a crumpled visiting-card crushed in his clenched right hand.

--------

# CHAPTER XI

## MR. SANRACK VISITS THE HOTEL ASTORIA

Mr. J. J. Oppner and his daughter sat at breakfast the next morning at the Astoria. Oppner was deeply interested in the *Gleaner*.

"Zoe," he said suddenly. "This is junk—joss—ponk!"

His voice had a tone quality which suggested that it had passed through hot sand.

Zoe looked up. Zoe Oppner was said to be the prettiest girl in the United States. Allowing that discount necessary in the case of John Jacob Oppner's daughter, Zoe still was undeniably very pretty indeed. She looked charming this morning in a loose wrap from Paris, which had cost rather more than an ordinary, fairly well-to-do young lady, residing, say, at Hampstead, expends upon her entire toilette in twelve months.

"What's that, Pa?" she inquired.

"What but this Séverac Bablon business!"

Assisted by her father, she had diligently searched that morning through stacks of daily papers for news of the robbery in Victoria Street. But in vain.

"Guess it's a false alarm, Zoe!" Mr. Oppner had drawled, in his dusty fashion. "Some humorist got a big hustle on him last night. Like enough Mr. Megger was guyed by the same comic that sent *me* on a pie-chase!"

Zoe thought otherwise, preferring to believe that Inspector Pepys had suppressed the news; now she wondered if, after all, they had overlooked it.

"Is there something about Séverac Bablon in the paper?" she asked interestedly. "*I* can't find anything."

"Nope?" drawled Oppner. "Nope? H'm! Then what about all this front page, with Julius Rohscheimer sitting in his *pie*-jams and the Marquess of Evershed talking at him? Ain't that Séverac Bablon? Sure! Did you think that Julius found it good for his health to part up a cool hundred thou.? And look at Hague up in the corner—and Elschild in the other corner! There's only one way to open the cheque-books of either of them guys; with a gun!"

"Oh!" cried Zoe—"how exciting!"

"I'm with you," drawled her father. "It's as thrilling as having all your front teeth out."

"Do you mean, Pa, that this is something to do with the card——"

"There's me and Jesson to shell out yet. That's what I mean! He's raised two hundred thousand. I'm richer'n any of 'em and he'll mulct me on my Canadian investments for the balance of half a million! Or maybe he'll split it between me and Jesson and Hohsmann!"

"Oh!" said Zoe, "what a pity! And I was going to ask you to buy me two new hats!"

Her father looked at her long and earnestly.

"You haven't got any proper kind of balance where money is concerned, Zoe," he drawled. "Your brain pod ain't burstin' with financial genius. You don't seem to care worth a baked bean that I'm bein' fleeced of thousands! That hog Bablon cleaned me out a level million dollars when he burned the Runek Mills, and now I know, plain as if I saw him, he's got me booked for another pile! Where d'you suppose money comes from? D'you think I can grab out like a coin manipulator, and my hand comes back full of dollars?"

Zoe made no reply. She was staring, absently, over her father's head, into a dream-world. Had Mr. Oppner been endowed with the power to read from another's eyes, he would have found a startling story written in the beautiful book fringed by Zoe's dark lashes. She was thinking of Séverac Bablon; thinking of him, not as a felon, but as he had been depicted to her by the strange man whom she had met at Lord Vignoles'—the man who pursued him, yet condoned his sins.

Her father's sandy voice broke in upon her reverie:

"Where I'm tied up—same with Rohscheimer and the rest—I don't know this thief Bablon when I see him."

"No," said Zoe. "Of course."

Mr. Oppner stared. His daughter's attitude was oddly unemotional, wholly detached and impersonal.

"H'm!" he grunted dryly. "I've got to see Alden, the Agency boy, upstairs. I'll be pushing off."

He "pushed off."

Almost immediately afterwards, Zoe's maid entered. There was a gentleman to see her. He would not give his card.

"Show him into the next room," said Zoe, full of excitement, "and if Mr. Oppner comes back, tell him I am engaged."

She entered the cosy reception-room, feeling that she was about to be admitted behind the scenes, and, woman-like, delightfully curious. A moment later, her visitor arrived.

"I have kept my promise, Miss Oppner!"

She turned, to greet him—and a little, quick cry escaped her.

For this was not Detective-Inspector Pepys who stood, smiling, in the doorway!

It was a man who was, or who seemed to be, taller than he; a slim man, having but one thing in common with the detective: his black morning-coat fitted him as perfectly as the dress-coat had fitted the inspector. An irreproachably attired man is a greater rarity than most people realise; and Zoe Oppner wondered why, even in that moment of amazement, she noted this fact.

Her visitor was singularly handsome. She knew, instantly, that she had never seen one so handsome before. He was of a puzzling type, wholly unlike any European she had met, though no darker of complexion than many Americans. With his waving black hair, extraordinarily perfect features, and the light of conscious power in his large eyes, he awoke something within her that was half memory—yet not wholly so.

She was vaguely afraid, but strongly attracted towards this mysterious stranger.

"But," she said, staring the while as one fascinated, "you—are not Inspector Pepys!"

"True!" he answered smilingly. "I am not Inspector Pepys; nor is there any such person!"

The voice was different, yet somehow reminiscent. Only now, a faint, indefinable accent had crept into it.

"What do you mean?"

Zoe, at the idea that she had been imposed upon, grew regally indignant. She was a lovely woman, and accustomed to the homage which mankind pays to beauty. Her naturally frank, laughter-loving nature made her a charming companion; but she could be distant, scornful—could crush the most presumptuous with a glance of her eyes.

Now she looked at her strange visitor with frigid dignity, and he merely smiled amusedly, as one smiles at a pretty child.

"Be good enough to explain yourself. If you dared to impose upon Lady Vignoles last night—if you are not really a detective—what are you?"

"That question would take too long to answer, Miss Oppner!"

"I demand an answer! Who are you?"

"That is another question," replied the stranger, in his soft, musical voice, "and I will try to answer it. At dinner last night I told you of a man whose fathers saw the Great Pyramid built, whose race was old when that pyramid was new. I told you of an unbroken line of kings—of kings who wore no crowns, whose throne was lost in the long ago."

She closed and re-opened her right hand nervously, and a new light came into her eyes. His words had touched again, as the night before, the hidden deeps of her nature, quickening into life the mysticism that lay there. She would have spoken, but he quietly motioned her to silence—and she was silent.

"I said that the time approached when that ancient line again should claim place among the monarchies of the world. I said that millions of men and women, in every habitable quarter of the globe, owed allegiance to that man who was, by divine right, their king!"

His face lighted up with a wild enthusiasm. To the beautiful girl who listened, spell-bound, he seemed as one inspired.

"Upon his people lay a cloud—a tainting shadow grown black through the centuries. He must disperse it, proclaiming to the world that his was a noble people, a nation with a mighty soul! The evil came not from without but from within. The worst enemies of the Jews are the Jews. In attacking those enemies of his people, inevitably he would come into collision with many governments. But he would do them no wrong, save in showing them powerless to protect the traitors from his righteous wrath!"

For a long moment she watched him, and no words came to her. That this splendid man was mad flashed through her mind as a possible thing; but that thought she dismissed, and remained bewildered.

"Is it true?" she asked, in a pleading voice; "or are you jesting with me?"

He smiled, having resumed his habitual calm.

"It is true!" he answered. "Upon the word of a rogue—a thief—upon the honour of Séverac Bablon!"

Zoe started, yet she was not afraid; for something had told her almost from his entrance that this was he—the man whose name at that very hour glared from countless placards, upon a great part of the civilised world;

whose deeds at that moment were being babbled of in every tongue from Chinese to Italian.

"But, if you are that man, and——" She hesitated. "You are wrong, I am sure! Oh! indeed, truly, I think you are wrong! Not in your aims, but in making so many new enemies! You have placed yourself outside all laws! You may be arrested at any hour!"

"That phase of my campaign will pass. I shall meet the Ministers of all the Powers upon equality—as the plenipotentiary of eight million people! All that I have done will be forgotten in the light of what I *shall* do!"

"I cannot understand about last night. Your presence was an accident——"

He laughed softly.

"I knew that Lady Vignoles' party numbered fourteen. I caused your father to be detained. One of my friends—I will not name him—suggested a novel mode of seeking a guest: I caused Megger's man to be absent whilst another of my friends, imitating his speech, sent the telephone message! Is that accident?"

"It is——"

"Unworthy, you would say? The work of a common cracksman? But, by those lowly means I secured proof that Bernard Megger, director of the Uitland Rands Consolidated Mines Syndicate, and Isaac Jacobsen, the Kimberley mail robber, were one and the same! He has escaped the laws of England, but he cannot escape me!"

She shrank involuntarily, her now frightened eyes fixed upon the face of this man, whose patriotism, whose zeal, whose incredibly lofty purpose she did not, could not, doubt, but whose methods she could, not condone—by whose will her own father had suffered. Then, in a quickly imperious yet kindly manner, he placed both his hands upon her shoulders, looking, with earnest, searching eyes, deep into her own.

"What would you desire me to do that half a million pounds can compass?" he asked.

"Return it to those it belongs to, if you can, and, with any that you cannot return, endow homes by the shore for sick slum children!"

He moved his left hand, and she saw dully gleaming upon his finger, a great green stone, bearing a strange device. In some weird fashion it seemed to convey a message to her—intimate, convincing. Within those green depths there dwelt a mystery. She felt that the ring was incalculably old, and that its wearer must wield almost limitless power. It was an uncanny idea, but she lived to know that her instincts had not wholly misled her.

"It shall be done!" said Séverac Bablon. "And you will be my friend?"

"I will try!" whispered Zoe, "if you wish. But, oh, believe me! You are wrong! You are wrong! There is, there *must* be some better way!"

As he removed his hands from her shoulders she turned aside and glanced through the open window, seeing nothing of the panorama of London below, but seeing only a great throne, and upon it a regal figure, his head crowned with the ancient crown of the Jewish kings. When she turned again her father stood behind her. But Séverac Bablon was gone!

"Thought you had a visitor, Zoe?" said Mr. Oppner. "There's a gentleman here would like to have a look at him!"

He turned to a big, burly man, dressed in neat serge, who bowed awkwardly and immediately took a sharp look around the room. Mr. Oppner eyed his daughter with grim suspicion.

"Inspector Sheffield would like to ask you something!"

"Sorry to trouble you, miss," said the inspector, misinterpreting the sudden, strained look that had come into her eyes, and smiling in kindly fashion. "But I've been following a man all the morning, and I rather think he came into this hotel! Also—please excuse me if I'm wrong—I rather fancy he came up here!"

"What is he like—this—man?" she asked mechanically, looking away from the detective.

"This morning he was like the handsomest gentleman in Europe, miss! But he may have altered since I saw him last! He's the latest thing in quick-change artists I've met to date!"

"What do you want him for?"

Sheffield raised his eyebrows.

"He's Séverac Bablon!" he said simply. "Does your late visitor answer to the description?"

"My visitor was a gentleman who wanted funds for building a home for invalid children!"

"You're sure it wasn't our man, miss?"

("And you will be my friend" he had asked. "I will try," had been her promise.)

"I am quite sure my visitor was not a criminal of any kind!" she answered. "You have made a strange mistake!"

The inspector bowed and quitted the room immediately. Mr. Oppner stood for some moments watching his daughter—and then followed the officer. Zoe went to her room, and allowed her maid to dress her, without proposing a solitary alteration in the scheme. She was very preoccupied. In the lounge she found her father deep in conversation with a clean-shaven man who had the features and complexion of a Sioux, and wore a tweed suit which to British eyes must have appeared several sizes too large for him. His Stetson was tilted well to the rear of his skull, and he lay back smoking a black cheroot. This was Aloys X. Alden of Pinkerton's. Zoe hesitated. The conversation clearly was a business one.

And, at that moment, a tall figure appeared beside her.

Zoe drew a sharp breath—almost a breath of pain. She glanced toward the group of two in the distant corner. They were discussing, as she knew quite well, various plans for the apprehension of the man who had become a nightmare to certain capitalists. They were devising, or seeking to devise, schemes for penetrating the secret of his real identity—for peering beneath the mask of the real man.

And here, by her side, stood Séverac Bablon!

"Pray, pray go!" she whispered tremulously. "I thought you had left the hotel. For your own sake, if not for mine, you should have done so."

"But if it happens that I am staying here?"

"Please go! There—with my father—is a detective——"

"I know him well!" was the reply. Séverac Bablon's melodious voice was calm. He smiled serenely. "But, fortunately, he does not know me! My name, then, for the present, is Mr. Sanrack; and I have taken this risk—though believe me it is not so great as you deem it—because I have something more to say. I was interrupted by the arrival of Inspector Sheffield."

"He may come in at any moment!"

"Then, *I* shall go out! But first I wish to tell you that I consider it my duty to force your father's hand in regard to a large sum of money!"

Zoe's little foot tapped the floor nervously.

"How do you dare?" she said. "How do you dare to tell *me* such a thing?"

"I dare, because what I do is right and just," he resumed; "and because, although I know that its justice will be apparent to you, I am anxious to have your personal assurance upon that point."

"My assurance that I think you are right in robbing my father!"

"I could scarcely expect that; I certainly should not ask for it. But you know that despite enormous benefactions, the Jews as a race bear the stigma of cupidity and meanness. It is wholly undeserved. The sums annually devoted to charitable purposes, by such a family as the Elschilds—my very good friends—are truly stupendous. But the Elschilds do not seek the limelight. Mr. Rohscheimer, Baron Hague, Sir Leopold Jesson, Mr. Hohsmann—and your father, are celebrated only for their unscrupulous commercial methods in the formation of combines. They do not distribute their wealth. Is it not true?"

Zoe nodded. Vaguely, she felt indignant, but Séverac Bablon was entirely unanswerable. Then:

"Heavens!" she whispered—"here comes my father!"

It was true. Mr. Oppner and the detective were approaching.

"I wish to meet your father," whispered Séverac Bablon. "Remember, I am Mr. Sanrack!"

As he spoke, he watched her keenly. It was a crucial test, and both knew it. Zoe was slightly pale. She fully realised that to conform now to Séverac Bablon's wishes was tantamount to becoming a member of his organisation (which operated against her father!)—was to take a possibly irrevocable step in the dark.

Whilst in many respects she disagreed with Séverac Bablon's wildly unlawful methods, yet, knowing something of his exalted aims she could not—despite all—withhold her sympathy. In some strange fashion, the wishes of this fugitive from the law partook of the nature of commands. But she could have wished to be spared this trial.

Oppner came up.

"Oh, father," began Zoe, striving to veil her confusion, "I don't think you have met Mr. Sanrack before? This is my father, Mr. Sanrack—Mr. Alden."

The millionaire stared, ere nodding shortly. The detective showed no emotion whatever.

"There is something which I am particularly anxious to explain to you, Mr. Oppner," began Sanrack, having acknowledged the introductions with easy courtesy. "It has reference to Séverac Bablon!"

Zoe held her breath. Alden moved his cheroot from the left corner of his mouth to the right. Mr. Oppner wrinkled up his eyes and scrutinised the speaker with a blank astonishment.

"I hold no brief for Séverac Bablon," continued the fascinating voice.

"Nope?" drawled Oppner.

"His deeds must speak for themselves. But on behalf of an important financial group I have a proposition to make."

Mr. Oppner took a step forward.

"What group's that?"

"Shall I say, simply, the most influential in Europe?"

"The Elschilds?"

"If you consider them to be so, you may construe my words in that way."

"Mr. Antony Elschild has been pulling my leg with some fool proposition about whitewashing the millionaire, or something to that effect. It's always seemed to me he's got more money than sense. He's passed out a cheque to this *Gleaner* fund big enough to build a soap factory!"

"So has Mr. Rohscheimer, and so has Baron Hague!"

"I'm not laughin'! They were held up! Why they don't say so, straight out, is their business. Jesson and Hohsmann will part out next, I suppose, if it ain't me. But if I subscribe it will be because I had a gun screwed in my ear while I wrote the cheque!"

"That is what my friends so deeply lament!"

"It is, eh? Yep? They'd like to see me paperin' all the workhouses with ten-dollar bills, I reckon? Mr. Ransack, I've got better uses for my money. It ain't my line of business buyin' caviare for loafers, and I don't consider it's up to me to buy airships for Great Britain! When you see me start in buyin' airships it's time to smother me! It means I'm too old and silly to be trusted with money!"

"My friends and myself—for I take a keen interest in everything appertaining to the Jewish nation—are anxious to save you from the ignominy of being compelled to subscribe!"

"That's thoughtful! Can your friends and yourself find any reason why a United States citizen should buy airships for England? If I got a rush of dollars to the head and was anxious to be bled of half a million, I might as well buy submarines for China, for all the good it'd do me!"

"On the contrary! So far as my knowledge goes you derive no part of your income from China, whereas your interests throughout Greater Britain are extensive. Thus, by becoming a subscriber, you would be indirectly protecting yourself, in addition to establishing a reputation which, speaking sordidly, would be of inestimable value to you throughout the British dominions."

Mr. Oppner nodded.

"It's good of you to drop in and deputise for my Dutch uncle!" he said. "Though no more than I might expect from a friend of my daughter's. But your arguments strike me as the foolishest I ever heard out of any man's mouth. As an old advertiser, I reckon your proposition ain't worth a rat's whiskers!"

Mr. Sanrack smiled. Alden was closely observing him.

"You are quite entitled to your opinion. My friends are anxious to learn if there be any purely philanthropic cause you would prefer to support. The mere interest on your capital, Mr. Oppner, is more than you can ever hope to spend, however lavish your mode of living."

"Thanks," drawled Oppner. "For a brand-new acquaintance you're nice and chatty and confidential. Your friends are such experts at spending their own money that it's not surprisin' they'd like to teach me a thing or two. But during the last forty years I haven't found any cause better worthy of support than my own. Give my love to Mr. Elschild. Good morning!"

He moved off, with the stoical Alden.

"You see," said Séverac Bablon to Zoe, who lingered, "your father is impervious to the demands of Charity!"

"Is that why you did this? Were you anxious to bring out Pa's meanness as a sort of excuse for what you contemplate?"

"Partly, that was my motive. A demand upon an American citizen to found a British air fleet is extravagant—in a sense, absurd. But I was anxious to offer Mr. Oppner one more opportunity of distributing some of the vast sum which he has locked up for his own amusement—financial chess."

"You have placed me in an impossible situation."

"Why? If you consider me to be what I have been accused of being—a thief—an incendiary—an iconoclast—denounce me—to whom you will! At any time I will see you, and any friend you may care to bring, be it Inspector Sheffield of New Scotland Yard, at Laurel Cottage, Dulwich Village. I impose no yoke upon you that you cannot shake off!"

But as Zoe Oppner looked into the great luminous eyes she knew that he had imposed upon her the yoke of a mysterious sovereignty.

From the foyer came a sound, unfamiliar enough in the Astoria—the sound of someone whistling. Even as Zoe started, wondering if she could trust her ears, Séverac Bablon took both her hands, in the impulsive and strangely imperious way she knew.

"Good-bye," he said. "Perhaps I am wrong and you are right. Time will reveal that. If you ever wish to see me, you know where I may be found. Good-bye!"

He turned abruptly and ascended the stairs. He had but just disappeared when Inspector Sheffield entered!

Zoe felt that her face turned pale; but she bravely smiled as the Scotland Yard man approached her.

"You see, I am back again, Miss Oppner! Do you know if Mr. Oppner has gone out?"

"I am not sure. But I think he went out with Mr. Alden."

Sheffield's face clouded. This employment of a private detective was a sore point with the Inspector. It seemed strangely like a slight upon the official service. Not that Sheffield was on bad terms with Alden. He was too keen a diplomat for that. But he went in hourly dread that the Pinkerton man would forestall Scotland Yard.

To Sheffield it appeared impossible that Séverac Bablon could much longer evade arrest. In fact, it was incomprehensible to him how this elusive character had thus far remained at large. Slowly, and by painful degrees, Sheffield was learning that Séverac Bablon's organisation was more elaborate and far-reaching, and embraced more highly placed persons, than at one time he could have credited.

It would appear that there were Government officials in the group which surrounded this man, pointing to ramifications which sometimes the detective despaired of following. News from Paris, received only that morning, would seem to indicate that a similar state of affairs prevailed in the French capital. With whom, Sheffield asked himself, had he to deal? Who *was* Séverac Bablon? That he was in some way associated with Jewish people and Jewish interests the Yard man was convinced. But he could not determine, to his own satisfaction, if Séverac Bablon's activities were inimical to Juda or otherwise. It was a bewildering case.

"I hope Mr. Oppner hasn't gone out," he said, after a pause. "I particularly wanted to see him again."

"Is there some new clue?" asked Zoe eagerly.

Inspector Sheffield was nonplussed. Here was the daughter of J. J. Oppner, the last girl in the world whom any sane man would suspect of complicity in the Séverac Bablon outrages; yet, for reasons of his own, Sheffield wondered if she were as wholly ignorant of Bablon's identity as the rest of the world. He distrusted everyone. He had said to Detective-Sergeant Harborne, who was associated with him in the case, "Where Séverac Bablon is concerned, I wouldn't trust the Lord Mayor of London—no, nor the Archbishop of Canterbury."

Accordingly, he replied, "I think not, Miss Oppner. I'll just run upstairs and see if there's anybody about."

# CHAPTER XII

## LOVE, LUCRE AND MR. ALDEN

Zoe was waiting for Lady Mary Evershed. Lady Mary was late—an unremarkable circumstance, since Lady Mary was a woman, and less remarkable than ordinarily for the reason that Lady Mary had met Sir Richard Haredale on the way. At the time she should have been at the Astoria she was pacing slowly through St. James's Park, beside Haredale.

"My position is becoming impossible, Mary," he said, with painful distinctness. "Every day seems to see the time more distant, instead of nearer, when I can say good-bye to Mr. Julius Rohscheimer. My situation is little better than that of his secretary. By hard work, and it *is* hard work to act as Rohscheimer's social Virgil!—and by harder self-repression, I have struggled to earn enough to enable me to cry quits with the other rogues who preyed upon me, when—before I knew you. I've scarcely a shred of self-respect left, Mary!"

She looked down at the gravelled path and made no answer to his self-accusation.

"It is only my sense of humour that has saved me. But one day I shall break out! It is inevitable. I cannot pander for ever to Rohscheimer's social ambitions. Yet, if I show fight, he will break me! Saving the prospect—with a hale and hearty uncle intervening, and one of the best; may he live to be a hundred!—of the title, and all that goes with it, what have I to offer you, Mary? I am a man sailing under false colours. Practically, I am a salaried servant of Rohscheimer's. I don't actually draw my salary; but in recognition of my services in popularising his wife's entertainments, he keeps the vultures at bay! Bah! I despise myself!"

Mary looked up to him, tenderly reproachful.

"You silly boy!" she said. "There is nothing dishonourable in what you do!"

"Possibly not. But how would your father like to know of my position."

She lowered her eyes again.

"Is my father indebted to Julius Rohscheimer in any way, Dick?" she asked suddenly.

Haredale laughed nervously.

"Rohscheimer does not honour me with the whole of his confidence in financial matters," he replied. "It is a question Adeler would be better able to answer."

"Mr. Adeler, yes. What a singular man! Do you know, Dick, in spite of father's ideas respecting our old English aristocracy, I have sometimes felt, in Mr. Adeler's presence, that he, though a Jew, was a thousand times more of an aristocrat than I?"

Haredale glanced at her oddly.

"I have at times been conscious of a similar feeling!" he said. "No doubt one's instincts are true enough. Adeler's pedigree conceivably may go back to Jewish nobles who entertained monarchs in their marble palaces when the Eversheds and Haredales considered several streaks of red ochre an adequate costume for the most important functions."

He laughed boyishly at his own words.

"Oh, Dick!" said Mary. "How absurd of you. It is impossible to imagine an Evershed in such a condition. But yet, you are right. How singular that most people should overlook so obvious a fact; that there is a Jewish aristocracy, possibly one of the most ancient in the world."

"The Jews are an Eastern people," replied Haredale. "That is the fact which is generally overlooked. They are, excepting one, the most remarkable people in the modern world."

"Do you know," said the girl, unconsciously lowering her voice, "I have sometimes thought that Séverac Bablon was in some way connected——"

"Yes?"

"With the ancient history of the Jews!"

"What do you mean exactly?"

"I can hardly explain. But at the Rohscheimers, on the night of the ball, Séverac Bablon was masked, of course; yet it seemed to me——"

"Mary," interrupted Haredale, "don't tell me that you believe the romantic stories circulating about the man!"

"What stories, Dick?"

"Why, about his holding the Seal of Suleyman, whatever that may be——"

"But Mrs. Elschild says he *does*!"

Haredale started.

"How can she possibly know?"

A flush tinged Lady Mary's clear complexion for a moment, and left it paler than it was wont to be. She despised a woman who could not preserve a secret (and therefore must have had a poor opinion of her sex), yet she had nearly allowed her own tongue to betray her. Whatever Mrs. Elschild had told her had been told in confidence, and under the seal of friendship.

"Perhaps she does not know. Someone may have told her."

"It's all over London," said Haredale; "in the clubs, everywhere! I wonder you have not heard it before. There seems to be an organised attempt to glorify this man, who, after all, is no more than an up-to-date highwayman. Someone has spread the absurd story that he is of Jewish royal blood; whereas the royal line of the Jews must have been extinct for untold generations!"

"Why must it? You have just said that the Jews are an Eastern people. And all Eastern peoples are subtle and secretive. I invariably lose half of my self-importance in Egypt, for instance. There is something in the eye of the meanest *fellah* which is painfully like patronage!"

Haredale shrugged his shoulders.

"What a thing it is," he said humorously, "to be born with black hair, flashing eyes and an olive skin! One can then be any kind of mountebank or robber, and yet rest assured of the ladies' homage."

They walked on in silence for awhile. Then—

"Heaven knows what happened to Rohscheimer," said Haredale abruptly, "to have frightened him into writing such a stupendous cheque! I may hear, later, but thus far he is too sore to touch upon the matter!"

"My father has visited him."

"At last—yes! Do you remember when Rohscheimer offered me five hundred pounds if I could induce the Marquess to come to dinner? Gad! He came perilously near to a just retribution that day! I think if I had been in uniform I should have run him through!"

"These extraordinary donations of course are the sequel to the mysterious business of the card and the unseen hand?"

"Certainly. Séverac Bablon is at the bottom of the whole business. I described the device, introducing two triangles, do you remember, which appeared on the cards, to a chap at the club who is rather a learned Orientalist, and he assured me that, so far as he could judge from my description, it corresponded with that of the supposed seal of Solomon. I was unable to remember part of the design, of course. But, at any rate, this merely goes to prove that Bablon is an accomplished showman."

"I am afraid I must be going, Dick. I have to meet Zoe Oppner."

"Let's go and find a cab, then. But it was so delightful to have you all to myself, Mary, if only for a very little while."

The boyishness had gone out of his voice again, and Lady Mary knew all too well of what he was thinking. She took his arm and pressed it hard.

"I don't think anyone was ever in such a dreadful position in the world before, Dick!" she declared. "To tolerate it seems impossible, seems wrong. But to defy Rohscheimer, with your affairs as they are, means—what does it mean, Dick?"

"I dare not think what it means, Mary," he replied. "Not when *you* are with me. But one day—soon, I am afraid—it will all be taken out of my hands. I shall tell Mr. Julius Rohscheimer exactly what I think of him, and there will be an end of the whole arrangement."

They said no more until the girl was entering the cab. Then:

"*I* understand, Dick," she whispered, "and nobody else knows, so try to be diplomatic for a little longer."

Holding her hand, he looked into her eyes. Then, without another word between them, the cab moved off, and Haredale stood looking after it until it was lost amid the traffic. He started to walk across to Park Lane.

At the Astoria Zoe was waiting patiently. But when, at last, Mary found herself in her friend's room, the gloomy companionship of the thoughts with which she had been alone since leaving Haredale, proved too grievous to be borne alone. She threw herself on to a cushioned settee, and her troubles found vent in tears.

"Mary, dear!" cried Zoe, all that was maternal protective in her nature, asserting itself. "Tell me all about it."

The unruly mop of her brown hair mingled with the gold of her friend's, and presently, between sobs, the story was told—an old, old story enough.

"He will have to resign his commission," she sobbed. "And then he will have to go abroad! Oh, Zoe! I know it must come soon. Even *I* cannot expect him, nor wish him to dance attendance on that odious Julius Rohscheimer for ever! And he makes so little headway."

Zoe's little foot beat a soft tatoo upon the carpet.

"I wonder—will there always be a Julius Rohscheimer for him to dance attendance upon!" she said softly.

Mary raised her tearful eyes.

"What do you mean, Zoe?"

"Has it never occurred to you that—Séverac Bablon will ultimately make a poor man of Rohscheimer?"

"Oh! I should not like to think that, because——"

"If he went that far, he might do the same for Pa. I can't believe that, Mary. Pa's awful mean, but after all his money is cleaner than Rohscheimer's."

Mary dried her eyes.

"I hardly know whether to regard that strange man, Séverac Bablon, as a friend or a foe," she said. "He certainly seems to confine his outrages to those who have plenty but object to spending it."

"Except on themselves! He's a friend right enough, Mary. I believe he is anxious to reveal all these rich people in a new light, to whitewash them. If only they would change their ideas and do some good with their money, I don't think they would be troubled any more by Séverac Bablon. You never hear of Mr. Elschild being robbed by him—nor any of the family suffering in any way."

"Mr. Elschild received one of the mysterious cards, and he has sent a big cheque to the *Gleaner* fund."

"He has to keep up appearances, Mary, don't you see? But it is certain that he sent the money quite voluntarily. He did not wait to be squeezed. I wish Pa would come to his senses. If, instead of spending a small fortune on private detectives, he would start to use his money for good, he would have no further need for the Pinkerton men. Certainly he would not be made to buy airships for England!"

A smile dawned upon Lady Mary's face.

"Isn't it preposterous!" she said. "The idea of raising money for such a purpose from people like Baron Hague!"

"Baron Hague left for Berlin this morning. We shall probably never know under what circumstances he issued his cheque for fifty thousand pounds! Doesn't it seem just awful, with all this money floating about, that poor Sir Richard is nearly stranded for quite a trifle!"

"Oh, it is dreadful! And I can see no way out."

"No," murmured Zoe. "Yet there must be a way."

She walked to the window, and stood looking out thoughtfully upon the Embankment far below.

What a strange, complex drama moved about her! It was impossible even to determine for what parts some of the players were cast. Where, she wondered, was Inspector Sheffield now? And where was Séverac Bablon? So far as she was aware, both were actually in the Astoria. There was something almost uncanny in the elusiveness of Séverac Bablon. His disdain of all attempts to compass his downfall betokened something more than bravado. He must *know* himself immune.

Why?

If what he had rather hinted than declared were true—and never for a moment did she doubt his sincerity—then his accomplices, his friends, his subjects (she knew not how to name them), must be numberless. Was she, herself, not of their ranks?

Of the thousands who moved beneath her, upon trams, in cabs, in cars, on foot, how many were servants of that mysterious master? It was fascinating, yet terrifying, this inside knowledge of a giant conspiracy, of which, at that moment, the civilised world was talking. Mary Evershed's voice broke in upon her musing:

"Come along, Zoe. We shall never be back in time for lunch if we don't hurry."

They descended in the lift and walked out to where Mr. Oppner's big car awaited them. A moment later, as the man turned out into the Strand, Sheard passed close by upon the pavement. He raised his hat to the two pretty travellers. Clearly, he was bound for the Astoria.

And a few yards further on, unobtrusively walking behind a very large German tourist, appeared the person of Mr. A. X. Alden.

"Why!" whispered Zoe. "I believe he is following Mr. Sheard."

Her surmise was correct. The astute Mr. Alden had found himself at a loss to account for some of the exclusive items respecting the doings of Séverac Bablon which latterly had been appearing in the *Gleaner*. By dint of judiciously oiling the tongue of a chatty compositor, he had learned that the unique copy was contributed by Mr. H. T. Sheard. Mr. Oppner had advised him to keep a close watch upon the movements of Mr. Antony Elschild. Although Alden found it hard to credit the idea that the great Elschild family should be in any way associated with the campaign of brigandage, Mr. Oppner was more open-minded.

Now Alden, too, was beginning to wonder. There seemed to be a friendship between Elschild and the pressman; and Sheard, from some source evidently unopen to his fellow copy-hunters, obtained much curious information anent Séverac Bablon. One of Alden's American colleagues accordingly was devoting some unobtrusive attention to whomsoever came and went at the Elschild establishment in Lombard Street, whilst Alden addressed himself to the task of shadowing Sheard.

When the latter walked into the lobby of the Astoria, Mr. Alden was not far away.

"Has Mr. Gale of New York arrived yet?" was the pressman's inquiry.

Yes. Mr. Gale of New York had arrived.

Upon learning which, Sheard seemed to hesitate, glancing about him as if suspicious of espionage. Mr. Alden, deeply engaged, or so it appeared, in selecting a cigar at the stall, was all ears—and through a mirror before which he had intentionally placed himself, he could watch Sheard's movements whilst standing with his back towards him.

At last Sheard took out his notebook and hastily scribbled something therein. Tearing out the leaf, he asked for an envelope, which the boy procured for him. With the closed book as a writing-pad, he addressed the envelope. Then, enclosing the note, carefully sealed up the message, and handed it to the boy, glancing about him the while with a palpable apprehension.

Finally, lighting a cigarette with an air of nonchalance but ill assumed, Sheard strolled out of the hotel.

He had not passed the door ere Alden was clamouring for an hotel envelope. The boy was just about to enter a lift as the detective darted across the lobby and entered with him. Short as the time at his disposal had been, Mr. Alden had scrawled some illegible initial followed by "Gale, Esq.," upon the envelope, and had stuck down the flap.

The boy quitted the lift on the fourth floor. So did Alden. One or two passengers joined at that landing, but the unsuspecting boy went on his way along the corridor, turned to the right and rapped on a door numbered 63.

"Come in," he was instructed.

He entered, tray in hand. A tanned and bearded gentleman who was busily engaged unpacking a large steamer trunk, looked up inquiringly.

"Gentleman couldn't wait, sir," said the boy, and proffered the message.

The bearded man took the envelope, drew his brows together in an endeavour to recognise the scrawly handwriting; failed, and tore the envelope open.

It was empty!

"See here, boy! What's the game?"

He threw the envelope on the floor beside him and stared hard at the page.

"Excuse me, sir"—the boy was frightened—"excuse me, sir; but I saw the gentleman put a note in!"

"Did you!" laughed the American, readily perceiving that whoever the joker might be the boy was innocent of complicity. "You mean, you thought you did! See here, what was he like?"

The boy described Sheard, and described him so aptly that he was recognised.

"That's Sheard," muttered the recipient of the empty envelope. "It's Sheard, sure! Right oh! I'll ring him up at the office in a minute and see what sort of game he's playing. Here boy, stick that in your pocket; you might make a descriptive writer, but you'll never shine at sleight of hand! You didn't watch that envelope half close enough!"

Thus, the man to whom the note was addressed. Let us glance at Mr. Alden again.

Having effected the substitution with the ease of a David Devant, he hastened to a quiet corner to inspect his haul. He was not unduly elated. He had been prompt and clever, but in justice to him, it must be admitted that he was a clever man. Therefore he regarded the incident merely as part of the day's work. His success wrought no quickening of the pulse.

In a little palmy balcony which overlooked the lobby he took the envelope from his pocket. It bore the inscription:

RADLEY GALE, ESQ.

Quietly, his cheroot stuck in a corner of his mouth, he opened it—tearing the end off as all Americans do. He pulled out the scribbled note, and read as follows:

"MY DEAR GALE,—Don't forget that we're expecting your wife and yourself along about 7. I will say no more as I rather think an impudent American detective (?) is going to purloin this note.

"SHEARD."

Mr. Alden carefully replaced the torn leaf in the envelope, and the envelope in his case. He rolled his smoke from the left corner of his mouth to the right, and, his hands thrust deep in his pockets, walked slowly downstairs. He was not offended. Mr. Aloys. X. Alden was a Stoic who had known for many years that he was not the only clever man in the world.

# CHAPTER XIII

## THE LISTENER

Sheard sat with both elbows resting upon his writing-table. A suburban quietude reigned about him, for the hour was long past midnight. Before him was spread out the final edition of the *Gleaner* and prominent upon the front page appeared:—

SIR LEOPOLD JESSON AND MR. HOHSMANN FALL INTO LINE

With a tact which was inspired by private information from a certain source, the *Gleaner* had pooh-poohed the story of the mysterious cards received by the guests at Julius Rohscheimer's. The story had leaked out, of course, but Sheard was in no way responsible for the leakage.

Frantically, representatives of the *Gleaner's* rivals had sought for confirmation from the lips of the victims; but, as had been foreseen by the astute Sheard, no confirmation was forthcoming. There had been an informal council held at the urgent request of Rohscheimer, whereat it had been decided that for the latter to appear, now, in the light of a victim of Séverac Bablon, would be for him to throw away such advantages as might accrue—to throw a potential peerage after his lost £100,000!

Baron Hague had been coerced into silence, and had left for Berlin without seeing a single newspaper man. Mr. Elschild had persisted that his donation was entirely a voluntary one. Jesson had been most urgent for placing the true facts before Scotland Yard, but had finally fallen in with Rohscheimer's wishes.

"You see, Jesson," the latter had argued, "I'll never get my money back. It's gone as completely as if I'd burnt it! All I've got to hope for is a peerage; and I'd lose that if I started crying."

"I agree," Antony Elschild had contributed, "Rohscheimer had suddenly become a popular hero! So that a title is all the return he is ever likely to get for his money. It is popularly expected that Hohsmann and yourself will also subscribe. You must remember that owing to the attitude of a section of the Press it is not generally believed that Séverac Bablon has anything to do with this burst of generosity!"

Jesson had muttered something about "the *Gleaner*," and a decision had been arrived at to organise a private campaign against Séverac Bablon whilst professing, publicly, that he was in no way concerned in the swelling of the *Gleaner* fund.

Now, Jesson and Hohsmann had both sent huge cheques to the paper, and interviews with the philanthropic and patriotic capitalists appeared upon the front page. Sheard had not done either interview.

Encouraged by their amazing donations, the general public was responding in an unheard-of manner to the *Gleaner's* appeal. The Marquess of Evershed had contributed a long personal letter, which was reproduced in the centre of the first page of every issue. The Imperialistic spirit ran rampant throughout Great Britain.

Meanwhile, Mr. Oppner's detectives were everywhere. Inspector Sheffield, C.I.D., was not idle. And Sheard found his position at times a dangerous one.

He stood up, walked to the grate, and knocked out his pipe. Having refilled and lighted it, he tiptoed upstairs, and from a convenient window surveyed the empty road. So far as he could judge, its emptiness was real enough. Yet on looking out a quarter of an hour earlier, he had detected, or thought he had detected, a lurking form under the trees some hundred yards beyond his gate.

His visit to the Astoria, the morning before, had been in response to an invitation from Séverac Bablon, but divining that he was closely watched, he had sent the message to Gale—an American friend whom he knew to have just arrived—which had fallen into the hands of Mr. Aloys. X. Alden. Sheard had actually had an appointment with Gale, and had rung him up later in the morning—gaining confirmation of his suspicions, in the form of Gale's story of the empty envelope.

Then, at night, his American friend had been followed to the house and followed back again to the hotel. This had been merely humorous; but to-night there existed more real cause of apprehension. Sheard had received a plain correspondence card, bearing the following, in a small neat hand:

"Do not bolt your front door. Expect me at about one o'clock A.M."

For a time it had been exciting, absorbingly interesting, to know himself behind the scenes of this mystery play which had all the world for an audience. But it was a situation of quite unique danger. Séverac Bablon was opposed to tremendous interests. Apart from the activity of the ordinary authorities, there were those in the field against this man of mystery to whom money, in furtherance of their end, was no object.

Sheard realised, at times—and these were uncomfortable times—that his strange acquaintance with Séverac Bablon quite conceivably might end in Brixton Prison.

Yet there are some respects wherein the copy-hunter and the scalp-hunter tally. The thrill of the New Journalism has enlisted in the ranks of the Fleet Street army some who, in a former age, must have sought their fortune with the less mighty weapon. A love of adventure was some part of the complement of Sheard; and now, suspecting that a Pinkerton man lurked in the neighbourhood, and uncertain if his wife slept, he awaited his visitor, with nerves tensely strung. But there was an exquisite delight tingling through his veins—an appreciation of his peril wholly pleasurable.

Faintly, he heard a key grate in the lock of the front door. The door was opened, and gently closed.

Sheard stood up.

Into the study walked Séverac Bablon.

He was perfectly attired, as usual; wore evening-dress, and a heavy fur-lined coat. His silk hat he held in his hand. As he stood within the doorway, where the rays from the shaded lamp failed to touch his features, he seemed, in the semi-light, a man more than humanly handsome.

"The house is watched," began Sheard—and broke off.

A shadow had showed, momentarily, upon the cream of the drawn casement-curtains. Someone was crouching on the lawn, under the study window.

"Did you see that?" jerked the pressman. "Somebody looked in! The curtain isn't quite drawn to at that corner."

"My dear Sheard"—Séverac Bablon's musical voice was untroubled by any trace of apprehension—"there is no occasion to worry! Mr. Aloys. X. Alden looked in!"

"But——"

"Had it been Inspector Sheffield there had been some cause for excitement. Inspector Sheffield, if I am rightly informed, holds a warrant for my arrest. Mr. Alden is an unofficial investigator."

"But he can call a constable!"

"Reflect, Sheard. If he calls a constable, what happens?"

"You are arrested!"

"Not so; but I will grant you that much for the sake of argument. To whom would the credit fall?"

"Patently, Mr. Alden."

"Wrong! You know that it is wrong! The official service would reap every gain! Believe me, Sheard, Mr. Alden will not reveal my presence here to a living soul! He may try to trap me when I leave, but there will be no clamouring on the door by members of the Metropolitan Police force, as you seemingly apprehend!"

Séverac Bablon threw himself into the big arm-chair, and lighted a cigarette—a yellow cigarette.

"The trick you played upon Alden yesterday was such as no man with a sense of humour could well have resisted," he said. "But it was indiscreet."

"I know."

"Suspicion pointed to you as the perpetrator of the card trick at Rohscheimer's. You must not run unnecessary risks."

"It was a thrilling moment for me, when I leant over to Miss Hohsmann, my right hand extended for the salt or something of the kind, and my left stretched behind her chair!"

"Jesson, of course, was looking in the opposite direction?"

"I selected a moment when he was talking to Lady Vignoles, and those shaded table lights helped me very much. I could just reach the table, and I intentionally touched Salome's hand with mine, in laying down the card."

"She actually saw your hand!"

"I fancy not. She felt my fingers touch hers, I think. She turned so quickly that Jesson turned, too, and just as she was taking the card up."

"Critical moment."

"Not in the least. My object would have been as well served if the card had gone no further. But my infernal sense of humour prompted me to make a bid for complicating the mystery. I dropped my arm, of course, as Jesson turned to her, and it never occurred to Salome that the hand which had placed the card beside her was any other than that of her neighbour on the left, Jesson. Before she could address him, or he address her, I inquired if I might examine the card. Jesson continued his conversation with Lady Vignoles, and the 'second notice' passed all around the table."

"Excellent! Do you know, Sheard, these childish little conjuring tricks help me immensely! Can you picture Julius Rohscheimer cowering throughout a whole night before the rod of a trousers-stretcher projecting from a wardrobe door!"

"Was that the solution of the 'patriotic' mystery?"

"Certainly. Adeler, who was concealed in the wardrobe, armed with the necessary written threats, made his escape directly Rohscheimer's cheque was in his hand—leaving the rod to mount guard whilst you got the announcement into print and induced the Marquess to pay an early morning visit."

Séverac Bablon's handsome face looked almost boyish as he related how the financier had been forced to play the part of a patriot. Sheard, watching him, found new matter for wonderment.

This was the man who claimed to command the destinies of eight million people—the man who claimed to wield the power of a Solomon. This was Séverac Bablon, the most inscrutably mysterious being who had ever sown wonderment throughout the continents, the man who juggled with vast fortunes as Cinquevalli juggles with billiard-balls! This was the man whose great velvety eyes could gleam with uncanny force, whose will could enthrall hypnotically, for whom the police of the world searched, for whose apprehension huge rewards were offered, whose abode was unknown, whose accomplices were unnumbered, to whom no door was locked, from whose all-seeing gaze no secret was secret!

It was difficult, all but impossible, to realise.

"Yet I am he," said the melodious voice.

Sheard started as though a viper had touched him. He stared at his visitor in wide-eyed amazement.

"Heavens! Was I thinking aloud?"

"Practically. Your mind was so intensely concentrated upon certain incidents in my career—see, your pipe is out—that, in a broad sense, I could hear you thinking!"

Sheard laughed dryly, and relighted his pipe. Séverac Bablon's trick of replying to unspoken questions was too singular to be forgotten lightly.

"Mr. Hohsmann is now of my friends," continued the strange visitor. "You received the paragraph? Ah! I see it appears in your later edition."

"But Jesson?"

"Sir Leopold can never be my friend, nor do I desire it. There is an incident in his career——You understand? I do not reproach him with it. It should never have been recalled to him had he held his purse-strings less tightly.

But it served as a lever. It was a poor one, for, though he does not know it, I would cast stones at no man. But it served. He has made his contribution. I begin to achieve something, Sheard. The *Times* has a leader in the press showing how the Jews are the backbone of British prosperity, and truer patriots than any whose fathers crossed with Norman William."

He ceased speaking, abruptly, and with his eyes, drew Sheard's attention again to the window. Since Séverac Bablon's arrival, indeed, the journalist had glanced thither often enough. But, now, he perceived something which made him wonder.

There was a street lamp at the corner of the road, and, his own table-lamp leaving the further window in shade, it was possible to detect the presence of anything immediately outside by its faint shadow.

Something round was pressed upon a corner of the lower pane.

Séverac Bablon stepped to the table and scribbled upon a sheet of paper:—

"He has some kind of portable telephonic arrangement designed for the purpose, attached to the glass. No doubt he can follow our conversation. He may attempt to hold me up as I leave the house. He cannot enter, of course, or we could arrest him on a charge of housebreaking! You have a back gate. If you will permit me to pass through your domestic offices and your garden, I will leave by that exit. Continue to talk for some minutes after I am gone. Do not fear that there is any evidence of my having been here. Alden can prove nothing."

Replacing the pencil on the tray:

"I want you to join me at a little supper on Wednesday evening," said Séverac Bablon. "Practically all our influential friends will be present——"

He ignored Sheard's head-shakes and expressive nods directed towards the window.

"There is an old house which I have rented for a time at Richmond. It is known as 'The Cedars,' and overlooks the Thames. The grounds are fairly extensive, and bordered by two very quiet roads. In fact, it is an ideal spot for my purpose. I will send you further particulars"—he glanced towards the window—"in writing. We meet there on Wednesday at nine-thirty. Can I rely upon you?"

"Yes," said Sheard, wondering at the other's indiscretion, "unless I wire you to the contrary. I might be unable to turn up at the last moment, of course."

"You are nervous!" Séverac Bablon smiled, and slipped from the room.

"On the contrary," said Sheard, addressing the window. "There is nothing I enjoy better than an evening in a haunted house!"

(Perhaps, he argued, Alden was not absolutely certain of his visitor's identity. He did not know at what point in the conversation the telephone device had come into action. It was a pity to waste words; he might as well endeavour to throw the eavesdropper off the scent, in addition to covering Séverac Bablon's retreat.)

"Let us hope, Professor," he resumed, with this laudable intention, "that the Society for Psychical Research will be the richer in knowledge for our experiment on Wednesday evening!"

Mr. Aloys. X. Alden, with his ear to the ingenious little "electric eavesdropper," experienced an unpleasant chill upon hearing the visitor within addressed as "Professor."

He had conceived the idea that Sheard—whom he strongly suspected, might hold interviews with the mysterious and elusive Séverac Bablon in the small hours of the morning, at his own house, when the rest of the household were retired.

Mr. Alden had watched for five nights when he knew the pressman to be at home. On four of them Sheard's light had been extinguished before midnight. To-night, the fifth, it had remained burning, and long vigilance had been rewarded.

A car had drawn up at some distance from the house, and its occupant had proceeded forward on foot. He had been admitted so rapidly that Alden had been unable to ascertain by whom. The car, too, had been driven off immediately. He had had no chance of taking the number; but was astute enough to know that in any event it would have availed him little, since, if the car were Bablon's the number would almost certainly be a false one.

For once in a way, Mr. Alden became excited. Whom could so late a visitor be, save one who wished to keep secret his visit? In attaching his eavesdropper he had clumsily raised his head above the level of the window-ledge, but he had hoped that this gross error of strategy had passed unnoticed. For a time he had failed to pick up the conversation until his ear became attuned to the subdued tone in which it was conducted. Thus, he had lost the key to its purport and had had to improvise one.

But, even so, words had passed which had amply confirmed his suspicions; so much so that, whilst he listened, all but breathlessly, he was devising a scheme for capturing Sheard's visitor, single-handed, as he left the house. Furthermore, he was devising a way out of the difficulty in the event of the captive proving to be another than Séverac Bablon.

The latter part of the duologue had puzzled him badly. The visitor seemed to have ceased talking altogether, and Sheard's remarks had in some inexplicable way drifted into quite a different channel. They appeared to appertain to what had preceded them but remotely. The relation seemed forced.

Still the visitor said nothing. Sheard continued to talk, and in upon the mind of the detective shone a light of inspiration.

He detached the cunning little instrument, crawled across the lawn and slunk out at the gate. Then he *ran* around to the rear of the house. A narrow lane there was, and into its black mouth he plunged without hesitation.

The gate of the tradesmen's entrance was unbolted.

Alden was perfectly familiar with the nightly customs of the Sheard establishment, and knew this to be irregular. He tilted his hat back and scratched his head reflectively.

Then, from somewhere down the road, on the other side of the house, came the sound of a curious whistle, an eerie minor whistle.

Like an Indian, Alden set off running. He rounded the corner as a car whirled into view five hundred yards further along, and from the next turning on the right. It stopped. One of its doors slammed.

It was off again. It had vanished.

Mr. Alden carefully extracted a cheroot from his case and lighted it with loving care.

---

# CHAPTER XIV

## ZOE DREAMS

If you know the Astoria, you will remember that all around the north-west side of the arcade-like structure, which opens on the Old Supper Room, the Rajah Suite, the Louis Ballroom, the Edwardian Banqueting Hall, and the Persian Lounge, are tiny cosy-corners. In one of these you may smoke your secluded cigar, cigarette or pipe, wholly aloof from the bustle, with its marked New Yorkist note, which characterises the more public apartments of the giant *caravanserai*.

There is a nicely shaded light, if you wish to read, or to write, at night. But you control this by a switch, conveniently placed, so that the darkness which aids reflection is also at your command. Then there is the window, opening right down to the floor, from which, if it please you, you may study the activity of the roofless ant-hill beneath, the restless febrility of West End London.

To such a nook Zoe Oppner retired, after a dinner but little enjoyed in solitary splendour amid the gaiety of one of the public dining-rooms. Her father had been called away by some mysterious business, too late in the evening for her to make other arrangements. So she had descended and dined, a charming, but lonely figure, at the little corner table.

In some strange way, she had more than half anticipated that Séverac Bablon would be there. But, although there were a number of people present whom she knew, the audacious Mr. Sanrack was not one of them.

Zoe had nodded to a number of acquaintances, but had not encouraged any of them to disturb her solitude. The long and tiresome meal dealt with, she had fled to the nook I have mentioned, and, with an Egyptian cigarette between her lips, lay back watching, from the perfumed darkness, the lights of London below.

The idea of calling upon Mary Evershed had occurred to her. Then she had remembered that Mary was at some semi-official function of her uncle's, Mr. Belford's. Sheila Vignoles would be at home, but Zoe began to feel too deliciously lazy to think seriously of driving even so short a distance.

In a big, cane lounge-chair packed with cushions she curled up luxuriously and began to reflect.

Her reflections, it is needless to say, centred around Séverac Bablon. Why, she asked herself, despite his deeds, did she admire and respect him? Her mind refused to face the problem, but she felt a hot blush rise to her cheeks. She was a traitor to her father; she could not deny it. But at any rate she was a frank traitor, if such a state be possible. Only that morning she had explained her position to him.

"Séverac Bablon," she had maintained, "only makes you rich men do what you ought to do with some of your money! Even if the object weren't a good one, even were it a ridiculous one, like making Dutchmen and Americans buy British airships, it does make you *spend* something. And that's a change!"

Mr. Oppner was used to these outspoken critcisms from his daughter. He had smiled grimly, wryly.

"I guess," had been his comment, "you'd stand up for the Bablon man, then, if he ever came your way?"

"Sure!" Zoe had cried. "You spend too much on me, and on Pinkertons, and not enough on people who really want it."

"You ought to join the staff of the *Gleaner*, Zoe! They specialise in that brand of junk, and they're in the popular market at the moment, too. They'll win the next election hands down, I'm told."

"Why don't you start a fund for Canadian emigrants?" Zoe had proceeded. "You've made a heap of money out of Canada. Then you wouldn't have to buy any airships, maybe!"

"I don't have to! No Roman Emperor was watched closer'n me! If that guy gets me held up he's earnin' his money! Zoe, you're a durned unnatural daughter!"

The thought of that conversation made her smile. To her it seemed so ridiculous that her father should guard his expenditure like one who has but a few dollars between himself and starvation. The gold fever was an incomprehensible disease to the daughter of the man who was more savagely bitten with it than almost any other living plutocrat.

Musing upon these matters, Zoe slept, and dreamed.

She dreamed that she stood in the gateway of an ancient city, amid a throng of people attired in the picturesque garb of the East. About her, the city was *en fête*. Before her stretched the desert, an undulating ocean of greyness, a dry ocean parched by a merciless sun.

Barbaric music sounded; the clashing of cymbals and quiver of strange instruments rendering it unlike any music she had ever heard. A procession was issuing from the gateway with much pomp. There were venerable, white-bearded priests, and there were girls, too, arrayed in festive garb, their hair bedecked with flowers. Their gay ranks, amid which the slow-pacing patriarchs struck a sombre note, passed out across the sands.

They were met by what seemed to be the advance guard of a great army. A man whose golden armour glittered hotly in the blazing sun descended from a chariot to receive them.

Then, amid music and shouting and the beating of drums, the procession returned, surrounding the chariot in which the golden one rode. It was filled to the brim with flowers.

As it passed in at the gate, the occupant stooped, took up a huge lily and threw it to Zoe. His eyes met hers. And, amid that panoply of long-ago, she recognised Séverac Bablon.

She dreamed on.

She lay in a huge temple, prone upon its marble floor, in the shadow of a pillar curiously carven. The lily lay beside her. Two men stood upon the other side of the pillar. She was invisible from where they were, and in low voices they spoke together, and Zoe listened.

"It overlooks the river," said one. "Two sides of the garden are on streets as lonely as the middle of the Atlantic. A narrow lane joins and runs right down the back. We want six or eight men, as well as you and I."

"What," inquired the other (his voice seemed strangely familiar), "is the matter with Scotland Yard?"

A moment's silence followed. Then:

"I didn't want to call them in. Largely, I'm out for reputation."

"Mostly," came a drawling reply, "I'm out for business!"

A veil seemed to have taken the place of the carven pillar, a thin, dream-veil. Although, in her curious mental state, Zoe could not know it, this was the veil which separated dreamland from reality.

"Martin can come with us. The other two boys will have to hang on to the tails of Mr. Elschild and Sheard. We mustn't neglect the rest of the programme because this item looks like a top-liner. I asked Sullivan if he could draft me half-a-dozen smart boys for Wednesday evening, and he said yep."

"More expense! What do you want to go and get men from a private detective agency for, when there's official police whose business it is to do it for nothing?"

"I thought there'd be people there, maybe, with big names. If we're in charge we can hush up what we like. If Scotland Yard had the job in hand there'd be a big scandal."

"You weren't thinkin' of that so much as huggin' all the credit! This blame man'll ruin me anyway. I can see it. What have you found out about this house?"

"It's called 'The Cedars' and it fronts on J—— Road. It's just been leased to a Dr. Ignatius Phillips, who's supposed to be a brain specialist. I've weighed up every inch of ground and my plan's this: Two boys come along directly after dusk, and take up their posts behind the hedge of the back lane; ten minutes after, two more make themselves scarce on the west side and two more on the towing-path. There's a thick clump of trees with some railings around, right opposite the door. You and I will hide there with Martin. We'll see who goes in. There's just a short, crescent-shaped drive, and only a low hedge. When everybody has arrived, *we* march up to the front door. As soon as it's opened, in we go, a whole crush of us! The house will be surrounded——"

"It sounds a bit on the dangerous side!"

"There'll be plenty of us—four or five."

"Make it six. He's got such a crowd of accomplices!"

"Six of us, then——"

"I wish you'd let Scotland Yard take it in hand."

"As you please. It's for you to say. But they have made so many blunders——"

"You're right! Hang the expense! I'll see to this business myself!"

"Then we shall want rather more men than I'd arranged for. Suppose we go and ring up Sullivan's?"

Zoe was wide awake now. A door shut. She sat up with a start. The darkness was redolent of strong tobacco-smoke, the smoke of a cheroot. She realised, instantly, what had happened—

Her father and Alden had entered the little room for an undisturbed chat and had not troubled to switch the light on. Many people like to talk in the dark; J.J. Oppner was one of them. Hidden amid the cushions of the big chair, she had not been seen. Since they had found the room in darkness, her presence had not been suspected. And what had she thus overheard?

A plot to capture Séverac Bablon!

Now, indeed, she was face to face with the hard facts of her situation. What should she do? What *could* she do?

He must be warned. It was impossible to think of seeing him a prisoner— seeing him in the dock like a common felon. It was impossible to think of meeting his eyes, his grave, luminous eyes, and reading reproach there!

But how should she act? This was Tuesday, and they had spoken of Wednesday as the day when the attempt was to be made. If only she had a confidant! It was so hard to come, unaided, to a decision respecting the right course to follow.

Laurel Cottage, Dulwich Village, that was the address which he had confided to her. But how should she get there? To go in the car was tantamount to taking the chauffeur into her confidence. She must go, then, in a cab.

Zoe was a member of that branch of American society which laughs at the theory of chaperons. There was nothing to prevent her going where she pleased, when she pleased, and how she pleased. Her mind, then, was made up very quickly.

She ran to her room, and without troubling her maid, quickly changed into a dark tweed costume and put on one of those simple, apparently untrimmed hats which the masculine mind values at about three-and-nine, but which actually cost as much as a masculine dress suit.

Fearful of meeting her father in the lifts, she went down by the stair, and slipped out of the hotel unnoticed.

"A cab, madam?"

She nodded. Then, just as the man raised his whistle, she shook her head.

"No thanks," she said. "I think I'll walk."

She passed out across the courtyard and mingled with the stream of pedestrians. Right at the beginning of her adventure she had nearly blundered. She laughed, with a certain glee. It was novel and exhilarating, this conspiracy against the powers that be. There was something that appealed to the adventurous within her in thus being under the necessity of covering her tracks.

Certainly, she was a novice. It would never have done to lay a trail right from the hotel door to Laurel Cottage.

She walked into Charing Cross Station and approached the driver of the first vacant taxi that offered.

"I want to go to Dulwich Village."

The man pulled a wry face. If he undertook that journey it would mean that he would in all probability have to run back empty, and then he would miss the theatre people.

"Sorry, miss. But I don't think I've got enough petrol!"

"Oh, how tiresome."

The American accent, now suddenly pronounced, induced him to change his mind.

"Should you want me to bring you back, miss?"

"Sure! I don't want to be left there!"

"All right, miss. Jump in."

"But I thought you hadn't enough petrol?"

The man grinned.

"I didn't want to be stranded right out there with no chance of a fare, miss!" he confessed.

Zoe laughed, good-naturedly, and entered the cab.

The man set off, and soon Zoe found herself upon unfamiliar ground. Through slummish localities they passed, and through popular suburbs, where all the activity of the West End prevailed without its fascinating, cosmopolitan glitter.

Dulwich Village was reached at last, and the cab was drawn up on a corner bearing a signpost.

"Which house did you want, miss?"

"I want Laurel Cottage."

The taxi-man scratched his head.

"You see, some of the houses in the village aren't numbered," he said; "and I don't know this part very well. I never heard of Laurel Cottage. Any idea which way it lies?"

"Not the slightest. Do you think you could find out for me?"

A policeman was standing on the opposite corner, and, crossing, the taxi-man held some conversation with him. He returned very shortly.

"It's round at the back of the College buildings, miss," he reported.

Again the cab proceeded onward. This was a curiously lonely spot, more lonely than Zoe could have believed to exist within so short a distance from the ever-throbbing heart of London. She began to wish that she had shared her secret with another; that she had a companion. After all, how little, how very little, she knew of Séverac Bablon. With all her romantic and mystic qualities Zoe was at heart a shrewd American girl, and not one to be readily beguiled by any man, however fascinating. She was not afraid, but she admitted to herself that the expedition was compromising, if not dangerous. If she ever had occasion to come again, she would confide in Mary and come in her company.

"This road isn't paved, miss. I don't think I can get any further."

The cab, after jolting horribly, had come to a stand-still. Zoe got out.

"Is Laurel Cottage much farther on?"

"It stands all alone, on the left, about a hundred yards along."

"Thank you. Please wait here."

Zoe walked ahead. It was a very lonely spot. The cab had stopped before some partially-constructed houses. Beyond that lay vacant lots, on either side. In front, showed a clump of trees, and, at the back of them on a slight acclivity, a big house.

The night was fine but moonless. Save for the taxi-man and herself, it would seem that nothing moved anywhere about. She came up level with the trees. There was a kind of very small lodge among them, closely invested with ragged shrubs and overshadowed by heavier foliage.

Beyond, farther along the road, showed nothing but uninviting darkness, solitude and vacancy. This then must be the place.

Zoe peered between the bars of the gate. No light was anywhere to be seen. The house appeared to be deserted. Could the cabman have made a mistake or have been misinformed?

Zoe carried a little case, containing, amongst a number of other things, a tiny matchbox. She extracted and lighted a match. There was no breeze, or she must certainly have failed to accomplish the operation.

Shading the light with her gloved hands, she bent and examined some half-defaced white characters which adorned the top bar of the gate; by which means she made out the words:—

LAUREL COTTAGE

There had been no mistake, then. She opened the gate, and by a narrow, moss-grown path through the bushes, came to the door. All was still. It was impossible to suppose the place inhabited.

No bell was to be found, but an iron knocker hung upon the low door.

Zoe knocked.

The way in which the sound echoed through the little cottage almost frightened her. It seemed to point to emptiness. Surely Laurel Cottage must be unfurnished.

There was no reply, no sign of life.

She knocked again. She knocked a third time.

Then the stillness of the place, and the darkness of the long avenue away up where the trees met in a verdant arch, became intolerable. She turned and walked quickly out on to the road again.

---

# CHAPTER XV

## AT "THE CEDARS"

Zoe was nonplussed. She was unable to believe that this deserted place was the spot referred to by Séverac Bablon. She still clung to the idea that there must be some mistake, though she had the evidence of her own eyes that the cottage was called Laurel Cottage.

The notion of writing a note and slipping it through the letter-box came to her. But she remembered that there was no letter-box. Then, such a course might be dangerous.

She looked gratefully towards the beam of light from the cab lamps. The solitude was getting on her nerves. Yes, she determined, she *would* write a note, and put it under the door. She need not sign it.

With that determination, she returned to where the taxi-man waited.

"Find it all right, miss?"

"Yes, but there's no one at home. I want to write a note and I should like you to go and slip it under the door for me. It is so lonely there, it has made me feel quite nervous. I can mind the cab!"

The man smiled and touched his cap. Taxi-men are possessed of intuitions; and this one knew perfectly well that he had a good fare and one that would pay him well enough for his trouble.

"Certainly, miss, with pleasure."

"Have you a piece of paper and a pencil?"

The man tore a leaf from a notebook and handed Zoe a pencil. Using the book as a pad, she, by the light of the near-side lamp, wrote:

"Your meeting at The Cedars known to Mr. Alden. Don't go."

"It is such a tiny piece of paper," she said. "He—they may not see it."

"I believe I've got an envelope somewhere, miss. It's got the company's name and address printed on it, and it won't be extra clean, but——"

"Oh, thank you! If you could find it——"

It was found, and proved to be even more dirty than the man's words had indicated. Zoe enclosed the note, wetted a finger of her glove, and stuck down the lapel.

"Will you please put it under the door?"

"Yes, miss. Shan't be a minute."

He was absent but a few moments.

"Back to Charing Cross Station," directed Zoe, and got into the cab again.

She had done her best. But, throughout the whole of the journey to the Strand, her mind was occupied with dire possibilities. It almost alarmed her, this too keen interest which she found herself taking in the fortunes of Séverac Bablon.

At Charing Cross the taxi-man received a sovereign. It was more than double his fare. He knew, then, that his professional instincts had not misled him, but that he had been driving an American millionairess.

In the foyer of the Astoria, Mary Evershed was waiting, with Mrs. Wellington Lacey in stately attendance. Mary was simply radiant. She sprang forward to meet Zoe, both hands outstretched.

"Wherever have you been?" she cried.

"Picture show!" said Zoe, with composed mendacity, glancing at the aristocratic chaperon.

"I could not possibly wait until the morning," Mary ran on, her eyes sparkling with excitement. "I had to run along here straight from horrid, stuffy Downing Street to tell you. Dick has inherited a fortune."

"What!" said Zoe, and grasped both her friend's hands. "Inherited a fortune!"

"Well—not quite a fortune, perhaps—five thousand pounds."

And John Jacob Oppner's daughter, a real chum to the core, never even smiled. For she knew what five thousand pounds meant to these two, knew that it meant more than five *hundred* thousands meant to her; since it meant the difference between union and parting, between love and loss, meant that Sir Richard Haredale could now shake off the fetters that bound him, and look the world in the face.

"Oh, Mary," she said, and her pretty eyes were quite tearful. "How very, very glad I am! Isn't it just great! It sounds almost too good to be true! Come right upstairs and tell me all about it!"

In Zoe's cosy room the story was told, not a romantic one in its essentials, but romantic enough in its potential sequel. A remote aunt was the benefactress; and her death, news of which had been communicated to Sir Richard that evening, had enriched him by five thousand pounds and served to acquaint him, at its termination, with the existence of a relation whom he had never met and rarely heard of.

Mr. Oppner came in towards the close of the story, and offered dry congratulations in that singular voice which seemed to have been preserved, for generations, in sand.

"He ought to invest it," he said. "Runeks are a good thing."

"You see," explained Mary. "He hasn't actually got it yet, only the solicitor's letter. And he says he will be unable to believe in his good luck until the money is actually in the bank!"

"Never let money lie idle," preached Oppner. "Banks fatten on such foolishness. Look at Hague. Ain't *he* fat?"

Though it must have been imperceptible to another, Zoe detected, in her father's manner, a suppressed excitement; and augured from it a belief that the capture of Séverac Bablon was imminent.

However, when Mary was gone, Mr. Oppner said nothing of the matter which, doubtless, occupied his mind, and Zoe felt too guilty to broach the subject. They retired at last, without having mentioned the name of Séverac Bablon.

Zoe found sleep to be impossible, and lay reading until long past one o'clock. But when the book dropped from her hands, she slept soundly and dreamlessly.

In the morning she scanned her mail anxiously. But there was nothing to show that her warning had been received. Could it be that Séverac Bablon had suddenly deserted the cottage for some reason, and that he would to-night walk, blindly, into the trap prepared for him?

She was anxious to see her father. And his manner, at breakfast, but dimly veiled an evident exultation. He ate very little, leaving her at the table, with one of his dry though not unkindly apologies, to go off with the stoical Mr. Alden.

If only she had a friend in whom she might confide, whose advice she might seek. Zoe laughed a little to think how excited she was on behalf of Séverac Bablon and how placidly she surveyed the possibility of her father's being relieved of a huge sum of money.

"That's the worst of knowing Pa's so rich!" she mused philosophically.

The morning dragged wearily on. Noon came. Nothing and nobody interested Zoe. She went to be measured for a gown and could not support the tedium of the operation.

"Send someone to the Astoria to-morrow," she said. "I just can't stand here any longer."

In the afternoon she called upon Sheila Vignoles, but everyone, from Lord Vignoles to the butler, irritated her. She came away with a headache. With the falling of dusk, her condition grew all but insupportable. Her father had been absent all day. She had met no one who would be likely to know anything about the night's expedition.

She sat looking out from her window at the Embankment, where lights were now glowing, point after point, through the deepening gloom.

It was as she stood there, vainly wondering what was going forward, that her father, his spare figure enveloped in a big motor coat, his cap pulled down upon his brow, walked along Richmond High Street beside Mr. Alden.

"By the time we get there," said the latter, rolling the inevitable cheroot from one corner of his mouth to the other, "it will be dark enough for our purpose. It's a warm night, and dry, which is fortunate, and I've marked a place right opposite the gate where we can lie all snug until we're wanted."

"Can you rely on Sullivan's men?"

"He's sending eight of the best. At his office, this afternoon I went over a plan of the place with them. It's impossible to march a troop up to the house to reconnoitre. They know exactly what they've got to do. It will be covered all around. A cat won't be able to come out of The Cedars, sir, without being noted!"

"Yep. And when we march up to the door?"

"Directly it's opened," explained Alden patiently, "I'll *hold* it open! Then, in go five Sullivan men, Martin and you. But there'll still be a man covering every egress from the house. If anybody tries to get out there'll be someone to hold him up and to whistle for more help if it's needed."

"Seems all right," said Oppner; "if we don't get loaded up with lead. Is this place much further? We seem to have been walkin' up this blame hill for hours."

"See that white milestone? Well, the first gate is fifty yards beyond, on the right."

"Have the crowd arrived yet?"

"Some of them. They're drafting up singly and in couples. There ought to be four on the river side of the place by now, and Martin waiting somewhere around the front."

"Four to come, yet?"

"Yep. Two for the other gate of the drive, and two for the lane that leads down to the river."

They plodded on in silence. Abreast of the milestone, but without stopping, Alden whistled softly.

He was answered from somewhere among the trees bordering the left of the road.

"That's Martin!" he said. "Come on, Mr. Oppner, through this gap in the fence."

Mr. Oppner crawled, in undignified silence, through the gap indicated.

"You see," explained Alden's voice out of the gloom, "farther along are open rails and dense bushes. That's where we're going to watch from. We'll see every soul that comes up."

"You're stone sure it's to-night they arranged?"

Patiently, Alden replied: "Stone sure."

"Because," drawled Oppner, stumbling along in the darkness, "this is not in my line."

"*Sss!*" came from close at hand.

Mr. Oppner started.

"That you, Martin?" from Alden.

"Yes; no one has gone in yet. But a ground floor room is lighted up, and also the conservatory."

"Right."

There was a momentary faint gleam of light. Mr. Alden was consulting his electrically-lighted watch.

"Time they were all posted," he said. "Martin, do the rounds. Hustle!"

Martin was heard slipping away through the bushes. Then came silence. Oppner and Alden were now at a point directly opposite a gate, and in full view of the house. Many of the windows were illuminated.

"Does the lawn slope down to the towpath?" came Oppner's voice.

"Sure. There are men on the towpath."

Silence fell once more. From somewhere down the road, in the direction of Richmond, was wafted a faint tinkling sound. Oppner heard Alden moving.

"I'll have to leave you for a minute," said the detective. "Don't be scared if Martin comes back."

Without waiting for a reply, Alden departed. Mr. Oppner heard him brushing against the bushes in passing. Crouching there uncomfortably, and looking out across the road to the gateway of The Cedars, Oppner saw a singular thing, a thing that made him wonder.

He saw Alden run swiftly across from the gap in the fence by which they had entered their hiding-place, to the gate opposite. He saw him run in. Then he disappeared. Whilst Oppner was thrashing his brains for a solution to this man[oe]uvre, a faint rattling sound drew his gaze down the hill.

Someone was approaching on a bicycle!

Almost holding his breath, he watched. Nearer came the rider, and nearer. Immediately before the gate of The Cedars he dismounted. He was a telegraph messenger.

At that moment Alden came strolling out, smoking his cigar and pulling on a pair of gloves.

"Hullo, boy!" he said; his voice was clearly audible to the listening Oppner. "Got a wire for me? I've been expecting it all the evening."

The boy opened his wallet, but with some hesitation.

"Dr. Phillips," continued Alden, "that right?"

The boy hesitated no longer.

"Phillips, yes, sir," he said, and handed the telegram to Alden.

With a nonchalant air which excited Mr. Oppner's admiration, Alden walked to a lamp some little distance away, tore open the yellow envelope, and read the message.

"All right, boy," he said. "No reply. Here, catch!"

He tossed the boy a coin, and with a touch of genius which showed him to be a really great detective, halted a moment, scratched his chin, and as the boy again mounted his bicycle, re-entered the gate of The Cedars.

"That's real cute!" murmured Oppner.

The boy having ridden off, Alden slipped warily out on to the road, ran across, and was lost to view. Presently a rustling in the bushes told of his return to Oppner's side.

"It's from Sheard," whispered the detective. "Our man must have written him further particulars, same as he said he'd do. It just reads: 'Detained. S.' But it was handed in at Fleet Street, and I haven't any doubt who sent it."

"He's smart, is Sheard," said Mr. Oppner. "He smelled trouble, or maybe he got wise to us——"

"*Sss!*"

"That you, Martin?"—from Alden.

"All right. Everybody seems to be posted. They're all finely out of sight, too."

"Good. The newspaper man isn't coming. See me get the wire?"

"Yes. I wonder if the rest will come."

"Hope so. I don't want to have to open the ball, because until some visitors have gone in we haven't got any real evidence that Séverac Bablon is there himself."

"Quiet," said Martin.

A measured tread proclaimed itself, drew nearer, and a policeman passed their hiding-place. When the regular footsteps had died away again:

"If *he* knew who's leased The Cedars," murmured Alden, "he'd be a sergeant sooner than he expects."

Which remark was the last contributed by any of the party for some considerable time. Alden's description of the road before The Cedars as a lonely one was fully justified. From the time of Martin's return until that when the big car drove up and turned into the drive, not a solitary pedestrian passed their hiding-place.

A laggard moon sailed out from a cloud-bank and painted the road white as far as the eye could follow it. Then came a breeze from the river, to sing drearily through the trees. In the intervals, when the breeze was still, its absence seemed in some way, to stimulate the watchers' power of hearing, so that they could detect vague sounds which proceeded from the river. The creak of oars told of a late rower on the stream—a voice was wafted up to them, to be drowned in the sighing of the leaves set swaying by the new breeze.

Then came the car.

The whirr of the motor announced its coming from afar off; but, so swiftly did it travel, that it was upon them a moment later. As it swung around and on to the drive of The Cedars its number showed clearly.

"3509," said Martin. "That's Mr. Antony Elschild!"

"Gee!" said Oppner, and his sandy voice shook somewhat, perhaps owing to the chill of the breeze. "This is getting real exciting!"

The car was delayed some little time before the door of the house, then driven around, and out at the further gate of the drive. It returned by the way it had come, racing down the hill at something considerably exceeding the legal speed. The *thud-thud-thud* of the motor died away, and became inaudible.

"I'm glad the police aren't with us, and yet sorry," said Oppner. "This is a whole-hog conspiracy properly. No wonder he was so hard to catch; look at the class of people he's got in with him! Think of Elschild! Gee! There's goin' to be a scene in a minute."

"For the present," said Alden, "we'll make no move; we'll just sit tight. There's maybe a lot to arrive yet."

Just before the breeze came creeping up from the river again, *thud-thud-thud* was borne to their ears. Another car was approaching.

# CHAPTER XVI

## THE LAMP AND THE MASK

"10761," said Alden. "I wonder whose car that is."

None of the watchful trio had any idea. But whomever was within it, the second car performed exactly the same man[oe]uvres as the first, and, a few moments after its appearance, was lost to sight and hearing once more.

But a matter of seconds later, came the familiar *thud-thud-thud*; and a third car plunged up the hill and went swinging around the drive. Again, no one of the three was able to recognise the number. Out by the further gate of the drive it passed, turned, and flashed by them in the darkness, to go leaping down the slope.

"Three," said Alden. "I wonder if there's any more."

His tone was thoughtful.

"Say," began Mr. Oppner, "we'd better get on with it now, because——"

"I know," Alden interrupted, "there may be only one more to come? You're thinking that, after all those expected have arrived, there'll be trouble in getting the door to open?"

"I was thinking that, too," said Martin. "Maybe they're all arrived as it is; but we stand a still worse chance if we wait."

"Come on," said Mr. Oppner, with a rising excitement evident in his voice. "We know there's one big fish in the net, anyway!"

*Thud-thud-thud!*

"There's another car coming," cried Alden. "Hurry up, Mr. Oppner! This way. Mind your head through this broken part. We'll be on the steps as the car comes around the drive!"

They crept through the gap below and ran across the road, Oppner as actively as either of his companions. Already, the white beam of the headlight was cutting-the gloom, below, where the road was heavily bordered with trees.

"Just in time!"

Past the gate they ran, and pattered on to the drive. Behind them, a big car was just spinning past the gate. As it came leaping along the drive Alden ran up the four stone steps to the door and jammed his thumb hard against the bell button.

At the same moment, Martin whistled shrilly, three times.

Whereupon affairs began to move in meteoric fashion.

Several people came bundling out of the car. From the gloom all about it there sounded the scamper of hurrying feet.

The door was thrown open, and a blaze of light swept the steps.

Alden leapt over the threshold, pistol in hand, yelling at the same time:

"Follow me, boys!"

Like the swoop of heated play to a goal burst a human wave upon the steps. Oppner and Martin were swept irresistibly upward and inward. They were surrounded, penned in. Then:

"Break away, you goldarned idiot!" rose Alden's angry voice ahead.

The lights went out. The door slammed.

"Alden!" cried Mr. Oppner. "Alden!"

Someone pinioned him from behind.

"There's a mistake, you blamed ass!" he screamed. "I ain't one of 'em! Alden! Martin!"

A hand was pressed firmly over his mouth, and with veins swelling up and eyes starting from his head in impotent fury, Mr. Oppner was hustled forward through the darkness.

Around him a number of people seemed to be moving, and when he found his feet upon stairs, several unseen hands were outstretched to thrust him upward. The darkness was impenetrable.

Apparently the stair was uncarpeted, as likewise was the corridor along which he presently found himself proceeding. The echo of many footsteps rang through the house. It sounded shell-like, empty. Then it seemed to him that not so many were about him. He felt his revolver slide from his hip-pocket. He was pushed gently forward, and a door closed behind him. The sound of footsteps died away with that of whispering voices.

Came a sudden angry roar, muffled, distant, he thought in the voice of Alden. It was stifled, cut off ere it had come to full crescendo, in a very significant manner. Silence, then, fell about him, the chill silence of an empty house.

Cautiously he turned and felt for the door, which he knew to be close behind him. He was obsessed by a childish, though not unnatural, fear of falling through some trap.

He touched the door-knob, turned it. As he had anticipated, the door was locked. He wondered if there were any windows to this strangely dark apartment. With his fingers touching the wall, he crept slowly forward, halting at every other step to listen; but the night gave up no sound.

The tenth pace brought him to a corner. He turned off at right angles, still pursuing the wall, and came upon shutters, closely barred. He pressed on, came to another corner; proceeded, another; and finally touched the door-knob again.

This was a square room, apparently, and unfurnished. But what might not yawn for him in the middle of the floor? He remembered that the river ran at the end of the garden.

Pressing his ear to the door, he listened intently.

Without, absolutely nothing stirred. He drew a quick, sibilant breath, and turned, planting his back against the door and clenching his fists.

Suddenly it had been borne in upon his mind that something, someone, was in the room with him!

Vainly he sought to peer through the darkness. His throat was parched.

A dim glow was born in the heart of the gloom. Scarce able to draw breath, fearing what he might see, yet more greatly fearing to look away, even for an instant, Mr. Oppner stared and stared. His eyes ached.

Brighter became the glow, and proclaimed itself a ball of light. It illuminated the face that was but a few inches removed from it. In the midst of that absolute darkness the effect was indescribably weird. Nothing for some moments was visible but just that ball of light and the dark face with the piercing eyes gleaming out from slits in a silk mask.

Then the ball became fully illuminated, and Oppner saw that it was some unfamiliar kind of lamp, and that it rested in a sort of metal tripod upon a plain deal table, otherwise absolutely bare.

Save for this table, the lamp, and a chair, the room was entirely innocent of furniture. Upon the chair, with his elbows resting on the table, sat a man in evening dress. He was very dark, very well groomed, and seemingly very handsome; but the black silk half-mask effectually disguised him. His eyes were arresting. Mr. Oppner did not move, and he could not look away.

For he knew that he stood in the presence of Séverac Bablon.

The latter pushed something across the table in Oppner's direction.

"Your cheque-book," he said, "and a fountain pen."

Mr. Oppner gulped; did not stir, did not speak. Séverac Bablon's voice was vaguely familiar to him.

"You are the second richest man in the United States," he continued, "and the first in parsimony. I shall mulct you in one hundred thousand pounds!"

"You'll never get it!" rasped Oppner.

"No? Well let us weigh the possibilities, one against the other. There have been protests, from rival journals, against the *Gleaner's* acceptance of foreign money for British national purposes. This I had anticipated, but such donations have had the effect of stimulating the British public. If the cheques already received, and your own, which you are about to draw, are not directly devoted to the purpose for which they are intended, I can guarantee that you shall not be humiliated by their return!"

"Ah!" sighed Oppner.

"The *Gleaner* newspaper has made all arrangements with an important English firm to construct several air vessels. The materials and the workmanship will be British throughout, and the vessels will be placed at the disposal of the authorities. The source of the *Gleaner's* fund thus becomes immaterial. But, in recognition of the subscribers, the vessels will be named 'Oppner I.,' 'Oppner II.,' 'Hague I.,' etc."

"Yep?"

"At some future time we may understand one another better, Mr. Oppner. For the present I shall make no overtures. I have no desire unduly to mystify you, however. The men whom Mr. Martin of Pinkerton's, found surrounding this house were not the men from Sullivan's Agency, but friends of my own. Sullivans were informed at the last moment that the raid had been abandoned. The car, again, which you observed, is my own. I caused it to be driven to and fro between here and Richmond Bridge for your especial amusement, altering the number on each occasion. Finally, any outcry you may care to raise will pass unnoticed, as The Cedars has been leased for the purpose of a private establishment for the care of mental cases."

"You're holding me to ransom?"

"In a sense. But you would not remain here. I should remove you to a safer place. My car is waiting."

"You can't hold me for ever." Mr. Oppner was gathering courage. This interview was so very businesslike, so dissimilar from the methods of American brigandage, that his keen, commercial instincts were coming to the surface. "Any time I get out I can tell the truth and demand my money back."

"It is so. But on the day that you act in that manner, within an hour from the time, your New York mansion will be burned to a shell, without loss of life, but with destruction of property considerably exceeding in value the amount of your donation to the *Gleaner* fund. I may add that I shall continue to force your expenditures in this way, Mr. Oppner, until such time as I bring you to see the falsity of your views. On that day we shall become friends."

"Ah!"

"You may wonder why I have gone to the trouble to make a captive of you, here, when by means of such a menace alone I might have achieved my object; I reply that you possess that stubborn type of disposition which only succumbs to *force majeure*. Your letter to the *Gleaner* explaining your views respecting the Dominion, and proposing that an air-vessel be christened 'The Canada,' is here, typed; you have only to sign it. The future, immediate, and distant is entirely in your own hands, Mr. Oppner. You will remain my guest until I have your cheque and your signature to this letter. You will always be open to sudden demands upon your capital, from me, so long as you continue, by your wrongful employment of the power of wealth, to blacken the Jewish name. For it is because you are a Jew that I require these things of you."

# CHAPTER XVII

## THE DAMASCUS CURTAIN

The British public poured contributions into the air-fleet fund with a lavishness that has never been equalled in history. For, after the stupendous sums, each one a big fortune in itself, which the Jewish financiers had subscribed, every man who called himself a Britisher (and who thought that Britain really needed airships) came forward with his dole.

There was a special service held at the Great Synagogue in Aldgate, and Juda was exalted in public estimation to a dizzy pinnacle.

One morning, whilst the enthusiasm was at its height, Mr. Oppner rose from the breakfast table upon hearing the 'phone bell ring.

"Zoe," he said, "if that's a reporter, tell him I'm ill in bed."

He shuffled from the room. Since the night of the abortive raid upon The Cedars he had showed a marked aversion from the society of newspaper men. Regarding the facts of his donation to the fund he had vouchsafed no word to Zoe. Closely had the story of his doings at Richmond been hushed up; as closely as a bottomless purse can achieve such silencing, but, nevertheless, Zoe knew the truth.

Sheard was shown in.

"Excuse me," he said hastily, "but I wanted to ask Mr. Oppner if there is anything in this article"—he held out a proof slip—"that he would like altered. It's for the *Magazine of Empire*. They're having full-page photographs of all the Aero Millionaires, that's what they call them now!"

"Can you leave it?" asked Zoe. "He is dressing—and not in a very good temper."

"Right!" said Sheard promptly, and laid the slip on the table. "'Phone me if there is anything to come out. Good-bye."

Zoe was reading the proof when her father came in again.

"Newspaper men been here?" he drawled. "Thought so. What a poor old addle-pated martyr I am."

"Listen," began Zoe, "this is an article all about you! It quotes Dr. Herman Hertz, that is to say, it represents you as quoting him! It says:—

"'The true Jew is an integral part of the life and spiritual endeavour of every nation where Providence has allotted his home. And as for the Jews of this Empire, which is earth's nearest realisation hitherto of justice coupled with humanity, finely has a noble Anglo-Jewish soldier, Colonel Goldschmidt, expressed it: "Loyalty to the flag for which the sun once stood still can only deepen our devotion to the flag on which the sun never sets."' Is that all right?"

"H'm!" said Oppner. "Have Rohscheimer and Jesson seen this article?"

"Don't know!" answered Zoe.

"Because," explained Oppner, "they've showed their blame devotion to the flag on which the sun don't set, same as me, and if *they* can stand it, my hide's as tough as theirs, I reckon."

It was whilst Mr. Oppner was thus expressing himself that Sheard, who, having left the proof at the Astoria, had raced back to the club to keep an appointment, quitted the club again (his man had disappointed him), and walked down the court to Fleet Street.

Mr. Aloys. X. Alden, arrayed in his capacious tweed suit, a Stetson felt hat, and a pair of brogues with eloquent Broadway welts, liquidated the business that had detained him in the "Cheshire Cheese" and drifted idly in the same direction.

A taxi-driver questioned Sheard with his eyebrows, but the pressman, after a moment's hesitancy, shook his head, and, suddenly running out into the stream of traffic, swung himself on a westward bound bus. Pausing in the act of lighting a Havana cigarette, Alden hailed the disappointed taxi-driver and gave him rapid instructions. The broad-brimmed Stetson disappeared within the cab, and the cab darted off in the wake of the westward bound bus.

Such was the price that Mr. Thomas Sheard must pay for the reputation won by his inspired articles upon Séverac Bablon. For what he had learnt of him during their brief association had enabled that clever journalist to invest his copy with an atmosphere of "exclusiveness" which had attracted universal attention.

As a less pleasant result, the staff of the *Gleaner*—and Sheard in particular—were being kept under strict surveillance.

Sheard occupied an outside seat, and as the bus travelled rapidly westward, Fleet Street and the Strand offered to his gratified gaze one long vista of placards:

"M. DUQUESNE IN LONDON."

That item was exclusive to the *Gleaner*, and had been communicated to Sheard upon a plain correspondence card, such as he had learnt to associate with Séverac Bablon. The *Gleaner*, amongst all London's news-sheets, alone could inform a public, strung to a tense pitch of excitement, that M. Duquesne, of the Paris police, was staying at the Hotel Astoria, in connection with the Séverac Bablon case.

As the bus stopped outside Charing Cross Station, Sheard took a quick and anxious look back down the Strand. A taxi standing near the gates attracted his attention, for, although he could not see the Stetson inside, he noted that the cab was engaged, and, therefore, possibly occupied. It was sufficient, in these days of constant surveillance, to arouse his suspicion; it was more than sufficient to-day to set his brain working upon a plan to elude the hypothetical pursuer. He had become, latterly, an expert in detecting detectives, and now his wits must be taxed to the utmost.

For he had a correspondence card in his pocket which differed from those he was used to, in that it bore the address, 70A Finchley Road, and invited him to lunch with Séverac Bablon that day!

With the detectives of New York and London busy, and, now, with the famous Duquesne in town, Sheard well might survey the Strand behind, carefully, anxiously, distrustfully.

Séverac Bablon, so far as he was aware, no longer had any actual hold upon him. There was no substantial reason why he should not hand the invitation—bearing that address which one man, alone, in London at that hour cheerfully would have given a thousand pounds to know—to the proper authorities. But Séverac Bablon had appealed strongly, irresistibly, to something within Sheard that had responded with warmth and friendship. Despite his reckless, lawless deeds, the pressman no more would have thought of betraying him than of betraying the most sacred charge. In fact, as has appeared, he did not hesitate to aid and abet him in his most outrageous projects. But yet he wondered at the great, the incredible audacity of this super-audacious man who now had entrusted to him the secret of his residence.

Hastily descending from the bus, he walked quickly forward to the nearest tobacconist's and turned in the entrance to note if the man who might be in the taxi would betray his presence.

He did.

The Stetson appeared from the window, and a pair of keen grey eyes fixed themselves upon the door wherein Sheard was lurking.

A rapid calculation showed the pressman where lay his best chance. Darting across the road, he dived, rabbit-like, into the burrow of the Tube, got his ticket smartly, and ran to the stairway. With his head on a level with the floor of the booking-offices he paused.

An instant later the canoe-shaped brogues came clattering down from above. The American took in the people in the hall with one comprehensive glance, got a ticket without a moment's delay, and jumped into a lift that was about to descend.

Two minutes afterwards Sheard was in a cab bound for the house of Séverac Bablon. The New Journalism is an exciting vocation.

He discharged the cabman at the corner of Finchley Road, and walked along to No. 70A.

Opening the monastic looking gate, he passed around a trim lawn and stood in the porch of one of those small and picturesque houses which survive in some parts of red-brick London.

A man who wore conventional black, but who looked like an Ababdeh Arab, opened the door before he had time to ring. He confirmed Sheard's guess at his Eastern nationality by the manner of his silent salutation. Without a word of inquiry he conducted the visitor to a small room on the left of the hall and retired in the same noiseless fashion.

The journalist had anticipated a curious taste in decoration, and he was not disappointed. For this apartment could not well be termed a room; it was a mere cell.

The floor was composed of blocks—or perhaps only faced with layers of red granite; the walls showed a surface of smooth plaster. An unglazed window which opened on a garden afforded ample light, and, presumably for illumination at night, an odd-looking antique lamp stood in a niche. A littered table, black with great age and heavily carved, and a chair to match, stood upon a rough fibre mat. There was no fireplace. The only luxurious touch in the strange place was afforded by a richly Damascened curtain, draped before a recess at the farther end.

From the table arose Séverac Bablon, wearing a novel garment strangely like a bernouse.

"My dear Sheard," he said warmly and familiarly, "I am really delighted to see you again."

Sheard shook his hand heartily. Séverac Bablon was as irresistible as ever.

"Take the arm-chair," he continued, "and try to overlook the peculiarities of my study. Believe me, they are not intended for mere effect. Every item of my arrangements has its peculiar note of inspiration, I assure you."

Sheard turned, and found that a deep-seated, heavily-cushioned chair, also antique, and which he had overlooked, stood close behind him. An odd perfume hung in the air.

"Ah," said Séverac Bablon, in his softly musical voice, "you have detected my vice."

He passed an ebony box to his visitor, containing cigarettes of a dark yellow colour. Sheard lighted one, and discovered it possessed a peculiar aromatic flavour, which he found very fascinating. Séverac Bablon watched him with a quizzical smile upon his wonderfully handsome face.

"I am afraid there is opium in them," he said.

Sheard started.

"Do not fear," laughed the other. "You cannot develop the vice, for these cigarettes are unobtainable in London. Their history serves to disprove the popular theory that the use of tobacco was introduced from Mexico in the sixteenth century. These were known in the East generations earlier."

And so, with the mere melody of his voice, he re-established his sovereignty over Sheard's mind. His extraordinary knowledge of extraordinary matters occasioned the pressman's constant amazement. From the preparations made for the reception of the Queen of Sheba at Solomon's court in 980 B.C. he passed to the internal organisation of the Criminal Investigation Department.

"I should mention," said Sheard at this point, "that an attempt was made to follow me here."

Séverac Bablon waved a long white hand carelessly.

"Never mind," he replied soothingly. "It is annoying for you, but I give you my word that you shall not be compromised by *me*—come, luncheon is waiting. I will show you the only three men in Europe and America who might associate the bandit, the incendiary, with him who calls himself Séverac Bablon."

He stood up and gazed abstractedly in the direction of the garden. In silence he stood looking, not at the garden, but beyond it, into some vaster garden of his fancy. Sheard studied him with earnest curiosity.

"Will you never tell me," he began abruptly, "who you are really, what is the source of your influence, and what is your aim in all this wild business?"

Séverac Bablon turned and regarded him fixedly.

"I will," he said, "when the day comes—if ever it does come." A shadow crept over his mobile features.

"I am a dreamer, Sheard," he continued, "and perhaps a trifle mad. I am trying to wield a weapon that my fathers were content to let rust in its scabbard. For the source of the influence you speak of—its emblem lies there."

He pointed a long, thin finger to the recess veiled with its heavy Damascus curtain.

"May I see it?"

The quizzical smile returned to the fine face.

"Oh, thou of the copy-hunting soul," exclaimed Séverac Bablon. "A day may come. But it is not to-day."

He seized Sheard by the arm and led him out into the hall.

"Look at these three portraits," he directed. "The three great practical investigators of the world. Mr. Brinsley Monro, of Dearborn Street, Chicago; Mr. Paul Harley, of Chancery Lane; and last, but greatest, M. Victor Lemage, of Paris."

"Is Duquesne acting under his instructions?"

"M. Lemage took charge of the case this morning."

Sheard looked hard at Séverac Bablon. Victor Lemage, inventor of the anthroposcopic system of identification, the greatest living authority upon criminology, was a man to be feared.

Séverac Bablon smiled, clapped both hands upon his shoulders, and looked into his eyes.

"It is the lighter side of my strange warfare," he said. "I revel in it, Sheard. It refreshes me for more serious things. This evening you must arrange to meet me for a few moments. I shall have a 'scoop' to offer you for the *Gleaner*. Do not fail me. It will leave you ample time to get on to Downing Street afterwards. You see, I knew you were going to Downing Street to-night! Am I not a magician? I shall wire you. If, when you ring at the door of the house to which you will be directed, no one replies, go away at once. I will then communicate the news later. And now—lunch."

# CHAPTER XVIII

## A WHITE ORCHID

Whoever could have taken a peep into a certain bare-looking room at Scotland Yard some three hours after Sheard had left Finchley Road must have been drawn to the conclusion that the net was closing more tightly about Séverac Bablon than he supposed.

Behind a large, bare table, upon which were some sheets of foolscap, a metal inkpot, and pens, sat Chief Inspector Sheffield. On three uncomfortable-looking chairs were disposed Detective Sergeant Harborne, he of the Stetson and brogues, and M. Duquesne, of Paris. Stetson and brogues, as became a non-official, observed much outward deference towards the Chief Inspector in whose room he found himself.

"We may take it, then," said Sheffield, with a keen glance of his shrewd, kindly eyes towards the American and the celebrated little Frenchman, "that Bablon, when he isn't made up, is a man so extremely handsome and of such marked personality that he'd be spotted anywhere. We have some reason to believe that he's a Jew. The head of the greatest Jewish house in Europe has declined to deny, according to M. Duquesne, that he knows who he is, and"—consulting a sheet of foolscap—"Mr. Alden, here, from New York, volunteers the information that H. T. Sheard, of the *Gleaner*, went to see Bablon this morning. We are aware, from information by Sir Leopold Jesson, that this newspaper man is acquainted with B. But we can't act on it. We understand that Bablon has a house in or near to London. None of us"—looking hard at Alden—"have any idea of the locality. There are two rewards privately offered, totalling £3,000—which is of more interest to Mr. Alden than to the rest of us—and M. Duquesne is advised this morning that his Chief is coming over at once. Now, we're all as wise as one another"—with a second hard look at his French confrère and Alden—"so we can all set about the job again in our own ways."

After this interesting conference, whereof each member had but sought to pump the others, M. Duquesne, entering Whitehall, almost ran into a tall man, wearing a most unusual and conspicuous caped overcoat, silk lined; whose haughty, downward glance revealed his possession of very large, dark eyes; whose face was so handsome that the little Frenchman caught his breath; whose carriage was that of a monarch or of one of the musketeers of Louis XIII.

With the ease of long practice, M. Duquesne formed an unseen escort for this distinguished stranger.

Arriving at Charing Cross, the latter, without hesitation, entered the telegraph office. M. Duquesne also recollected an important matter that called for a telegram. In quest of a better pen he leaned over to the compartment occupied by the handsome man, but was unable to get so much as a glimpse of what he was writing. Having handed in his message in such a manner that the ingenious Frenchman was foiled again, he strode out, the observed of everyone in the place, but particularly of M. Duquesne.

To the latter's unbounded astonishment, at the door he turned and raised his hat to him ironically.

Familiar with the characteristic bravado of French criminals, that decided the detective's next move. He stepped quickly back to the counter as the polite stranger disappeared.

"I am Duquesne of Paris," he said in his fluent English to the clerk who had taken the message, and showed his card. "On official business I wish to inspect the last telegram which you received."

The clerk shook his head.

"Can't be done. Only for Scotland Yard."

Duquesne was a man of action. He wasted not a precious moment in feckless argument. It was hard that he should have to share this treasure with another. But in seven minutes he was at New Scotland Yard, and in fifteen he was back again to his great good fortune, with Inspector Sheffield.

The matter was adjusted. In the notebooks of Messrs Duquesne and Sheffield the following was written:

"Sheard, *Gleaner*, Tudor Street. Laurel Cottage, Dulwich Village, eight to-night."

Returning to the Astoria to make arrangements for the evening's expedition, Duquesne upon entering his room, found there a large-boned man, with a great, sparsely-covered skull, and a thin, untidy beard. He sat writing by the window, and, at the other's entrance, cast a slow glance from heavy-lidded eyes across his shoulder.

M. Duquesne bowed profoundly, hat in hand.

It was the great Lemage.

There were overwhelming forces about to take the field. France, England and the United States were combining against Séverac Bablon. It seemed that at Laurel Cottage he was like to meet his Waterloo.

At twenty-five minutes to seven that evening a smart plain-clothes constable reported in Chief Inspector Sheffield's room.

"Well, Dawson?" said the inspector, looking up from his writing.

"Laurel Cottage, Dulwich, was let by the Old College authorities, sir, to a Mr. Sanrack a month ago."

"What is he like, this Mr. Sanrack?"

"A tall, dark gentleman. Very handsome. Looks like an actor."

"Sanrack—Séverac," mused Sheffield. "Daring! All right, Dawson, you can go. You know where to wait."

Fifteen minutes later arrived M. Duquesne. He had been carpeted by his chief for invoking the aid of the London police in the matter of the telegram.

"Five methods occur to me instantly, stupid pig," the great Lemage had said, "whereby you might have learnt its contents alone!"

Heavy with a sense of his own dull powers of invention—for he found himself unable to conceive one, much less five such schemes—M. Duquesne came into the inspector's room.

"Does your chief join us to-night?" inquired Sheffield, on learning that the famous investigator was in London.

"He may do so, m'sieur; but his plans are uncertain."

Almost immediately afterwards they were joined by Harborne, and all three, entering one of the taxi-cabs that always are in waiting in the Yard, set out for Dulwich Village.

The night was very dark, with ample promise of early rain, and as the cab ran past Westminster Abbey a car ahead swung sharply around Sanctuary Corner. Harborne, whose business it was to know all about smart society, reported:

"Old Oppner's big Panhard in front. Going our way—Embankment is 'up.' I wonder what his Agency men are driving at? Alden's got something up his sleeve, I'll swear."

"I'd like a peep inside that car," said Sheffield.

Harborne took up the speaking-tube as the cab, in turn, rounded into Great Smith Street.

"Switch off this inside light," he called to the driver, "and get up as close alongside that Panhard ahead as you dare. She's not moving fast. Stick there till I tell you to drop back."

The man nodded, and immediately the gear snatched the cab ahead with a violent jerk. At a high speed they leapt forward upon the narrow road, swung out to the off-side to avoid a bus, and closed up to the brilliantly-lighted car.

It was occupied by two women in picturesque evening toilettes. One of them was a frizzy haired soubrette and the other a blonde. Both were conspicuously pretty. The fair girl wore a snow white orchid, splashed with deepest crimson, pinned at her breast. Her companion, who lounged in the near corner, her cloak negligently cast about her and one rounded shoulder against the window, was reading a letter; and Harborne, who found himself not a foot removed from her, was trying vainly to focus his gaze upon the writing when the fair girl looked up and started to find the cab so close. The light of a sudden suspicion leapt into her eyes as, obedient to the detective's order, the taxi-driver slowed down and permitted the car to pass. Almost immediately the big Panhard leapt to renewed speed, and quickly disappeared ahead.

Harborne turned to Inspector Sheffield.

"That was Miss Zoe Oppner, the old man's daughter."

"I know," said Sheffield sharply. "Read any of the letter?"

"No," admitted Harborne; "we were bumping too much. But there's a political affair on to-night in Downing Street. I should guess she's going to be there."

"Why? Who was the fair girl?"

"Lady Mary Evershed," answered Harborne. "It's her father's 'do' to-night. We want to keep an eye on Miss Oppner, after the Astoria Hotel business. Wish we had a list of guests."

"If Séverac Bablon is down," replied Sheffield; grimly, "I don't think she'll have the pleasure of seeing him this evening. But where on earth is she off to now?"

"Give it up," said Harborne, philosophically.

"Oh, she of the golden hair and the white *odontoglossum*," sighed the little Frenchman, rolling up his eyes. "What a perfection!"

They became silent as the cab rapidly bore them across Vauxhall Bridge and through south-west to south-east London, finally to Dulwich Village, that tiny and dwindling oasis in the stucco desert of Suburbia.

Talking to an officer on point duty at a corner, distinguished by the presence of a pillar-box, was P.C. Dawson in mufti. He and the other constable saluted as the three detectives left the cab and joined them.

"Been here long, Dawson?" asked Sheffield.

"No, sir. Just arrived."

"You and I will walk along on the far side from this Laurel Cottage," arranged the inspector, "and M. Duquesne might like a glass of wine, Harborne, until I've looked over the ground. Then we can distribute ourselves. We've got a full quarter of an hour."

It was arranged so, and Sheffield, guided by Dawson, proceeded to the end of the Village, turned to the left, past the College buildings, and found himself in a long, newly-cut road, with only a few unfinished houses. Towards the farther end a gloomy little cottage frowned upon the road. It looked deserted and lonely in its isolation amid marshy fields. In the background, upon a slight acclivity, a larger building might dimly be discerned. A clump of dismal poplars overhung the cottage on the west.

"It's been a gate lodge at some time, sir," explained Dawson. "You can see the old carriage sweep on the right. But the big house is to be pulled down, and they've let the lodge, temporarily, as a separate residence. There's no upstairs, only one door and very few windows. We can absolutely surround it!"

"H'm! Unpleasant looking place," muttered Sheffield, as the two walked by on the opposite side. "No lights. When we've passed this next tree, slip along and tuck yourself away under that fence on the left. Don't attempt any arrest until our man's well inside. Then, when you hear the whistle, close in on the door. I'll get back now."

Ten minutes later, though Laurel Cottage presented its usual sad and lonely aspect, it was efficiently surrounded by three detectives and a constable.

Sheffield's scientific dispositions were but just completed when a cursing taxi-man deposited Sheard half way up the road, having declined resolutely to bump over the ruts any further. Dismissing the man, the keenest copy-hunter in Fleet Street walked alone to the Cottage, all unaware that he did so under the scrutiny of four pairs of eyes. Finding a rusty bell-pull he rang three times. But none answered.

It was at the moment when he turned away that Mr. Alden and an Agency colleague, who—on this occasion successfully—had tracked him since he left the *Gleaner* office, turned the corner by the Village. Seeing him retracing his steps, they both darted up a plank into an unfinished house with the agility of true ferrets, and let him pass. As he re-entered the Village street one was at his heels. Mr. Alden strolled along to Laurel Cottage.

With but a moment's consideration, he, taking a rapid glance up and down the road, vaulted the low fence and disposed himself amongst the unkempt laurel bushes flanking the cottage on the west. The investing forces thus acquired a fifth member.

Then came the threatened rain.

Falling in a steady downpour, it sang its mournful song through poplar and shrub. Soon the grey tiled roof of the cottage poured its libation into spouting gutters, and every rut of the road became a miniature ditch. But, with dogged persistency, the five watchers stuck to their posts.

When Sheard had gone away again, Inspector Sheffield had found himself, temporarily, in a dilemma. It was something he had not foreseen. But, weighing the chances, he had come to the conclusion to give the others no signal, but to wait.

At seven minutes past eight, by Mr. Alden's electrically lighted timepiece, a car or a cab—it was impossible, at that distance, to determine which—dropped a passenger at the Village end of the road. A tall figure, completely enveloped in a huge, caped coat, and wearing a dripping silk hat, walked with a swinging stride towards the ambush—and entered the gate of the cottage.

M. Duquesne, who, from his damp post in a clump of rhododendrons on the left of the door had watched him approach, rubbed his wet hands delightedly. Without the peculiar coat that majestic walk was sufficient.

"It is he!" he muttered. "The Séverac!"

With a key which he must have held ready in his hand, the new-comer opened the door and entered the cottage. Acting upon a pre-arranged plan, the watchers closed in upon the four sides of the building, and Sheffield told himself triumphantly that he had shown sound generalship. With a grim nod of recognition to Alden, who appeared from the laurel thicket, he walked up to the door and rang smartly.

This had one notable result. A door banged inside.

Again he rang—and again.

Nothing stirred within. Only the steady drone of the falling rain broke the chilling silence.

Sheffield whistled shrilly.

At that signal M. Duquesne immediately broke the window which he was guarding, and stripping off his coat, he laid it over the jagged points of glass along the sashes and through the thickness of the cloth forced back the catch. Throwing up the glassless frame, he stepped into the dark room beyond.

To the crash which he had made, an answering crash had told him that Detective-sergeant Harborne had effected an entrance by the east window.

Cautiously he stepped forward in the darkness, a revolver in one hand; with the other he fumbled for the electric lamp in his breast pocket.

As his fingers closed upon it a slight noise behind him brought him right-about in a flash.

The figure of a man who was climbing in over the low ledge was silhouetted vaguely in the frame of the broken window.

"*Ah!*" hissed Duquesne. "Quick! speak! Who is that?"

"Ssh! my Duquesne!" came a thick voice. "Do you think, then, I can leave so beautiful a case to anyone?"

Duquesne turned the beam of the lantern on the speaker.

It was Victor Lemage.

Duquesne bowed, lantern in hand.

"Waste no moment," snapped Lemage. "Try that door!" pointing to the only one in the room.

As the other stepped forward to obey, the famous investigator made a comprehensive survey of the little kitchen, for such it was. Save for its few and simple appointments, it was quite empty.

"The door is locked."

"Ah, yes. I thought so."

"Hullo!" came Sheffield's voice through the window, "who's there, Duquesne?"

"It is M. Lemage. M'sieur, allow me to make known the great Scotland Yard Inspector Sheffield."

With a queer parody of politeness, Duquesne turned the light of his lantern alternately upon the face of each, as he mentioned his name.

Sheffield bowed awkwardly. For he knew that he stood in the presence of the undisputed head of his profession—the first detective in Europe.

"You have not left the front door unguarded, M'sieur the Inspector?" inquired Lemage sharply.

"No, Mr. Lemage," snapped Sheffield, "I have not. My man Dawson is there, with an Agency man, too."

"Then we surround completely the room in which he is," declared Lemage.

Such was the case, as a glance at the following plan will show.

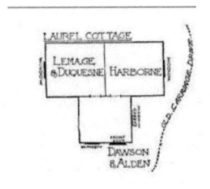

"There are, then, three ways," said Lemage. "We may break into the front room from here, or from the room where is m'sieur your colleague. There is, no doubt, a door corresponding to this one. The other way is to go in by the window of that front room, for I have made the observation that its other window, that opens on the old drive to the east, is barred most heavily. Do I accord with the views of m'sieur?"

"Quite," said Sheffield crisply. "We'll work through the front window. Hullo, Harborne!"

"Hullo!" came the latter's voice from the next room.

"Nobody in there?"

"No. Empty room. Door's locked. What's up on your side?"

"Nothing. Mr. Lemage has joined us. Stand by for squalls. I'm going round to get in at the front-room window."

He paused and listened. They all listened.

The rain droned monotonously on the roof, but there was no other sound.

Sheffield climbed out and passed around by the poplars and through the laurel bushes to the front. Dawson and Alden stood by the door. With a pair of handcuffs the inspector broke the glass, and, adopting the same method as the Frenchman, used his coat to protect his hands from the splintered pieces in forcing the catch. The rain came down in torrents. He was drenched to the skin.

Seizing the yellow blind, he tore it from the roller, and also pulled down the curtains. By the light of the bull's-eye lantern which Dawson carried he surveyed the little sitting-room. Next, with a muttered exclamation, he leapt through and searched the one hiding-place—beneath a large sofa—which the room afforded.

On the common oval walnut table lay a caped overcoat and a rain-soaked silk hat.

The two doors—other than that guarded by Dawson and Alden—gave (1) on the room occupied by Harborne; (2) on the room occupied by Duquesne and Lemage. The keys were missing. The one window, other than that by which he had entered, was heavily barred, and in any case, visible from the front door of the cottage.

All five had seen their man enter; all had heard the banging door when Sheffield knocked. No possible exit had been unwatched for a single instant.

But the place was empty.

When the others, having searched painfully every inch of ground, joined the inspector in the front room, Harborne, taking up the silk-lined caped overcoat, observed something lying on the polished walnut beneath.

He uttered a hasty exclamation.

"Damn!" cried Duquesne at his elbow, characteristically saying the right thing at the wrong time. "A white *odontoglossum crispum*, with crimson spots!"

Across the table all exchanged glances.

"He is very handsome," sighed the little Frenchman.

"That is an extreme privilege," said his chief, shrugging composedly and lighting a cigarette. "It is so interesting to the women, and they are so useful. It was the women who restored your English Charles II.—but they were his ruin in the end. It is a clue, this white orchid, that inspires in me two solutions immediately."

M. Duquesne suffered, temporarily, from a slight catarrh, occasioned, no doubt, by his wetting. But he lacked the courage to meet the drooping eye of his chief.

They were some distance from Laurel Cottage when Harborne, who carried the caped coat on his arm, exclaimed:

"By the way, who *has* the orchid?"

No one had it.

"M. Duquesne," said Lemage calmly, "of all the stupid pigs you are the more complete."

Sheffield ran back. Dawson had been left on duty outside the cottage. The inspector passed him and climbed back through the broken window. He looked on the table and searched, on hands and knees, about the floor.

"Dawson!"

"Sir?"

"You have heard or seen nothing suspicious since we left?"

Dawson, through the window, stared uncomprehendingly.

"Nothing, sir."

The white orchid was missing.

# CHAPTER XIX

## THREE LETTERS

Sheard did not remain many minutes in Downing Street that night. The rooms were uncomfortably crowded and insupportably stuffy. A vague idea which his common sense was impotent to combat successfully, that he would see or hear from Séverac Bablon amidst that political crush proved to be fallacious—as common sense had argued. He wondered why his extraordinary friend—for as a friend he had come to regard him—had been unable to keep his appointment. He wondered when the promised news would be communicated.

That one of the Americans, or two, to whose presence he was becoming painfully familiar, had followed him since he had left the office he was well aware. But, as he had thrown off the man who had tried to follow him to Finchley Road, he was untroubled now. They had probably secured the Dulwich address; but that was due to no fault of his own, and, in any case, Bablon seemed to regard all their efforts with complete indifference. So, presumably, it did not matter.

On his way out he met two hot and burly gentlemen, rather ill-dressed, who were hastening in. Instinctively he knew them for detective officers. Hailing a cab at the corner, he sank restfully into the seat and felt in his pocket for his cigarette-case. There was a letter there also, which he did not recollect to have been there before he entered Downing Street.

In some excitement he took it out and opened the plain envelope.

It contained a correspondence-card and a letter. Both of these, and a third letter which reached its destination on the following morning, whilst all England and all France were discussing the amazing circumstances set forth in No. 2, are appended in full.

---

No. 1

"MY DEAR SHEARD,—I enclose the promised 'exclusive to the *Gleaner*.' It will appear in no other paper of London, but in two of Paris, to-morrow. Forgive me for sending you to Dulwich. I did so for a private purpose of my own, and rely upon your generous friendship to excuse the liberty. I write this prior to visiting Downing Street, where it will be quite impossible, amongst so many people, to speak to you. Do not fear that there exists any evidence of complicity between us. I assure you that you are safe."

---

No. 2

"To the Editor of the *Gleaner*.

"SIR,—I desire to show myself, as always, a man of honour, and presume to request the freedom of your most valuable columns for that purpose. I address myself to the British public through the medium of the *Gleaner* as the most liberal journal in London, and that most opposed to government by plutocracy.

As the inventor of the digital system of identification, of the anthroposcopic method, and of the *Code* which bears my name, I am known to your readers, as well as for my years of labour against criminals of all classes and of all nations. I have been called the head of my profession, and shall I be accused of vanity if, with my hand upon my heart, I acknowledge that tribute and say, 'It is well deserved'?

"Under date as above, I am resigning my office as Chief of that department which I have so long directed, being no more in a position to perform my duties as a man of honour, since I have been instructed to take charge of what is called 'the Séverac Bablon case.'

"It is the first time that my duty to France has run contrary to my duty to the great, the marvellous man whom you know by that name, and to whom I owe all that I have, all that I am; whose orders I may not and would not disregard.

"By his instructions I performed to-day a little deception upon the representatives of English law and upon one of my esteemed colleagues—a most capable and honourable man, for whom I cherish extreme regard, and whom I would wish to see in the office I now resign. He is not one of Us, and in every respect is a suitable candidate for that high post.

"I was honoured, then, by instructions to impersonate my Leader. No reference here to my powers of disguise is necessary. I took the place of him you call Séverac Bablon at a certain Laurel Cottage in Dulwich. I entered with the key he had entrusted to me, too quickly to be arrested, if any had tried, and none made the attempt, which was an error of strategy (see *Code*, pp. 336-43). All in the dark I placed his coat and hat upon the table. I overlooked something in the gloom, but no matter. I correct my errors; it is the Secret. I was not otherwise disguised. It was not necessary. I waited until one of those watching broke into the little room at the back. I stood beside the window. Noiseless as the leopard I stepped behind him as he entered. I could have slain him with ease. I did not do so. I proclaimed myself. *I* was entering, too!

"Why should I name the man to whom I thus offered the one great chance of a lifetime? No, I am so old at this game. He overlooked no more than another must have done—any more than I.

"But, although outside it poured with rain, my clothes were scarce wet. How had I watched and kept dry?

"He did not ask himself. No matter. I gave him his chance. We French, to-day, are sportsmen!

"I understand that my Leader brought about this *contretemps* with deliberation, in order to terminate my false position, and make prominent this statement, and I am instructed to remind my authorities that State secrets of international importance are in my possession and thus in his. But, lastly, I would assure France and the world that no blot of dishonour is upon my name because I have served two masters. My great Leader never did and never will employ this knowledge to any improper end. But he would have my Government know something—so very little—of his influence and of his power. He would have them recall those warrants for his apprehension that place him on a level with the Apache, the ruffian; that are an *insult* to a man who has never done wrong to a living soul, but who only has exercised the fundamental, the Divine, the Mosaic Law of *Justice*.

"I loved my work and I love France. But I grieve not. Other work will be given to me. I make my bow; I disappear. Adieu!

"I am, sir,

"Your obedient servant,"VICTOR LEMAGE"(late *Service de Sûreté*)."

---

No. 3

(Received by Lady Mary Evershed)

"When, in your brave generosity, you accompanied your friend and mine on her perilous journey to warn me that Mr. Oppner's detectives had a plan for my capture, I knew, on the instant when you stepped into Laurel Cottage, that Miss Oppner had made a wise selection in the companion who should share her secret. I did not regret having confided that address to her discretion.

The warning was unnecessary, but I valued it none the less. By an oversight, for which I reproach myself, a clue to your presence was left behind, when, but a few minutes before the police arrived, we left the cottage—which had served its purpose. But another of my good friends secured it, and I have it now. It is a white orchid. I have ventured to keep it, that it may remind me of the gratitude I owe to you both."

———————————————————————

# CHAPTER XX

## CLOSED DOORS

"Why can't they open the doors? I can see there are people inside!"

A muffled roar, like that of a nearing storm at sea, drowned the querulous voice.

"Move along here, please! Move on! Move on!"

The monotonous orders of the police rose above the loud drone of the angry crowd.

Motor-buses made perilous navigation through the narrow street. The hooting of horns on taxi-cabs played a brisk accompaniment to the mournful chant. Almost from the Courts to the trebly guarded entrance of the Chancery Legal Incorporated Credit Society Bank stretched that deep rank of victims. For, at the corner of Chancery Lane, the contents-bill of a daily paper thus displayed, in suitable order of precedence, the vital topics of the moment:

MISS PAULETTE DELOTUS *NOT* MARRIED

Australians' Plucky Fight

IS SÉVERAC BABLON IN VIENNA?

BIG CITY BANK SMASH

SLUMP IN NICARAGUAN RAILS

To some, those closed doors meant the sacrifice of jewellery, of some part of the luxury of life; to others, they meant—the drop-curtain that blacked out the future, the end of the act, the end of the play.

"Move along here, please! Move on! Move on!"

"All right, constable," said Sir Richard Haredale, smiling unmirthfully; "I'll move on—and move out!"

He extricated himself from the swaying, groaning, cursing multitude, and stepped across to the opposite side of the street. Lost in unpleasant meditation, he stood, a spruce, military figure, bearing upon his exterior nothing indicative of the ruined man. He was quite unaware of the approach of a graceful, fair girl, whose fresh English beauty already had enslaved the imaginations of some fifty lawyers' clerks returning from lunch. As ignorant of her train of conquests as Haredale was ignorant of her presence, she came up to him—and tears gleamed upon her lashes. She stood beside him, and he did not see her.

"Dick!"

The voice aroused him, and a flush came upon his tanned, healthy-looking face. A beam of gladness and admiration lost itself in a cloud, as mechanically he raised his hat, and, holding the girl's hand, glanced uneasily aside, fearing to meet the anxious tenderness in the blue eyes which, now, were deepened to something nearer violet.

"It is true, then?" she asked softly.

He nodded, his lips grimly compressed.

"Who told you," he questioned in turn, "that I had my poor scrapings in it?"

"Oh, I don't know," she said wearily. "And it doesn't matter much, does it?"

"Come away somewhere," Haredale suggested. "We can't stand here."

In silence they walked away from the clamouring crowd of depositors.

"Move along here, please! Move on! Move on!"

"Where can we go?" asked the girl.

"Anywhere," said Haredale, "where we can sit down. This will do."

They turned into a cheap café, and, finding a secluded table, took their seats there, Haredale drearily ordering tea, without asking his companion whether she wanted it or not. It was improbable that Lady Mary Evershed had patronised such a tea-shop before, but the novelty of the thing did not interest her in the least. It was only her pride, the priceless legacy of British womanhood, which enabled her to preserve her composure—which checked the hot tears that burned in her eyes. For the mute misery in Haredale's face was more than he could hide. With all his sang-froid, and all his training to back it, he was hard put to it to keep up even an appearance of unconcern.

Presently she managed to speak again, biting her lips between every few words.

"Had you—everything—there, Dick?"

He nodded.

"I was a fool, of course," he said. "I never did have the faintest idea of business. There are dozens of sound investments—but what's the good of whining? I have acted as unofficial secretary to Mr. Julius Rohscheimer for two years, and eaten my pride at every meal. But—I *cannot* begin all over again, Mary. I shall have to let him break me—and clear out."

He dropped his clenched fists upon his knees, and under the little table a hand crept to his. He grasped it hard and released it.

Mary, with a strained look in her eyes, was drumming gloved fingers on the table.

"I detest Julius Rohscheimer!" she flashed. "He is a perfect octopus. Even father fears him—I don't know why."

Haredale smiled grimly.

"But there is *someone* who could prevent him from ruining your life, Dick," she continued, glancing down at the table.

She did not look up for a few moments. Then, as Haredale kept silent, she was forced to do so. His grey eyes were fixed upon her face.

"Séverac Bablon? What do you know of him, Mary?"

She grew suddenly pale.

"I only know"—hesitating—"that is, I *think*, he is a man who, however misguided, has a love of justice."

Haredale watched her.

"He is an up-to-date Claude Duval," he said harshly. "It hurts me, rather, Mary, to hear you approve of him. Why do you do so? I have noticed something of this before. Do you forget that this man, for all the romance and mystery that surround him, still is no more than a common thief—a criminal?"

Mary's lips tightened.

"He is not," she said, meeting his eyes bravely. "That is a very narrow view, Dick-"

Then, seeing the pain in the grey eyes, and remembering that this man with whom she disputed had just lost his hopes in life—his hopes of *her*—she reached out impulsively and grasped his arm.

"Oh, Dick!" she said; "forgive me! But I am so utterly miserable, dear, that any poor little straw seems worth grasping at."

So we must leave them; it was a situation full of poor human pathos. The emotions surging within these two hearts would have afforded an interesting study for the magical pen of Charles Dickens.

But we cannot pause to essay it; the tide of our narrative bears us elsewhere.

Mr. J. J. Oppner, the pride of Wall Street, when, his fascinating daughter, Zoe, beside him, he rose to address his guests at the Hotel Astoria that evening, would have provided a study equally interesting to Charles Dickens or to the late Professor Darwin. It would have puzzled even the distinguished biologist to reconcile the two species, represented by Mr. Oppner and Zoe, with any common origin. The millionaire's seamed and yellow face looked like nothing so much as a magnified section of a walnut. Whilst the girl, with her cloud of copper-dusted brown hair trapped within an Oriental head-dress, her piquant beauty enhanced, if that were possible, by the softly shaded lights, and the bewitching curves revealed by her evening gown borrowing a more subtle witchery from their sombre environment of black-coated plutocrats, justified the most inspired panegyric that ever had poured from the fountain-pen of a New York reporter. Mr. Oppner said:

"Gentlemen,—We have met this evening for *a* special purpose. With everyone's *per*mission, we will *ad*journ to another room and see how we can fix things up for Mr. Séverac Bablon."

He led the way without loss of time, his small, dried figure lost between that of John Macready ("the King of Coolgardie"), a stalwart, iron-grey Irishman, and the unshapely bulk of Baron Hague, once more perilously adventured upon English soil.

Sir Leopold Jesson, trim, perfectly groomed, his high, bald cranium gleaming like the dome of Solomon's temple, followed, deep in conversation with a red, raw-boned Scotsman, whose features seemed badly out of drawing, and whose eyebrows suggested shrimps. This was Hector Murray, the millionaire who had built and endowed more public baths and institutions than any man since the Emperor Vespasian. Last of all, went Julius Rohscheimer, that gross figurehead of British finance, saying, with a satirish smile, to Haredale, who had made an eighth at dinner:

"You won't mind amusing Miss Oppner, Haredale, till we're through with this little job? It's out of your line; you'll be more at home here, I'm sure."

The room chosen for this important conference was a small one, having but a single door, which opened on a tiny antechamber; this, in turn, gave upon the corridor. When the six millionaires had entered, and Mr. Oppner had satisfied himself that suitable refreshments were placed in readiness, he returned to the corridor. Immediately outside the door stood Mr. Aloys. X. Alden.

"You'll sit right there," instructed Oppner. "The man's bringing a chair and smokes and liquor, and you'll let nobody in—*nobody*. We can't be heard out here, with the anteroom between and both doors shut; there's only one window, and this is the sixth storey. So I guess our Bablon palaver will be private, some."

Alden nodded, bit off the end of a cheroot, and settled himself against the wall. Mr. Oppner returned to his guests. In another room Zoe and Sir Richard Haredale struggled with a conversation upon sundry matters wherein neither was interested in the least. Suddenly Zoe said, in her impulsive, earnest way:

"Sir Richard, I know you won't be angry, but Mary is my very dearest friend; we were at school together, too; and—she told me all about it this afternoon. I understand what this loss means to you, and that it's quite impossible for you to remain with Mr. Rohscheimer any longer; that you mean to resign your commission and go abroad. It isn't necessary for me to say I am sorry."

He thanked her mutely, but it was with a certain expectancy that he awaited her next words. Rumour had linked Zoe Oppner's name with that of Séverac Bablon, extravagantly, as it seemed to Haredale; but everything connected with that extraordinary man *was* extravagant. He recalled how Mary, on more than one occasion, had exhibited traces of embarrassment when the topic was mooted, and how she had hinted that Séverac Bablon might be induced to interest himself in his, Haredale's, financial loss. Could it be that Mary—perhaps through her notoriously eccentric American friend—had met the elusive wonder-worker? Haredale, be it remembered, was hard hit, and completely down. This insane suspicion had found no harbourage in his mind at any other time; but now, he hugged it dejectedly, watching Zoe Oppner's pretty, expressive face for confirmatory evidence.

"Of course, the bank has failed for more than three millions," said the girl earnestly; "but, in your own case, can nothing be done?"

Haredale lighted a cigarette, slightly shaking his head.

"I shall have to clear out. That's all"

"Oh!—but—it's real hard to say what I want to say. But—my father has business relations with Mr. Rohscheimer. May I try to do something?"

Haredale's true, generous instincts got the upper hand at that. He told himself that he was behaving, mentally, like a cad.

"Miss Oppner," he said warmly, "you are all that Mary has assured me. You are a real chum. I can say no more. But it is quite impossible, believe me."

There was such finality in the words that she was silenced. Haredale abruptly changed the subject.

An hour passed.

Two hours passed.

Zoe began to grow concerned on her father's behalf. He was in poor health, and his physician's orders were imperative upon the point of avoiding business.

Half-way through the third hour she made up her mind.

"He has wasted his time long enough," she pronounced firmly—and the expression struck Haredale as oddly chosen. "I am going to inform him that his 'conference' is closed."

She passed out into the corridor to where Mr. Alden, his chair tilted at a comfortable angle, and his brogue-shod feet upon a coffee-table which bore also a decanter, a siphon, and a box of cigars, contentedly was pursuing his instructions. He stood up as she appeared.

"Mr. Alden," she said, "I wish to speak to Mr. Oppner."

The detective spread his hands significantly.

"I respect your scruples, Mr. Alden," Zoe continued, "but my father's orders did not apply to me. Will you please go in and request him to see me for a moment?"

Perceiving no alternative, Alden opened the door, crossed the little anteroom, and knocked softly at the inner door.

He received no reply to his knocking, and knocked again. He knocked a third, a fourth time. With a puzzled glance at Miss Oppner he opened the door and entered.

An unemotional man, he usually was guilty of nothing demonstrative. But the appearance of the room wrenched a hoarse exclamation from his stoic lips.

In the first place, it was in darkness; in the second, when, with the aid of the electric lantern which he was never without, he had dispersed this darkness—he saw that *it was empty*!

The scene of confusion that ensued upon this incredible discovery defies description.

All the telephones in the Astoria could not accommodate the frantic people who sought them. Messenger boys in troops appeared. Hundreds of guests ran upstairs and hundreds of guests ran downstairs. Every groaning lift, ere long, was bearing its freight of police and pressmen to the scene of the most astounding mystery that ever had set London agape.

Soon it was ascertained that the current had been disconnected in some way from the room where the six magnates had met. But how, otherwise than through the door, they had been spirited away from a sixth floor apartment, was a problem that no one appeared competent to tackle; that they had not made their exit via the door was sufficiently proven by the expression of stark perplexity which dwelt upon the face of Mr. Aloys. X. Alden.

Whilst others came and went, scribbling hasty notes in dog-eared notebooks, he, a human statue of Amaze, gazed at the open window, continuously and vacantly. Jostled by the crowds of curious and interested visitors, he stood, the most surprised man in the two hemispheres.

Short of an airship, he could conceive no device whereby the missing six could have made their silent departure. He was shaken out of his stupor by Haredale.

"Pull yourself together, Mr. Alden," cried the latter. "Can't we *do* something? Here's half Scotland Yard in the place and nobody with an intelligent proposal to offer."

Mr. Alden shook himself, like a heavy sleeper awakened.

"Where's Miss Oppner?" he jerked.

Haredale started.

"I don't know," was his reply; "but I can go and see."

He forced his way past the knot of people at the door, ignoring Inspector Sheffield, who sought to detain him. Rapidly he ran through the rooms composing the suite. In one he met Zoe's maid, wringing her hands with extravagant emotion.

"Where is your mistress?"

"She has gone out, m'sieur. I cannot tell where. I do not know."

Haredale's heart gave a leap—and seemed to pause.

He ran to the stairs, not waiting for the overworked lift, and down into the hall.

"Has Miss Oppner gone out?" he demanded of the porter.

"Two minutes ago, sir."

"In her car?"

"No, sir. It was not ready. In a cab."

"Did you hear her directions?"

"No, sir. But the boy will know."

The boy was found.

"Where was Miss Oppner going, boy?" rapped Haredale.

"Eccleston Square, sir," was the prompt reply.

The Marquess of Evershed's. Then his suspicions had not been unfounded. He saw, in a flash of inspiration, the truth. Zoe Oppner had seen in this disappearance the hand of Séverac Bablon—if, indeed, if she did not *know* it for his work. She was anxious about her father. She wished to appeal to Séverac Bablon upon his behalf. And she had gone—not direct to the man—but to Eccleston Square. Why? Clearly because it was Lady Mary, and not herself, who had influence with him.

Hatless, Haredale ran out into the courtyard. Rohscheimer's car was waiting, and he leapt in, his grey eyes feverish. "Lord Evershed's," he called to the man; "Eccleston Square."

———

# CHAPTER XXI

## A CORNER IN MILLIONAIRES

At the moment that Julius Rohscheimer's car turned into the Square, a girl, enveloped in a dark opera wrap, but whose fair hair gleamed as she passed the open door, came alone, out of Lord Evershed's house, and entering a waiting taxi-cab, was driven away.

"Stop!" ordered Haredale hoarsely through the tube.

The big car pulled up as the cab passed around on the other side.

"Follow that cab."

With which the pursuit commenced. And Haredale found himself trembling, so violent was the war of emotions that waged within him. His deductions were proving painfully correct. Through Mayfair and St. John's Wood the cab led the way; finally into Finchley Road. Fifty yards behind, Haredale stopped the car as the cab drew up before a gate set in a high wall.

Lady Mary stepped out, opened the gate, and disappeared within. Heedless of the taxi-driver's curious stare, Haredale, a conspicuous figure in evening dress, with no overcoat and no hat, entered almost immediately afterwards.

Striding up to the porch, he was searching for bell or knocker when the door opened silently, and an Arab in spotless white robes saluted him with dignified courtesy.

"Take my card to your master," snapped Haredale, striving to exhibit no surprise, and stepped inside rapidly.

The Arab waved him to a small reception room, furnished with a wealth of curios for which the visitor had no eyes, and retired. As the man withdrew Haredale moved to the door and listened. He admitted to himself that this was the part of a common spy; but his consuming jealousy would brook no restraint.

From somewhere farther along the hall he heard, though indistinctly, a familiar voice.

Without stopping to reflect he made for a draped door, knocked peremptorily, and entered.

He found himself in a small apartment, whose form and appointments, even to his perturbed mind, conveyed a vague surprise. It was, to all intents and purposes, a cell, with stone-paved floor and plaster walls. An antique lamp, wherein rested what appeared to be a small ball of light, unlike any illuminant he had seen, stood upon a massive table, which was littered with papers. Excepting a chair of peculiar design and a magnificently worked Oriental curtain which veiled either a second door or a recess in the wall, the place otherwise was unfurnished.

Before this curtain, and facing him, pale but composed, stood Lady Mary Evershed, a sweet picture in a bizarre setting.

"Has your friend run away, then?" said Haredale roughly.

The girl did not reply, but looked fully at him with something of scorn and much of reproach in her eyes.

"I know whose house this is," continued Haredale violently, "and why you have come. What is he to you? Why do you know him—visit him—shield him? Oh! my God! it only wanted this to complete my misery. I have, now, not one single happy memory to take away with me."

His voice shook upon those last words.

"Mary," he said sadly, and all his rage was turned to pleading—"what does it mean? Tell me. I *know* there is some simple explanation——"

"You shall hear it, Sir Richard," interrupted a softly musical voice.

He turned as though an adder had bitten him; the blasé composure which is the pride of every British officer had melted in the rays of those blue eyes that for years had been the stars of his worship. It was a very human young man, badly shaken and badly conscious of his display of weakness, who faced the tall figure in the tightly buttoned frock-coat that now stood in the open doorway.

The man who had interrupted him was one to arrest attention anywhere and in any company. With figure and face cast in a severely classic mould, his intense, concentrated gaze conveyed to Haredale a throbbing sense of *force*, in an uncanny degree.

"Séverac Bablon!" flashed through his mind.

"Himself, Sir Richard."

Haredale, who had not spoken, met the weird, fixed look, but with a consciousness of physical loss—an indefinable sensation, probably mental, of being drawn out of himself. No words came to help him.

"You have acted to-night," continued Séverac Bablon, and Haredale, knowing himself in the presence of the most notorious criminal in Europe, yet listened passively, as a schoolboy to the admonition of his Head, "you have acted to-night unworthily. I had noted you, Sir Richard, as a man whose friendship I had hoped to gain. Knowing your trials, and"—glancing at the girl's pale face—"with what object you suffered them, I had respected you, whilst desiring an opportunity to point out to you the falsity of your position. I had thought that a man who could win such a prize as has fallen to your lot must, essentially, be above all that was petty—all that was mean."

Haredale clenched his hands angrily. Never since his Eton days had such words been addressed to him. He glared at the over-presumptuous mountebank—for so he appraised him; he told himself that, save for a woman's presence, he would have knocked him down. He met the calm but imperious gaze—and did nothing, said nothing.

"A woman may be judged," continued the fascinating voice, "not by her capacity for love, but by her capacity for that rarer thing, friendship. A woman who, at her great personal peril, can befriend another woman is a pearl beyond price. Knowing me, you have ceased to fear me as a rival, Sir Richard." (To his mental amazement something that was not of his mind, it seemed, told Haredale that this was so.) "It remains only for you to hear that simple explanation. Here it is."

He handed a note to him. It was as follows:

"You have confided to me the secret of your residence, where I might see or communicate with you, and I was coming to see you to-night, but I have met with a slight accident—enough to prevent me. Lady Mary has volunteered to go alone. I will not betray your confidence, but our friendly acquaintance cannot continue unless you *instantly* release my father—for I know that you have done this outrageous thing. He is ill and it is very, very cruel. I beg of you to let him return at once. If you admire true friendship and unselfishness, as you profess, do this to repay Mary Evershed, who risks irretrievably compromising herself to take this note—

"ZOE OPPNER."

"Miss Oppner, descending the stairs at Lord Evershed's in too great haste," explained Séverac Bablon, and a new note, faint but perceptible, had crept into his voice, "had the misfortune to sustain a slight accident—I am happy to know, no more than slight. Lady Mary brought me her message. I commit no breach of trust in showing it to you. There is a telephone in the room at Lord Evershed's in which Miss Oppner remains at present, and, as you entered, I obtained her spoken consent to do what I have done."

"Mary," Haredale burst out, "I know it is taking a mean advantage to plead that if I had not been so unutterably wretched and depressed I never could have doubted, but—will you forgive me?"

Whatever its ethical merits or demerits, it was the right, the one appeal. And it served.

Séverac Bablon watched the reconciliation with a smile upon his handsome face. Though clearly but a young man, he could at will invest himself with the aloof but benevolent dignity of a father-confessor.

"The cloud has passed," he said. "I have a word for you, Sir Richard. You have learnt to-night some of my secrets—my appearance, my residence, and the identities of two of my friends. I do not regret this, although I am a 'wanted man.' Only to-night I have committed a gross outrage which, with the circulation of to-morrow's papers, will cry out for redress to the civilised world. You are at liberty to act as you see fit. I would wish, as a favour, that you grant me thirty-six hours' grace—as Miss Oppner already has done. On my word—if you care to accept it—I shall not run away. At the end of that time I will again offer you the choice of detaining me or of condoning what I have done and shall do. Which is it to be?"

Haredale did not feel sure of himself. In fact, the episodes of that night seemed, now, like happenings in a dream—a dream from which he yet was not fully awakened. He glanced from Mary to the incomprehensible man who was so completely different from anything he had pictured, from anything he ever had known. He looked about the bare, cell-like apartment, illuminated by the soft light of the globe upon the massive table. He thought of the Arab who had admitted him—of the entire absence of subterfuge where subterfuge was to be expected.

"I will wait," he said.

But in less than thirty-six hours the world had news of Séverac Bablon.

At a time roughly corresponding with that when Mr. Aloys. X. Alden was standing, temporarily petrified with astonishment, in a certain room of the Hotel Astoria, two gentlemen in evening attire burst into a Wandsworth police station. One was a very angry Irishman, the other a profane Scot, whose language, which struck respectful awe to the hearts of two constables, a sergeant, and an inspector—would have done credit to the most eloquent mate in the mercantile marine.

He fired off a volley of redundant but gorgeously florid adjectives, what time he peeled factitious whiskers from his face and shook their stickiness from his fingers. His Irish friend, with brilliant but less elaborate comments, struggled to depilate a Kaiser-like moustache from his upper lip.

"What are ye sittin' still for-r?" shouted the Scotsman, and banged a card on the desk. "I'm Hector Murray, and this is John Macready of Melbourne.

We've been held up by the highwaym'n Bablon. Turrn out the forrce. Turrn out the dom'd diveesion. Get a move on ye, mon!"

The accumulated power of the three names—Hector Murray, John Macready, and Séverac Bablon—galvanised the station into sudden activity, and an extraordinary story, a fabulous story, was gleaned from the excited gentlemen. It appeared in every paper on the following morning, so it cannot better be presented here than in the comparatively simple form wherein it met the eyes of readers of the *Gleaner's* next issue. Cuts have been made where the reporter's account overlaps the preceding, or where he has become purely rhetorical.

## SIX FAMOUS CAPITALISTS KIDNAPPED

### Séverac Bablon Active Again

## AMAZING OUTRAGE AT THE ASTORIA

Under these heads appeared a full and finely descriptive account of the happenings already noticed.

## DRAMATIC ESCAPE OF MR. MACREADY AND MR. HECTOR MURRAY

### Special Interview with Mr. Murray

## WHERE ARE THE MISSING MAGNATES?

### Is Scotland Yard Effete?

From Mr. Hector Murray ... our special representative obtained a full account of the outrage, which threw much light upon a mystery that otherwise appeared insoluble. After ... they entered the room at the Astoria, where they had agreed to discuss a plan of mutual action against the common enemy of Capital, Mr. Murray informed our representative that nothing unusual took place for some twenty minutes or half an hour. Baron Hague had just risen to make a proposal, when the lights were extinguished.

As it was a very black night, the room was plunged into complete darkness. Before anyone had time to ascertain the meaning of the occurrence, a voice, which our representative was informed seemed to proceed from the floor, uttered the following words:

"Let no one speak or move. Mr. Macready place your revolver upon the table." (Mr. Macready was the only member of the company who was armed, and, curiously enough, as the voice commenced he had drawn his revolver.) "Otherwise, your son's yacht, the *Savannah*, will be posted missing. Hear me out, every one of you, lest great misfortune befall those dear to you. Mr. Murray, your sister and niece will disappear from the Villa Marina, Monte Carlo, within four hours of any movement made by you without my express permission. Mr. Oppner, you have a daughter. Believe me, she and you are quite safe—at present. Baron Hague, Sir Leopold Jesson, and Mr. Rohscheimer, my agents have orders, which only I can recall to bring you to Carey Street. I threaten no more than I can carry out. Give the alarm if it please you ... but I have warned."

During this most extraordinary speech shadowy shapes seemed to be flitting about the room. The nature of the threats uttered had, for the time, quite unmanned the six gentlemen, which is no matter for surprise. Then, at a muttered command in what Mr. Murray informed our representative to have been Arabic, four lamps—or, rather, balls of fire—appeared at the four corners of the apartment. This bizarre scene, suggestive of nothing so much as an Eastern romance, was due to the presence of several Arabs in heavy robes, who had in some way entered in the darkness, and who now stood around the walls, four of their number holding in their brown hands these peculiar globular lights, which were of a kind quite new to those present. (An article by Mr. Pearce Baldry, of Messrs. Armiston, Baldry & Co., dealing with the possible construction of these lamps, appears on page 6.)

Immediately inside the open window stood a tall man in a closely buttoned frock-coat. He carried no arms, but wore a black silk half-mask. Mr. Rohscheimer at this juncture rendered the episode even more dramatic by exclaiming:

"Good heavens! It's Séverac Bablon!"

"It is, indeed, Mr. Rohscheimer," said that menace to civilised society; "so that no doubt you will respect my orders. Mr. Macready, I do not see your revolver upon the table. I have warned you twice."

Mr. Macready, who is not easily intimidated, evidently concluding that no good could come of resistance at that time, threw the revolver on to the table and folded his arms.

"I give you my word," concluded Séverac Bablon, "that no bodily harm shall come to any one of you so long as you attempt no resistance. What will now be done is done only by way of precaution. Any sound would be fatal."

At a signal to the Arabs the four lights were hidden, and each of the six gentlemen were seized in the darkness in such a manner that resistance was impossible. Each had a hand clapped over his mouth, whilst he was securely gagged and bound by men who evidently had the arts of the Thug at their fingers' ends. Mr. Murray informed our representative that so certain were they of Séverac Bablon's power to perform all that he had threatened that, in his opinion, no one struggled, with the exception of Mr. Macready, who, however, was promptly overpowered.

It was then that they learnt how the Arabs and their master had entered. For each of the distinguished company, commencing with Baron Hague, was lowered by a rope to a window on the fifth floor and drawn in by men who waited there.

There is no doubt that access had been gained by means of a short ladder from this lower window; indeed, Mr. Murray saw such a ladder in use when, all having descended through the darkness, the last to leave—an Arab—returned by that means. Such was the dispatch and perfect efficiency of this audacious man's Eastern gang, that Mr. Murray and his friends were all removed from the upper apartment to the lower in less than seven minutes. It will be remembered that the south wing of the Astoria has lately been faced with dark grey granite, that it was a moonless night, and that the daring operation could only have been visible, if visible at all, from the distant Embankment. No hitch occurred whatever; Séverac Bablon's Arabs exhibited all the agility and quickness of monkeys. It is illustrative of his brazen methods that he then removed the gags, and invited his victims to partake of some refreshments, "as they had a long drive before them."

Needless to say, they were all severely shaken by their perilous adventure; and this led to an angry outburst from Mr. Macready, who demanded a full explanation of the outrage.

"Sir," was the reply, "it is not for you to ask. As a final warning to you and to your friends—for the provisions I have made in your case are no more complete than those which I have made in the others—permit me to tell you that eight of the twelve men manning your son's boat including two officers—are under my orders. If any obstacle be placed in my way by you a wireless message will carry instructions, though I myself lie in detention, or dead, that the *Savannah* be laid upon a certain course. That course, Mr. Macready, will not bring her into any port known to the Board of Trade. Shall I nominate the crew? Or are your doubts dispersed?"

The insight thus afforded them to the far-reaching influence, the all-pervading power, of this arch-brigand whose presence in our midst is a disgrace to the police of the world, was sufficient to determine them upon a passive attitude. A gentleman who seemed very nervous then appeared, and skilfully disguised all six. Mr. Rohscheimer mentioned later to Mr. Murray that in this man he had recognised, beyond any shadow of doubt, a perruquier whose name is a household word. But this doubtless was but another clever trick of the master trickster.

In three parties of two, each accompanied by an Arab dressed in European clothes, but wearing a tarboosh, they left the hotel. Disguised beyond recognition, they were conducted to a roomy car of the "family" pattern, which was in waiting; the blinds were drawn down, and they were driven away.

At the end of a rapid drive of about an hour's duration, Messrs. Murray and Macready were requested by one of the three accompanying Arabs to alight, and were informed that Séverac Bablon desired to tender his sincere apologies for the inconvenience to which, unavoidably, he had put them, and for the evils with which—though only in the "most sacred interests"— he had been compelled to threaten them. They were absolved from all obligations and at liberty now to take what steps they thought fit. With which they were set down in a lonely spot, and the car was driven away. As our readers are already well aware, this lonely spot was upon Wandsworth Common.

It is almost impossible to credit the fact that six influential men of world-wide reputation could thus, publicly, be kidnapped from a London hotel. But in this connection two things must be remembered. Firstly, for reasons readily to be understood and appreciated, they offered no resistance; secondly, the presence of so many Orientals in the hotel occasioned no surprise. A Prince Said Abu-el-Ahzab had been residing for some time in the apartments below those occupied by Mr. J. J. Oppner, and the members of his numerous suite are familiar to all residents. He and his following have disappeared, but a cash payment of all outstanding accounts has been left behind. It has been discovered that the light was cut off from one of the rooms occupied by the ci-devant prince, and the police are at work upon several other important clues which point beyond doubt to the fact that "Prince Said Abu-el-Ahzab" was none other than Séverac Bablon.

During the next twenty-four hours the entire habitable world touched by cable service literally gasped at this latest stroke of the notorious Séverac Bablon. Despite the frantic and unflagging labours of every man that Scotland Yard could spare to the case nothing was accomplished. The wife or nearest kin of each of the missing men had received a typed card:

"Fear nothing. No harm shall befall a guest of Séverac Bablon."

These cards, which could be traced to no maker or stationer, all had been posted at Charing Cross.

Then, in the stop press of the *Gleaner's* final edition, appeared the following:

"Baron Hague, Sir L. Jesson, Messrs. Rohscheimer and Oppner have returned to their homes."

It is improbable that in the history of the newspaper business, even during war-time, there has ever been such a rush made for the papers as that which worked the trade to the point of general exhaustion on the following morning.

Without pausing here to consider the morning's news, let us return to the Chancery Legal Incorporated Credit Society Bank.

"Move along here, please. Move on. Move on."

Again the street is packed with emotional humanity. But what a different scene is this, although in its essentials so similar. For every face is flushed with excitement—joyful excitement. As once before, they press eagerly on toward the bank entrance; but this morning the doors are *open*. Almost every member of that crushed and crushing assembly holds a copy of the morning paper. Every man and every woman in the crowd knows that the missing financiers have declined, firmly, to afford any information whatever respecting their strange adventure—that they have refused, all four of them, point blank either to substantiate or to deny the sensational story of Messrs. Macready and Murray. "The incident is closed," Baron Hague is reported as declaring. But what care the depositors of the Chancery Legal Incorporated? For is it not announced, also, that this quartet of public benefactors, with a fifth philanthropist (who modestly remains anonymous) have put up between them no less a sum than three and a half million pounds to salve the wrecked bank?

"By your leave. Make way here. Stand back, *if* you please."

Someone starts a cheer, and it is feverishly taken up by the highly wrought throng, as an escorted van pulls slowly through the crowd. It is bullion from the Bank of England. Good red gold and crisp notes. It is dead hopes raised from the dust; happiness reborn, like a ph[oe]nix from the ashes of misery.

"Hip, hip, hip, hooray!"

Again and again, and yet again that joyous cheer awakes the echoes of the ancient Inns.

It was as a final cheer died away that Haredale, on the rim of the throng, felt himself tapped upon the shoulder.

He turned a flushed face and saw a tall man, irreproachably attired, standing smiling at his elbow. The large eyes, with their compelling light of command, held nothing now but a command to friendship.

"Séverac Bablon!"

"Well, Haredale!" The musical voice made itself audible above all the din. "These good people would rejoice to know the name of that anonymous friend who, with four other disinterested philanthropists, has sought to bring a little gladness into a grey world. Here am I. And there, on the bank steps, are police. Make your decision. Either give me in charge or give me your hand."

Haredale could not speak; but he took the outstretched hand of the most surprising bandit the world ever has known, and wrung it hard.

---

# CHAPTER XXII

## THE TURKISH YATAGHAN

It was about a fortnight later that a City medical man, Dr. Simons, in the dusk of a spring evening, might have been seen pressing his way through the crowd of excited people who thronged the hall of Moorgate Place, Moorgate Street.

Addressing himself to a portly, florid gentleman who exhibited signs of having suffered a recent nervous shock, he said crisply.

"My name, sir, is Simons. You 'phoned me?"

The florid gentleman, mopping his forehead with a Cambridge-blue silk handkerchief, replied rather pompously, if thickly:

"I'm Julius Rohscheimer. You'll have heard of me."

Everyone had heard of that financial magnate, and Dr. Simons bowed slightly.

The two, followed by a murmuring chorus, ascended the stairs.

"Stand back, please," rapped the physician tartly, turning upon their following. "Will someone send for the police and ring up Scotland Yard? This is not a peep-show."

Abashed, the curious ones fell back, and Simons and Rohscheimer went upstairs alone. Most of the people employed in those offices left sharp at six, but a little group of belated workers from an upper floor were nervously peeping in at an open door bearing the words:

DOUGLAS GRAHAM

They stood aside for the doctor, who entered briskly, Rohscheimer at his heels, and closed the door behind him. A chilly and indefinable something pervaded the atmosphere of Moorgate Place a something that floats, like a marsh mist, about the scene of a foul deed.

The outer office was in darkness, as was that opening off it on the left; but out from the inner sanctum poured a flood of light.

Douglas Graham's private office was similar to the private offices of a million other business men, but on this occasion it differed in one dread particular.

Stretched upon the fur rug before the American desk lay a heavily built figure, face downward. It was that of a fashionably dressed man, one who had been portly, no longer young, but who had received a murderous thrust behind the left shoulder-blade, and whose life had ebbed in the grim red stream that stained the fur beneath him.

With a sharp glance about him, the doctor bent, turned the body and made a rapid examination. He stood up almost immediately, shrugging slightly.

"Dead!"

Julius Rohscheimer wiped his forehead with the Cambridge silk.

"Poor Graham! How long?" he said huskily.

"Roughly, half an hour."

"Look! look! On the desk!"

The doctor turned sharply from the body and looked as directed.

Stuck upright amid the litter of papers was a long, curved dagger, with a richly ornamented hilt. Several documents were impaled by its crimson point, and upon the topmost the following had roughly and shakily been printed:

"VENGENCE IS MINE!

"SÉVERAC BABLON."

Dr. Simons started perceptibly, and looked about the place with a sudden apprehension. It seemed to Julius Rohscheimer that his face grew pale.

In the eerie silence of the dead man's room they faced one another.

The doctor, his straight brows drawn together, looked, again and again, from the ominous writing to the poor, lifeless thing on the rug.

"Then, indeed, his sins were great," he whispered.

Rohscheimer, with his eyes fixed on the dagger, shuddered violently.

"Let's get out, doctor," he quavered thickly. "My—my nerve's goin'."

Dr. Simons, though visibly shaken by this later discovery, raised his hand in protest. He was looking, for the twentieth time, at the words printed upon the bloodstained paper.

"One moment," he said, and opened his bag. "Here"—pouring out a draught into a little glass—"drink this. And favour me with two minutes' conversation before the police arrive."

Rohscheimer drank it off and followed the movements of the doctor, who stepped to the telephone and called up a Gerrard number.

"Doctor John Simons speaking," he said presently. "Come *at once* to Moorgate Place, Moorgate Street. Murder been committed by—Séverac Bablon. Most peculiar weapon used. The police, no doubt, would value an expert opinion. You *must* be here within ten minutes."

The arrival of a couple of constables frustrated whatever object Dr. Simons had had in detaining Mr. Rohscheimer, but the doctor lingered on, evidently awaiting whoever he had spoken to on the telephone. The police ascertained from Rohscheimer that he had held an interest in the "Douglas Graham" business, that this business was of an usurious character, that the dead man's real name was Paul Gottschalk, and that he, Rohscheimer, found the outer door fastened when he arrived at about seven o'clock, opened it with a key which he held, and saw Gottschalk as they saw him now. The office was in darkness. Apparently, valuables had been taken from the safe—which was open. The staff usually left at six.

This was the point reached when Detective Harborne put in an appearance and, with professional nonchalance, took over the investigation. Dr. Simons glanced at his watch and impatiently strode up and down the outside office.

A few minutes later came a loud knocking on the door. Simons opened it quickly, admitting a most strange old gentleman—tall and ramshackle—who was buttoned up in a chess-board inverness; whose trousers frayed out over his lustreless boots like much-defiled lace; whose coat-sleeves, protruding from the cape of his inverness, sought to make amends for the dullness of his footwear. He wore a turned-down collar and a large, black French knot. His hirsute face was tanned to the uniform hue of a coffee berry; his unkempt grey hair escaped in tufts from beneath a huge slouched hat; and his keen old eyes peered into the room through thickly pebbled spectacles.

"Dr. Lepardo!" cried Simons. "I am glad to see you, sir."

"Eh? Who's that?" said Harborne, looking out from the inner office, notebook in hand. "You should not have let anybody in, doctor."

"Excuse me, Mr. Harborne," replied Simons civilly, "but I have taken the liberty of asking Doctor Emmanuel Lepardo, whom I chanced to know was in London, to give an opinion upon the rather odd weapon with which this crime was perpetrated. He is one of the first authorities in Europe, and I thought you might welcome his assistance at this early stage of your inquiry."

"Oh," said the detective thoughtfully, "that's different. Thank you, sir," nodding to the new-comer. "I'm afraid your name isn't known to me, but if you can give us a tip or two I shall be grateful. I wish Inspector Sheffield were here. These cases are fair nightmares to me. And now it's got to murder, life won't be worth living at the Yard if we don't make an arrest."

"Yes, yes," said Dr. Lepardo, peering about him, speaking in a most peculiar, rumbling tone, and with a strong accent. "I would not have missed such a chance. Where is this dagger? I have just returned from the Izamal temples of Yucatan. I have brought some fine specimens to Europe. Obsidian knives. Sacrificial. Beautiful."

He shuffled jerkily into the private office, seemed to grasp its every detail in one comprehensive, peering glance, and pounced upon the dagger with a hoarse exclamation. The Scotland Yard man watched him with curiosity, and Julius Rohscheimer, in the open door, followed his movements with a newly awakened interest.

"True Damascus!" he muttered, running a long finger up the blade. "Hilt, Persian—not Kultwork—Persian. Yes. Can I pull it out? Yes? Damascened to within three inches. Very early."

He turned to the detective, dagger in hand.

"This is a Turkish yataghan."

No one appeared to be greatly enlightened.

"When I say a Turkish yataghan I mean that from a broken Damascus sword-blade and a Persian dagger handle, a yataghan of the Turkish pattern has been made. There are stones incrusted in the hilt but the blade is worth more. Very rare. This was made in Persia for the Turkish market."

"One of Séverac Bablon's Arabs," burst in Rohscheimer hoarsely, "has done this."

"Ah, yes. So? I read of him in Paris. He is in league with the chief of the Paris detective. Him? So. I meet him once."

"Eh?" cried Harborne, "Séverac Bablon?"

Julius Rohscheimer's eyes grew more prominent than usual.

"No, no. The great Lemage. Lemage of Paris—his accomplice. This dagger is worth two thousand francs. Let me see if a Turk has been in these rooms. I meet Victor Lemage on such another occasion with this. He say to me, 'Dr. Lepardo, come to the Rue So-and-such. A young person is stabbed with a new kind of knife.' I tell him, 'It is Afghan, M. Lemage.' He find one who had been in that country, arrest—and it is the assassin. There is no smell of a Turk here. Ah, yes. The Turk, he have a smell of his own, as have the negro, the Chinese, the Malay."

Pulling a magnifying-glass from one bulging pocket of his inverness, Dr. Lepardo went peering over the writing desk, passing with a grunt from the bloodstained paper bearing the name of Séverac Bablon to the other documents and books lying there; to the pigeon-holes; to the chair; to the rug; to the body. Crawling on all fours he went peering about the floor, scratching at the carpet with his long nails like some monstrous, restless cat.

Harborne glanced at Dr. Simons and tapped his forehead significantly.

"Humour my friend," whispered the physician. "He may appear mad, but he is a man of most curious information. Believe me, if any Oriental has been in these rooms within the last hour he will tell you so."

Dr. Lepardo from beneath a table rumbled hoarsely:

"There is a back stair. He went out that way as someone came in."

Julius Rohscheimer started violently.

"Good God! Then he was here when *I* came in!" he exclaimed.

"Who speaks?" rumbled Lepardo, crawling away into the outside office, and apparently following a trail visible only to himself.

"It is Mr. Julius Rohscheimer," explained Simons. "He was a partner, I understand, of the late Mr. Graham's. He entered with a key about seven o'clock and discovered the murder."

"As he came in our friend the assassin go out," cried Lepardo.

Harborne gave rapid orders to the two constables, both of whom immediately departed.

"Are you sure of that, sir?" he called.

Against the promptings of his common sense, the eccentric methods of the peculiar old traveller were beginning to impress him.

"Certainly. But look!"

Dr. Lepardo re-entered the inner office, carrying several files.

"See! He begins to destroy these letters. He has certainly taken many away. If you look you see that he has torn pages from the private accounts on the desk. He is disturbed by Mr. Someheimer. Can you know the address of his lady secretary-typist?"

Harborne's eyes sparkled appreciatively.

"You're pretty wide at this business, doctor," he confessed. "I'm looking after her myself. But Mr. Rohscheimer doesn't know, and all the staff have gone long ago."

"Ah!" rumbled Dr. Lepardo, dropping his glass into the sack-like pocket. "No Arab or such person has done this. He was one who wore gloves. So I no longer am interested. Here"—placing a small object on the desk beside the yataghan—"is new evidence I find for you. It is a boot-button—foreign. Ah! if the great Lemage could be here. It is his imagination that makes him supreme. In his imagination he would murder again the poor Graham with the yataghan. He would lose his boot-button. He would run away—as Mr. Heimar comes in—to some hiding-place, taking with him the bills and the letters he had stolen, and the notes from the safe. Once in his secret retreat, he would arrest himself—and behold, in an hour—in ten minutes—his hand would be upon the shoulder of the other assassin. Ah! such a case would be joy to him. He would revel. He would gloat."

Harborne nodded.

"If Mr. Lemage would come and revel with me for half an hour I wouldn't say no to learning from him," he said. "But it isn't likely—particularly considering that this is a Séverac Bablon case."

"Ah!" rumbled Dr. Lepardo, "you should travel, my friend. You would learn much of the imagination in the desert of Sahara, in the forests of Yucatan."

"You know," continued Harborne, turning to Simons, "these Séverac Bablon cases—I don't mind admitting it—are over my weight. They bristle with clues. We get to know of addresses he uses—people he's acquainted with—and what good does it do us? Not a ha'p'orth. Of course, it's a fact that he's had influential friends up to now, but this job, unless I'm mistaken, will alter the complexion of things. What d'you think Victor Lemage will say to *this*, Dr. Lepardo?"

But there was no one to answer, for the man from the forests of Yucatan had vanished.

The charwoman of Moorgate Place was the next person to encounter Dr. Lepardo, and his kindly manner completely won her heart. She had seen Miss Maitland—the dead man's secretary—regularly go to lunch and sometimes to tea with a young lady from Messrs. Bowden and Ralph's. The staff at this firm of stockbrokers was working late, and it was unlikely that the young lady had left, even yet. Dr. Lepardo expressed his anxiety to make her acquaintance, and was conducted by the garrulous old charwoman to an office in Copthall Avenue. The required young lady was found.

"My dear," said Dr. Lepardo, paternally, "I have a private matter of utmost importance to tell to Miss Maitland—to-night. Where shall I find her?"

She lived, he was informed, at No. —— Stockwell Road, S.W. He took his departure, leaving an excellent impression behind him and half a sovereign in the hand of the charwoman. A torpedo-like racing car was waiting near Lothbury corner, and therein, Dr. Lepardo very shortly was whirling southward. The chauffeur negotiated London Bridge in a manner that filled the hearts of a score of taxi drivers with awe and wonderment. Stockwell Road was reached in twelve and a half minutes.

A dingy maid informed Dr. Lepardo that Miss Maitland had just finished her dinner. Would he walk up?

Dr. Lepardo walked up and made himself known to the pretty brown-haired girl who rose to greet him. Miss Maitland clearly was surprised—and a little frightened—by this unexpected visit. Her glance strayed from the visitor to a silver-framed photograph on the mantelpiece and back again to Dr. Lepardo in a curiously wistful way.

"My dear," he said, and his kindly, paternal manner seemed to reassure her somewhat, "I have come to ask your help in a——"

He suddenly stepped to the mantelpiece and peered at the photograph. It was that of a rather odd-looking young man, and bore the inscription: "To Iris. Lawrence."

"Why, yes," he burst out; "surely this is my old friend! Can it be my old friend—Gardener—Gaston—ah! I have no memory for his name. The good boy, Lawrence Greely?"

The girl's eyes opened wildly.

"Guthrie!" she said, blushing. "You mean Guthrie?"

"Ah! Guthrie," cried the doctor, triumphantly. "You know my old friend, Lawrence Guthrie? He is in England?"

"He has never left it, to my knowledge," said the girl with sudden doubt.

"Foolish me," exclaimed Lepardo. "It was his father that lives abroad, in the East—Bagdad—Cairo."

"Constantinople," corrected Miss Maitland.

"Still the old foolish," rumbled her odd visitor. "Always the old fool. To be certain, it was Constantinople."

A curious gleam had crept into the keen eyes that twinkled behind the pebbles.

"He used to say to me, the Guthrie père, 'I send that boy Turkish pipes and ornaments and curiosities for his room. I wonder if that bad fellow'"—Dr. Lepardo poked a jesting finger at the girl—"'I wonder if he sell them.'"

"I'm *sure* he wouldn't," flashed Miss Maitland. Then came a sudden cloud upon the young face. "That is—I don't think he would—if he could help it."

"Ah, those money troubles," sighed the old doctor. "But I quite forgot my business, thinking of Lawrence. There has been an—accident at your office, my child. *He* is quite well. Do not be afraid. Tell me—when did you leave to-night?"

Iris Maitland retreated from him step by step, her eyes fixed affrightedly upon his face. She sank into an arm-chair. The pretty blush had fled now, and she was very pale.

"Why," she said tensely, "why have you asked me those questions? You do not know Lawrence. What has happened? Oh, what has happened?"

She was trembling now.

"Oh," she said, "I am afraid of you, Dr. Lepardo. I don't know what you want. Who are you? But I see now that you have made me tell you all about him. I will tell you no more."

"My dear," said Dr. Lepardo, and the rumbling of his voice was kindly, "a woman has that great gift, intuition. It is true. It is my rule, my dear, never to neglect opportunity, however slight. When I arrive, unexpected, you glance at his photograph. You associate him, then, with the unexpected. I experiment. Forgive me. It is by such leaps in the dark that great things are won. It is where a little intuition is worth much wisdom. You are a brave girl, and so I tell you—it is for you to save Lawrence. If the Scotland Yard Mr. Harborne knew so much as I, nothing, I fear, could save him. I can do it—*I*. You shall help me. I work, my child, as no man has worked before. For great things I work. I work against time—against the police. I aspire to do the all but impossible—the wonderful. Only what you call luck and what I call intuition can make me win. A bargain—you answer me my questions and I answer you yours?"

The girl nodded. Her fingers were clutching and releasing the arms of the chair. Through the odd mask of peering benevolence worn by the brown old traveller another, inspired, being momentarily had peeped forth.

"What time did you leave to-night?"

"A quarter past six."

"How many appointments had Mr. Graham afterwards? One with Lawrence. What other?"

"With Mr. Rohscheimer."

"No other?"

"No."

"What time Lawrence?"

"Directly I left."

"Mr. Graham did not know you two are acquainted, eh?"

"He did not."

"Had you access to his private accounts that he keep in his safe?"

"No."

"You keep the files?"

"Yes."

"Who is the most important creditor filed under G? Lawrence?"

The girl shook her head emphatically.

"Why, he only owed about fifty pounds," she said. "There were none of importance under G, except Garraway, the Hon. Claude Garraway and Count de Guise."

"Ah! Count de Guise. So quaint a name. He is rich, yes?"

"Awfully rich. He is selling all the things in his flat and going abroad for good. There is an advertisement in to-day's paper. His pictures and things are valued at no less than thirty thousand pounds. I don't know how his business stood with Mr. Graham; latterly, it had not passed through my hands at all."

"And his address?"

"59b Bedford Court Mansions."

"And I must see Lawrence too. Where shall I find him?"

"At Bart's—St. Bartholomew's Hospital. He is studying there. You are sure to find him there to-night. He is engaged there, I know, up to ten o'clock."

Dr. Lepardo took the girl's hand and pressed it soothingly.

"Do not faint; be a brave girl," he said. "Your employer was killed shortly after you left."

Deathly pale, she sat watching him.

"By—whom?"

"By Séverac Bablon, so it is written on his desk. It is unfortunate that Lawrence was there to-night; but I—I am your friend, my child. Are you going to faint—no?"

"No," said the girl, smiling bravely.

"Then good-night."

He pressed her hand again—and was gone.

# CHAPTER XXIII

## M. LEVI

The art of detection, in common with every other art, produces from time to time a genius; and a genius, whatever else he may be, emphatically is *not* a person having "an infinite capacity for taking pains." Such masters of criminology as Alphonse Bertillon or his famous compatriot, Victor Lemage, whose resignation so recently had stirred the wide world to wonder—achieve their results by painstaking labours, yes, but all those labours would be more or less futile without that elusive element of inspiration, intuition, luck—call it what you will—which constitutes genius, which alone distinguishes such men from the other capable plodders about them. A brief retrospective survey of the surprising results achieved by Dr. Lepardo within the space of an hour will show these to have been due to brilliant imagination, deep knowledge of human nature, foresight, unusual mental activity, and—that other capacity so hard to define.

Dr. Lepardo was studying the following paragraph marked by Miss Maitland:

FOR SALE.—Entire furniture, antique, of large flat, comprising pieces by Sheraton, Chippendale, Boule, etc. Paintings by Greuze, Murillo, Van Dyck, also modern masters. Pottery, Chinese, Sèvres, old English, etc. A collection of 500 pieces of early pewter, etc., etc., etc. The whole valued at over £30,000.

The torpedo-like car had dropped him at Bedford Court Mansions, and, shuffling up the steps into the hall, he addressed himself to the porter.

"Ah, my friend, has the Count de Guise gone out again?"

"I have not seen him go out, sir."

"Not since you saw him come in?"

"Not since then, sir—no."

"About half-past seven he came in, I think? Yes, about half-past."

"Quite right, sir."

Again the odd gleam came into the doctor's eyes, as it had come when, by one of his amazing leading questions he had learnt that Lawrence Guthrie's father resided in Constantinople. The doctor mounted to the first floor. He was about to ring the bell of No. 59b, when another idea struck him. He descended and again addressed the porter.

"The Count must be resting. He does not reply. He has, of course, discharged his servants?"

"Yes, sir. He leaves England next week."

"Ah, he is alone."

Upstairs once more.

He rang three times before the door was opened to him by a tall, slight man, arrayed in a blue silk dressing-gown. He had a most pleasant face, and wore his moustache and beard according to the latest Parisian mode. He looked about thirty years of age, was fair, blue-eyed, and handsome.

"I am sorry to trouble you so late, Count," said the old doctor, in perfect French; "but I think I can make you an offer for some, if not all, of your collection."

He hunted, peering through a case which apparently contained some dozens of cards, finally handing the Count the following:

ISIDOR LEVI

Fine Art Expert

*London and Paris.*

Count de Guise hesitated, glanced at his caller, glanced at his watch, cleared his throat—and still hesitated.

"If I approve," continued 'Isidor Levi,' "I will hand you a cheque on the Crédit Lyonnais."

The Count bowed.

"Enter, M. Levi. Your name, of course, is known to me."

Indeed it was a name familiar enough in art circles.

Dr. Lepardo entered.

The room into which the Count ushered him was most magnificently appointed. The visitor's feet sank into the carpet as into banked moss. Beautiful furniture stood about. Pictures by eminent artists graced the walls. Statuettes, vases, busts, choice antiques, were everywhere. It was the room of a wealthy connoisseur, of an æsthete whose delicacy of taste bordered upon the effeminate. The doctor stared hard at the Count without permitting the latter to observe that he did so. With his hands thrust deep in the sack-like pockets of his inverness he drifted from treasure to treasure—uninvited, from room to room—like some rudderless craft. The Count followed. In his handsome face it might be read that he resented the attitude of M. Levi, who behaved as though he found himself in the gallery of a dealer. Suddenly, before a Van Dyck portrait, the visitor cried:

"Ah, a forgery, m'sieur! Spurious."

Count de Guise leapt round upon him with perfect fury blazing in his blue eyes. The veins had sprung into prominence upon his forehead, and one throbbed—a virile blue cord—upon his left temple.

"M'sieur!"

He seemed to choke. His sudden passion was volcanic—terrible.

Dr. Lepardo, still peering, seemed not to heed him; then quickly:

"Ah, I apologise, I most sincerely apologise. I was misled by the unusual tone of the brown. But—no, it is undoubted. None other than Van Dyck painted that ruff."

The Count glared and quivered, his fine nostrils distended, a while longer, but swallowed his rage and bowed in acknowledgment of the apology. Dr. Lepardo was off again upon his voyage of discovery, drifting from picture to vase, from statuette to buhl cabinet.

"M'sieur," he rumbled, peering around at de Guise, who now stood by the fireplace of the room to which the visitor's driftings had led him, his hands locked behind him. "I think I can propose you for the entire collection. Is it agreeable?"

The Count bowed.

"Ah!"

M. Levi seated himself at the writing-table—for the room was a beautifully appointed study—and produced a cheque-book.

"Twenty thousand pounds, English?"

The Count laughed contemptuously.

"Twenty-two?"

"Do not jest, m'sieur. Nothing but thirty."

"Twenty-eight is final. It is the price I had determined upon."

De Guise considered, bit his lip, glanced at the open cheque-book—always a potent argument—and bowed in his grand fashion. Lepardo changed his spectacles for a larger pair, reached for a pen, peering, and overturned a massive inkstand. The ink poured in an oily black stream across the leathern top of the table.

"Ah, clumsy!" he cried. "Blotting-paper, quick."

The other took some from a drawer and sopped up the ink. Lepardo rumbled apologies, and, when the ink had been dried up, made out a cheque for £28,000, payable to "The Count de Guise, in settlement for the entire effects contained in his flat, No. 59b Bedford Court Mansions," signed it "I. Levi," and handed it to de Guise, who was surveying his inky hands, usually so spotless, with frowning disfavour.

The Count took the cheque, and Lepardo stood up.

"One moment, m'sieur."

Lepardo sat down again.

"You have dated this cheque 1928."

"Ah," cried the other, "always so absent. I had in mind the price, m'sieur. Believe me, I shall lose on this deal, but no matter. Give it back to me; I will write out another."

The second cheque made out, correctly, Lepardo shuffled to the door, refusing de Guise's offer of refreshments. He was about to pass out on to the landing when:

"Heavens! I am truly an absent fool. I wear my writing glasses and have left my street glasses on your table. One moment. No, I would not trouble you."

He shuffled quickly back to the study, to return almost immediately, glasses in hand.

"Will seven-thirty in the morning be too early for my men to commence an inventory?"

"Not at all."

"Good night, m'sieur le Comte."

"Good night, M. Levi."

So concluded an act in this strange comedy.

Let us glance for a moment at Thomas Sheard, of the *Gleaner*, who sat in his study, his head resting upon his clenched hand, his pipe cold.

Twelve o'clock, and the household sleeping. He had spent the early part of the night at Moorgate Place, had written his account of the murder, seen it consigned to the machines, and returned wearily home. Now, in the stillness, he was listening; every belated cab whose passing broke the silence of the night set his heart beating, for he was listening—listening for Séverac Bablon.

His faith was shaken.

He had been content to know himself the confidant of the man who had taken from Park Lane to give to the Embankment; of the man who had kidnapped four great millionaires and compelled them each to bear an equal share with himself, towards salving a wrecked bank; of the man, who assisted by M. Lemage, the first detective in Europe, had hoodwinked Scotland Yard. But the thought that he had called "friend" the man who had murdered, or caused to be murdered, Douglas Graham—whatever had been the dead man's character—was dreadful—terrifying.

It meant? It meant that if Séverac Bablon did not come, and come that night, to clear himself, then he, Sheard, must confess to his knowledge of him—must, at whatever personal cost, give every assistance in his power to those who sought to apprehend the murderer.

A key turned in the lock of the front door.

Sheard started to his feet. A soft step in the hall—and Séverac Bablon entered.

The journalist could find no words to greet him; but he stood watching the fine masterful face. There was a new, eager look in the long, dark eyes.

Séverac Bablon extended his hand. Sheard shook his head and resting his elbow on the mantelpiece, looked down into the dying embers of the fire.

"You, too, my friend?"

Sheard turned impulsively.

"Tell me you are in no way implicated in that ghastly crime!" he burst out. "Only tell me, and I shall be satisfied."

Séverac Bablon stepped quickly forward, grasped him by both shoulders and looked hard into his eyes with that strange, penetrating gaze that seemed to pierce through all pretence into the mind beyond.

"Sheard, in the pursuit of what I—and my poor wisdom may be no better than a wiser man's folly—of what I consider to be Nature's one law—Justice, I have braved the laws of man, risked my honour and my liberty. I have dared to hold the scales, to weigh in the balance some of the affairs of men. But life, be it that of the lowliest insect, of the vilest sinner against every code of mankind, is sacred. I—with all my egotism, with all my poor human vanity—would not dare to rob a fellow creature of that gift which only God can give, which only God may take back."

"Then——"

"You, who knew me, doubted?"

Sheard grasped the proffered hand.

"Forgive my fears," he said warmly; "I should have known. But this horrible thing has shaken me. I cannot survey murdered corpses with the calmly professional eye of the Sheffields and Harbornes."

"It was the work of an enemy, Sheard. There are men labouring, even now, piecing a false chain together, link by link; searching, spying, toiling in the dark to prove that the robber, the incendiary, the iconoclast, is also a murderer. I have need of all my friends to-night."

With a weary gesture, almost pathetic, he ran his fingers through his black hair. The shaded light struck greenly venomous sparks from his ring.

"This is such a coward's blow as I never had foreseen," he continued; "but, as I believe, my resources are equal even to this."

"What! You know the murderer?"

"If the wrong man is not arrested by some one of the agents of Scotland Yard, of Mr. Oppner, of Julius Rohscheimer, of Heaven alone knows how many others that seek, I have hopes that within a few hours, at most, of the world's learning I am an assassin, the world will learn that I am not. Can you be ready to accompany me at any hour after 5 A.M. that I may come for you?"

Sheard stared.

"Certainly."

"Then—to bed, oh, doughty copy-hunter. You still are my friend. That is all I wished to know. For that alone I came like a thief in the night. Until I return, au revoir."

# CHAPTER XXIV

## "V-E-N-G-E-N-C-E"

At half-past seven on the morning following M. Levi's visit the Count de Guise opened the door of 59b Bedford Court Mansions to that eccentric old art expert. M. Levi was accompanied by his partner, a tall, heavily bearded man, who looked like a Russian, and by two other strangers, one an alert-eyed, clean-shaven person in a tweed suit, the other a younger man, evidently Scotch, who carried a little brown bag. These two would commence an inventory, m'sieur being agreeable.

Entering the dining-room, with its massive old oak furniture, de Guise, who found something uncomfortably fascinating in the eye of the partner, lighted a cigarette and took up a position on the rug before the fire, hands characteristically locked behind him.

"This is the Greuze," said Dr. Lepardo, pointing.

The Count, with the others, turned to look at the picture.

*Click! Click!*

He was securely handcuffed.

With an animal scream of rage the Count turned upon Lepardo, the vein throbbing on his temple, his eyes glaring in maniacal fury. He sought to speak, but only a slight froth rose to his lips; no word could he utter.

"Sit down in that chair," said Dr Lepardo.

With a gurgling scream de Guise's fury found utterance.

"Release me immediately. What——"

*"Sit down!"*

De Guise ground his white teeth together. The pulsing vein on his brow seemed like to burst. He dropped into a chair, trembling and quivering with passionate anger.

"You—shall—pay for—this!"

"My friend," said Lepardo, turning to the man who had carried the bag, "this gentleman"—nodding at his companion in the tweed suit—"would like to hear who you are, and for what you visited Moorgate Place last evening."

"I am Lawrence Guthrie," explained the young man, "and yesterday, much against my inclinations, but to prevent Graham's exposing the state of my affairs to my father, I was forced to leave with him, as security for fifty pounds, a Turkish yataghan worth considerably more."

"Stop! When I came to your Bart's last night, what did I tell you?"

"That Graham had been murdered with my yataghan."

"Well?"

"You said that the crime looked like the work of an old hand, for the murderer had worn gloves. You told me that you had recognised, in one of the victim's most important creditors, a notorious French criminal, André Legun——"

The Count, deathly pale, his throbbing forehead wet as if douched, drew a long, hissing breath. His eyes stared glassily at Dr. Lepardo.

"By what means?"

"By certain facial peculiarities."

"Rule 85."

"And particularly by a vein in his left temple, only visible when he was roused. You had secured, by a trick——"

"Article Six."

"An imprint of his thumb upon a cheque. This you had compared with certain in your possession—and forwarded to Paris."

"Unnecessary, but a usual form."

"You had secured from the grate in his study a pocketful of ash, some scraps of torn leather—bloodstained—and some few other fragments. These you and I spent the night examining and arranging. Amongst the ashes was a patent glove button, also bloodstained."

"What have I yet to find?"

"A pair of boots."

"I depart to find them."

Dr. Lepardo quitted the room. Count de Guise followed him with his eyes until he had disappeared. No one spoke nor stirred until the brown old doctor returned, carrying a pair of glacé kid boots.

He placed them on the table beside the bag and pointed a long finger at a gap in one row of buttons.

"Scotland Yard can complete the set, André," he said with grim humour. "In this bag are the results of our examination. In your grate are more ashes and fragments for the English Home Office to check us by. In this bag is a complete account of how you came to Moorgate Place, knocked at Gottschalk's door and were admitted. I do not know how you had *meant* to kill him, but the yataghan, left on his table by Mr. Guthrie, was tempting, eh? You then commenced to collect certain letters and papers, André. You tore from his private book the page containing your little account. Then you tore out others, to blind us all. You had begun upon the letter files when you were interrupted by one entering with a key. That was fortunate. It was file G you had commenced upon, André. And one of the torn pages was G. So I knew that you were a G, too, my friend. With what you took from the safe and with the letters and other papers, you slipped down the back stair you knew of into Copthall Avenue. By my great good luck, and not by my skill, I get upon your trail. But by my skill I trap you."

The prisoner, whose handsome face now had assumed a leaden hue, whose eyes were set in a fixed stare of horror and hatred, spoke slowly, clearly.

"You talk nonsense. You taunt me, to drive me mad. I ask you—who are you? You are not Levi, you are some spy."

Dr. Lepardo, or M. Isidor Levi, removed a grey wig and a pair of spectacles and seemed by some relaxation of the facial muscles, to melt out of existence, leaving in his place a heavy-eyed man, with stained skin and thin, straggling hair.

De Guise, as though an unseen hand pushed him, stepped back—and back—and back—until a heavy oak chair prevented further retreat. There—like a mined fortress, hitherto staunch, defiant—he seemed to crumble up.

"The good God!" he whispered. "It is *Victor Lemage!*"

"André Legun—Chevalier d'Oysan—Comte de Guise," said the famous criminologist, "Paris wants you, but London now has a better claim. So, when I have stolen back my cheque from your pocket-book, I hand you over to London."

With the bravado of the true French criminal, Legun forced a smile to his lips.

"It is finished, Victor," he said, dropping his affected manner and speaking with an exaggerated low Paris accent. "I am glad it was you, and not some stupid policeman of England who took me. Well, who cares? I have had a short life but a merry one. You know, Victor, that my misfortune in being the son of an aristocrat has pursued me always. I have such refined tastes, and such a skill with the cards. You recall the little house near the fortifications? But the inevitable run of bad luck came. One question. Why"—he glanced at the Russian-looking man with something like fear creeping again into his bold eyes—"why do you hunt me down?"

The black beard and moustache were pulled off in a second by their wearer, revealing a face of severely classic beauty. Lawrence Guthrie stared hard.

"Mr. Guthrie," said the whilom Russian, "behold me at your mercy. You know me innocent of one, at least, of the sins ascribed to me. I am Séverac Bablon."

Guthrie hesitated for one tremendous moment; he looked from the handsome face of the most notorious man in Europe to that of his companion who wore the tweed suit, and whom he knew to be H. T. Sheard, the well-known member of the *Gleaner* staff. His decision was made. He stretched out his hand and took that of Séverac Bablon.

"You ask," said the latter sternly to Legun, "why we have hunted you down. I answer—first, in the sacred interest of Justice; second, because you imputed your vile crime to *me*."

"What! To *you*? No! never!"

Victor Lemage's eyelids lifted quickly.

"Spell vengeance."

"V-e-n-g-e-a-n-c-e."

"My friends," said Lemage, reaching for the wide-brimmed hat of Dr. Lepardo, "I all but have spoiled this, my greatest case, by a stupid blunder. I have an early call to make. Advance your packing in my absence. I shall shortly return."

And so it happened that Mr. Julius Rohscheimer, in Park Lane, was just arising when his man brought him a card:

*Detective-Inspector Sheffield C.I.D., New Scotland Yard.*

Rohscheimer, who looked as though he had spent a poor night, ordered that Inspector Sheffield be shown up without delay. Immediately afterwards there came in a tall, black-bearded man, wearing blue spectacles, an old rain-coat, and a dilapidated silk hat. The drive, though short, had been long enough to enable Victor Lemage, secure from observation behind the drawn blinds of Séverac Bablon's big car, to merge his personality into that of another man, distinct from Dr. Lepardo—unlike M. Levi.

"Who are you?" blustered Rohscheimer, changing colour, and drawing a brilliant dressing-gown more closely about him. "Who the blazes are you?"

"*Ssh!* I am Inspector Sheffield—disguised. You will excuse me if, even here, I continue to impersonate an eccentric French character. You place yourself within the reach of the law, my friend. You lay yourself open to the suspicion of murder."

Julius Rohscheimer swallowed noisily. His flabby face assumed a dingy hue; his eyes protruded to an unpleasant degree.

"Here, upon this, my card, write the words, 'Vengeance is mine.'"

Rohscheimer rose unsteadily; his puffy hands groped as if, feeling himself slipping, he sought for something to lay hold upon.

"I swear——"

"Write!"

Rohscheimer shakily wrote the words, "*Vengence is mine.*"

"No 'a,'" cried Lemage triumphantly, "no 'a'! Of all the stupid pigs I am he. But I had not given you the credit of such nerve, M. Rohscheimer. I had forgotten how once you lived the rough life in South Africa. It is so? I did not think you had the courage to write—though wobbly—those lying words in presence of the dead Gottschalk. Why did you do it, you bad, foolish fellow? The yataghan already was stuck in the desk, eh? That Legun is a fury when the blood thirst is upon him, when the big vein throb. And you saw the blank paper? Yes? Or you feared that you—you—the mighty Julius might be suspect? Yes, a little? Principally you hope that this will spur the police and that *he* will hang. You prefer that the real one—who slays your partner—shall go free, if *he* can be blackened. You throw sand in the eye of Justice, eh? Well—you have influence; you shall use it to get yourself made Scotch-free. Very good. You will now write in a few words how all this is. That or—I have men outside. It is a public removal to—Good, you will write."

---

At about that hour when, at thousands of breakfast tables, horrified readers learned that Séverac Bablon's Arabs had committed a ghastly crime in Moorgate Street, a cart drove up to New Scotland Yard, and two green-aproned individuals both of whom would have been improved artistically by a clean shave, dragged a heavy packing-case into the office, said it contained curiosities from Bedford Court Mansions and was for Inspector Sheffield.

When, half an hour later, the unwieldy box had been opened, out glared a bound and gagged man, upon whose left temple there pulsed and throbbed a dark blue vein!

Detailed evidence proving that this was the murderer of Gottschalk, his record, his measurements, his thumb-prints, his boots, a number of tubes containing scraps of stained leather, a number containing ashes, and all neatly labelled together with a written confession, signed "Julius Rohscheimer," to the authorship of the words "Vengeance is mine" were also in this box. Finally, there was the following note:

"DEAR INSPECTOR SHEFFIELD,

"I enclose herewith André Legun, the man who murdered Paul Gottschalk, together with sufficient evidence to ensure a conviction, and completely to exculpate myself. I claim no credit. We both are indebted to M. Victor Lemage, who not only has surpassed his own brilliant records in the conduct of this case, but who kindly assisted me to carry the result of his labours into the office at New Scotland Yard. We both regretted our inability to see you personally.

"SÉVERAC BABLON."

# CHAPTER XXV

## AN OFFICIAL CALL

The Home Secretary sat before the red-leathern expanse of his writing-table. Papers of unique political importance were strewn carelessly about that diplomatic battlefield, for at this famous table the Right Honourable Walter Belford played political chess. To the right honourable gentleman the game of politics was a pursuit only second in its fascinations to the culture of rare orchids. It ranked in that fine, if eccentric, mind about equal with the accumulating of rare editions, early printed works, illuminated missals, palimpsests, and other MSS., or with the delights of the higher photography—a hobby to which Mr. Belford devoted much attention.

Visitors to a well-known Sussex coast resort will need no introduction to Womsley Old Place, the charming seat of that charming man, the Right Hon. Walter Belford. With a frowning glance at a number of letters pinned neatly together, Mr. Belford leant back in his heavily padded chair, and, through his gold-rimmed pince-nez, allowed himself the momentary luxury of surveying the loaded shelves of the noted Circular Study wherein he now was seated. The great writing-table, with its priceless bronze head of Cicero and its luxurious appointments; the morocco, parchment, the vellum backs of the rare works about; the busts above the belles-lettres, afforded him visible, if æsthetic enjoyment. In a gap between two tall bookcases a Persian curtain partially concealed the glass doors of a huge conservatory. Mr. Belford liked his orchids near him when at work and not, as lesser men, when at play.

Sighing gently, he took up the bundle of letters, laid it down again, and pressed a button.

"I will see Inspector Sheffield," he said to the footman who came.

Almost immediately entered a big man, fresh complexioned and of modest bearing—a man, Mr. Belford determined after one shrewd glance, who, once he saw his duty clearly, would pursue it through fire and flood, but who frequently experienced some difficulty in this initial particular.

"Sit down, inspector," said the politician genially, and with the appearance of wishing to hasten a distasteful business. "You would like to see the three communications which I have received from this man Bablon?"

Sheffield, seated on the extreme edge of a big morocco-covered lounge-chair, nodded deferentially. Mr. Belford took up the bundle of letters.

"This," he said, passing one to the man from Scotland Yard, "is that which I received upon the 28th ultimo."

Chief-Inspector Sheffield bent forward to the shaded light and ran his eyes over the following, written in a neat hand upon a plain correspondence card:

"Séverac Bablon begs to present his compliments to His Majesty's Principal Secretary of State for the Home Department and to request the honour of a private interview, which, he begs to assure the right honourable gentleman, would be mutually advantageous. The words, 'Safe conduct.— W. B.,' together with time and place proposed, in the agony column of *The Times*, he will accept as a sufficient guarantee of the right honourable gentleman's intentions."

"And this," continued Mr. Belford, selecting a second, "reached me upon the 7th instant":

"Séverac Bablon begs to present his compliments to His Majesty's Principal Secretary of State for the Home Department and to urge upon him the absolute necessity of an immediate interview. He would respectfully assure the right honourable gentleman that high issues are at stake."

"Finally," continued the politician, as Sheffield laid the second card upon the table, "I received this upon the 13th instant—yesterday":

"Séverac Bablon begs to present his compliments to His Majesty's Principal Secretary of State for the Home Department and to inform the right honourable gentleman that he having failed to appoint a time of meeting, Séverac Bablon is forced by circumstances to make his own appointment, and will venture to present himself at Womsley Old Place on the evening of the 14th instant, between the hours of 8 and 9."

Mr. Belford leant back in his chair, turning it slightly that he might face the detective.

"My information is," he said, in his finely modulated voice, "that you are personally familiar with the appearance of this Séverac Bablon"—Sheffield nodded—"but that no one else, or—ah—no one whom we may call upon—is in a position to identify him. Now, apart from the fact that I have reason to fear his taking some improper measures to see me here, this singular case is rapidly assuming a political significance!" He made the impressive pause of the cultured elocutionist. "Unofficially, I am advised that there is some wave of afflated opinion passing through the Semitic races of the Near East—if, indeed, it has not touched the Moslems. The Secretary for Foreign Affairs anticipates—I speak as a member of the public—anticipates a letter from a certain quarter respecting the advisablity of seizing the person of this man without delay. Had such a letter actually reached my friend, I had had no alternative but to place the matter in the hands of the Secret Service."

Inspector Sheffield fidgeted.

"Excuse me, sir," he said; "but the S.S. could do no more than we are doing."

"That I grant you," replied the Home Secretary, with his genial smile; "but, in the event referred to, no choice would remain to me. Far from desiring the intervention of another agent, I should regret it, for—family reasons."

"Ah!" said the inspector; "I was about to—to—approach that side of the matter, sir."

Mr. Belford's emotions were under perfect control, but at those words he regarded the detective with a new interest.

"You have my respectful attention," he said.

"Well, sir,"—Sheffield was palpably embarrassed—"there's nothing to be gained by beating about the bush! Excuse me, sir! But I know, and you know, that Lady Mary Evershed—your niece, sir—and her American friend, Miss Zoe Oppner, are——"

"Yes, inspector?"

"Are acquainted with Séverac Bablon!"

Mr. Belford scrutinised Sheffield closely. There was more in the man than appeared at first sight.

"Is this regrettable fact so generally known?" he asked rather coldly.

"No, sir," replied the other; "but if the case went on the Secret Service Fund it might be compromising!"

"Do I understand you to mean, inspector, that the discretion of our political agents is not to be relied upon?"

"No, sir. But your—private information could hardly be withheld from them—as it has been withheld from us!"

Even the politician's studied reserve was not proof against that thrust. He started. Chief-Inspector Sheffield, after all, was a man to be counted with. A silence fell between them—to be broken by the Home Secretary.

"Your frankness pleases me, Inspector Sheffield."

The other bowed awkwardly.

"I perceive that you would make a bargain. I am to take you into my confidence, and you, in turn, hope to render any employment of the Fund unnecessary?"

"Whatever you tell me, sir, will go no farther—not to one other living. Better confide in me than in a political agent. Then, you can't have anything more incriminating than this."

He took a card from his pocket and placed it before Mr. Belford.

"TO LADY MARY EVERSHED.

"I shall always be indebted to you and to Miss Oppner, but I can assure you of Sir Richard's safety.

"SÉVERAC BABLON."

"No one has seen that but myself," continued the detective. "I know better! But anything further you can let me have, sir, will help me to get them out of the tangle: that's what I'm aiming at!"

Mr. Belford's expression had changed when the damning card was placed before him; but his decision was quickly come to. He opened a drawer of the writing table.

"Here," he said, passing a sheet of foolscap to the inspector, "is the plan of international co-operation which—I will return candour for candour—the increasing importance of the case renders expedient. It was drawn up by my friend the Foreign Secretary. It ensures secrecy, dispatch, and affords no loophole by which Bablon can escape us."

His manner had grown brisk. The dilettante was lost in the man of action.

Inspector Sheffield read carefully through the long document and returned it to Belford, frowning thoughtfully.

"Thank you, sir," he said; "and what else?"

Mr. Belford smiled thoughtfully.

"You are aware that, owing to the family complications referred to, I have been employing Mr. Paul Harley, the private detective?"

Sheffield nodded.

"He has secured other letters, incriminating a Mr. Sheard, of the staff of the *Gleaner*; Sir Richard Haredale, of the —— Guards; Miss Zoe Oppner; and ... well—you know the worst—my niece, again!" The inspector drew a long, deep breath.

"Next to Victor Lemage, who's also an accomplice," he said admiringly, "I don't mind admitting that Harley is the smartest man in the business. But in justice to us, sir, you must remember that our hands are tied. A C.I.D. man isn't allowed to do what Harley can do."

"I grant it, inspector. Now, having given you my confidence, I rely upon you to work with me—not against me."

"I am with you entirely, sir. May I have those letters?"

Mr. Belford hesitated.

"It is surely inconsistent with your duty to keep them private?"

"What about the one in my pocket, sir? That alone is sufficient, if I wanted to make a scandal. No; I give you my word that no other eye shall see them."

The Home Secretary shrugged his shoulders, and taking up the bundle from which already he had selected Séverac Bablon's three communications, he placed it in the detective's hands.

"I rely upon you to keep certain names out of the affair."

"I give you my word that they shall never be mentioned in connection with it. You have taken the only course which could ensure that, sir. May I see the photographs?"

If the Right Hon. Walter Belford had already revised his first estimate of Inspector Sheffield, this last request upset it altogether. He stared.

"I am glad to enjoy your co-operation, inspector," he said. "I prefer to know that a man of your calibre is of my camp! You are evidently aware that Harley has secured an elaborate series of snapshots of persons known to Miss Oppner and to my niece. Of the several hundreds of persons photographed, only one negative proved to be interesting. I have enlarged the photograph myself. Here it is!"

He took a photograph from the drawer.

"This gentleman," he continued, "was taken in the act of bowing to Lady Mary and Miss Oppner at the corner of Bond Street."

Sheffield glanced at the photograph. It represented a strikingly handsome man, with dark, curling hair and singularly flashing eyes, who was in the act of raising his hat.

"It's Séverac Bablon!" said the inspector simply.

"Ah!" cried Belford. "So I thought! So I thought!"

"May I take it with me?"

"I think not, inspector. You know the man; it is scarcely necessary." And with a certain displeasure he laid the enlargement upon the table.

The detective accepted his refusal with one of the awkward bows.

"Regarding your protection to-night, sir," he said, standing up and buttoning his coat, "there are six men on special duty round the house, and no one can possibly get in unseen."

The Home Secretary, smiling, glanced at his watch. "A quarter to nine!" he said. "He has fifteen minutes in which to make good his bluff. But I do not fear interruption."

Sheffield awkwardly returned the statesman's bow of dismissal, and withdrew under the patronage of a splendid footman. As the door closed, Mr. Belford, with a long sigh of relief, stepped to a bookcase and selected Petronius Arbiter's "*Satyricon.*"

Book in hand, he slid back the noiseless glass doors of the conservatory. A close smell of tropical plant life crept into the room, but this was as frankincense and myrrh to his nostrils. He passed through and seated himself in a cushioned cane chair amid the rare flora. Switching on a shaded lamp conveniently hung in this retreat, he settled down to read.

For it was a favourite relaxation of the right honourable gentleman's to bury himself amid exotic blooms, and in such congenial company as that of the Patrician æsthete, rekindle the torches of voluptuous Rome.

A few minutes later:

"Am I nowhere immune from interruption?" muttered Mr. Belford, with the nearest approach to irritability of which his equable temper was deemed capable.

But the next moment his genial smile dawned, as the charming face of his niece, Lady Mary Evershed, peeped through the foliage.

"Truman was afraid to interrupt you, uncle, as you were in your cell! But Inspector Sheffield is asking for you, and seems very excited."

"Dear me!" said her uncle, glancing at his watch; "but I saw him fifteen minutes ago! It has just gone nine." Then, recalling Séverac Bablon's boastful message: "He has not dared to attempt it! Unless—can it be that he is arrested? Tell Truman to send the inspector here, Mary."

The girl, with a little puzzled frown on her forehead, withdrew, and almost immediately a heavy step sounded in the library, and Chief-Inspector

Sheffield, pushing past the footman, burst unceremoniously into the conservatory. His face was flushed, and his eyes were angrily bright.

"We've been hoaxed, sir!" he cried. "We've been hoaxed!"

Mr. Belford raised a white hand.

"My dear inspector," he said, "be calm, I beg of you! Will you not take a seat and explain this matter to me?"

Sheffield dropped into a chair, but the flow of excited words would not be stayed nor dammed.

"He's tricked us again!" he burst out. "I suspect what he wanted, sir, and I rely on you to give me all the help you can! I know Paul Harley has got hold of evidence that we couldn't get; but a C.I.D. man can't spend a week making love to Lady Mary Evershed's maid——"

"But others are better able to devote that amount of time to my maid, I suppose?"

The interruption startled Mr. Belford out of his habitual calm, and startled the detective into sudden silence.

Lady Mary stood at the door of the conservatory.

"I am sorry to appear as an eavesdropper," she continued; "but, as a matter of fact, I had never left the study!"

"Er—Mary," began the Home Secretary, but for once in a way he was at a loss for words. He knew from experience that the most obstreperous friend "opposite" was easier to deal with than a pretty niece.

"Zoe is here with me, too," said Mary, and the frizzy head of Zoe Oppner appeared over her friend's shoulder. "We are sorry to have overheard Mr. Sheffield's words, but I think we have heard too much not to ask to hear more. Do I understand, inspector, that someone has been spying on my maid?"

Inspector Sheffield glanced at the Right Hon. Walter Belford, and read an appeal in the eyes behind the pince-nez. He squared his shoulders in a manner that had something admirably manly about it—and told a straightforward lie.

"One of the Pinkerton men engaged by Mr. Oppner tried to get some letters from your maid, I believe; but there's not a scrap of evidence on the market, so he must have failed!"

"Evidence of what?" asked Zoe Oppner sharply.

Mr. Belford nervously tapped his fingers upon the chair-arm.

"Of your friendship, and Lady Mary's with Séverac Bablon!" replied the inspector boldly.

Lady Mary was pale, and her eyes grew wide; but the American girl laughed with undisguised glee.

"Séverac Bablon has never done a dirty thing yet," she said. "If we knew him we should be proud of it! Come on, Mary! Mr. Belford, I'm almost ashamed of you! You're nearly as bad as pa!"

They withdrew, and Mr. Belford heaved a great sigh of relief.

"Thank you, inspector," he said. "Lady Mary would never understand that I sought only to save her from compromising herself. I am glad that the letters are in such safe hands as yours."

"But they're not!" cried Sheffield, leaping excitedly to his feet.

Gruffness had come into his voice, which the other ascribed to excitement.

"How so?"

An expression of blank wonderment was upon the politician's face.

"Because I never had them! Because I've never had a scrap of anything in black and white! Because I've been tied up in an old tool-shed in a turnip field for the past half-hour! And because the man who marched through my silly troop a while ago and came in here and got back I don't know what important evidence—*was Séverac Bablon!*"

It was a verbal thunderbolt. Mr. Belford sat with his eyes upon the detective's face—speechless. And now he perceived minor differences. The difference in voice he already had noted: now he saw that the eyes of the real Inspector Sheffield were many shades lighter than those of the spurious; that the red face was heavier and more rounded. It was almost incredible, but not quite. He had seen Tree play Falstaff, and the art of Séverac Bablon was only a shade greater.

"He's had months to study me!" explained the detective tersely. Then: "I'm stopping at the 'Golden Tiger,' in the village. I'd been over the ground in daylight, and I sent the men along first. They were round the house by half-past seven. Just as I turned the corner out of the High Street a big grey car overtook me; out jumped two fellows and had a jiu-jitsu hold on in a second! They gagged me and tied me up inside, all the time apologising and hoping they weren't hurting me! They drove me to this shed and left me there. It was five minutes to nine when one of them came back and untied my hands, giving himself a start while I undid the rest of the knots. Here I am! Where's Séverac Bablon?"

The Right Hon. Walter Belford became the man of action again. He pulled out his watch.

"Twenty-five minutes since he left the house," he said. "But he may not have taken the road at once."

He rang.

"Truman," he cried to the footman, "the limousine ready—immediately! This way, inspector!"

Off he went through the Circular Study, Sheffield following. At the door Mr. Belford paused—and turned back.

He bent over his writing-table, searching for his own careful enlargement of Séverac Bablon's photograph.

Séverac Bablon had not taken it with him, nor had he returned to the room.

But it was gone!

"Rome divided! Treason in the camp!" he said, *sotto voce*. Then, aloud: "This way, inspector!"

The tower of Womsley Old Place is a conspicuous landmark, to be seen from distant points in the surrounding country, and visible for some miles out to sea.

Mr. Belford raced up the many stairs at a speed which belied the story of his silver-grey hair, and which left Inspector Sheffield hopelessly in the rear. When at last the Scotland Yard man dragged weary feet into the little square chamber at the summit, he saw the Home Secretary with his eyes to the lens of a huge telescope, sweeping the country-side for signs of the daring fugitive.

An unclouded moon bathed the landscape in solemn light. To north, east, and west rolled the billows of the Downs, a verdant ocean. On the south the country was wooded, whilst in the south-east might be seen the gleaming expanse of the English Channel, a molten silver floor, its distant edge seemingly upholding the pure blue sky dome. Roads inland showed as white chalk lines, meadows as squares on a chess-board, houses and farmsteads as chess-men.

"If he has made for Eastbourne we have lost him!" muttered Mr. Belford. "If for Newhaven or Lewes we may not be too late. But there is a possibility——ah! Yes; it is! They are making for Tunbridge Wells— perhaps for London! Quick, inspector! Don't move the telescope. On the straight road leading to the Norman church tower! Is that the car?"

Sheffield lowered his eye to the glass, and after some little delay got a sight of a long-bodied, waspish, shape, creeping, insect-wise, along a white chalk mark. His eye growing more accustomed to the glass, he made it out for a grey car.

"There's a chance, sir. It looks about the right cut."

"This way, inspector! We will take the risk."

Down the tower stairs they sped, Sheffield stumbling and delaying in the dark and making better going where the light from a window showed the stairs clearly.

"If that is he," panted the Home Secretary, "the motor is not a powerful one. It is probably one hired for the occasion."

They came out from the tower into the hall and passed Lady Mary—who glanced away with an odd expression—and Zoe Oppner. Zoe's pretty face was flushed, and her breast rose and fell quickly. Her eyes were sparkling, but she lowered them as the excited pair ran by.

The chauffeur was ready to start, when Mr. Belford, hatless, leapt on to a footboard of the throbbing car with the agility of a sailor, Sheffield more slowly following suit, for he would have preferred an inside berth.

A man in a blue serge suit touched the inspector's arm.

"What shall we do, sir?"

"Wait here."

The limousine was off.

"Left! left!" directed Mr. Belford, and the man swung sharply round the curve and into the lane bordering the gardens of Womsley Old Place.

"Right!"

They leapt about again, and were humming along a chalky white road.

"Left! Straight ahead! Make for the church! Open her out!"

The pursuit had commenced!

Some dormant trait in the blood of His Majesty's Principal Secretary of State for the Home Department had risen above the surface of suave, polished courtesy which ordinarily passed for the character of the Right Hon. Walter Belford. The veneer was off, and this was a primitive Belford, kin of the Roger de Belfourd who had established the fortunes of the house. The eyes behind the pince-nez were hard and bright; the fine nostrils quivered with the joy of the chase; and the long, lean neck, protruding from the characteristically low collar, was strung up to whipcord tension.

"Let her go!" he shouted, his silvern hair streaming out grotesquely. "Cut through Church Lane!"

"It's an awful road, sir!" The chauffeur's voice was blown back in his teeth.

"Damn the road!" said the Right Hon. Walter Belford.

So, suddenly the powerful machine, spurning the solid earth like some huge, infuriated brute, leapt sideways, two tyres thrashing empty air, and went howling through an arch of verdure, between hedges which seemed to shrink to right and left from its devastating course.

The man was understood to say something about "Overweighted on her head."

"Scissors!" muttered Inspector Sheffield, wedging his bulk firmly against the front window and clutching at anything that offered. "I hope there are no police traps on this road!"

"He delayed for something!" yelled Belford through trumpeted hands. "We shall catch him by Grimsdyke Farm!"

Sheffield wondered what that vastly daring man had delayed for. Belford, with the fact of the missing photograph fresh in his mind, thought he knew.

The old Norman church tower came rushing now to meet them; looked down upon them, each venerable, lichened stone a mockery of this snorting, ephemeral thing of the Speed Age; and dropped behind to join the other vague memories which represented six miles of Sussex.

"Straight ahead now! Grimsdyke!"

Down swept the white road into a great bowl. Down shrieked the quivering limousine, and Inspector Sheffield crouched back with an uncomfortable sinking in the pit of the stomach, such as he had not known since he had adventured his weighty person on a "joy-ride" at an exhibition.

From the time they had left Womsley Old Place the speed had been consistently high, but now it rose to something enormous; increasing with every ten yards of the slope, it became terrific. The bottom was reached, and the climb began; but for some time little diminution was perceptible in their headlong progress. Then it began to tell, and presently they were mounting the long acclivity at what seemed a tortoise pace after the breathless drop into the valley.

The car rose to the brow, and Mr. Belford mounted recklessly beside the chauffeur, peering ahead under arched palms over the moon-bathed country-side.

"There they are! There they are! We shall overtake them at the old farm!"

His excitement was intensely contagious. Sheffield, who had been wedged upon the footboard, rose unsteadily, and, supporting himself with difficulty, looked along the gleaming ribbon of road.

There they were! The grey car was clearly discernible now, and even at that distance he could estimate something of her progress. He exulted to note that capture was becoming merely a question of minutes!

Then came a doubt. Suppose it should prove to be the wrong car!

Nearer they drew, and nearer.

The fugitives topped a slope, and against the blue sky was silhouetted a figure which stood upright in the car—the figure of a big man with raised arms and out-turned elbows. He was peering back, just as Belford was peering forward.

"Look at his bowler hat!" yelled Sheffield. "Why, it might be me!"

"It might!" shouted Mr. Belford; "but it isn't! It's Séverac Bablon!"

A wood dipped down to the roadside, and its shadows ate up their quarry; a breathless, nervous interval, and its glooms enveloped Mr. Belford's party in turn. From out of the darkness the road ahead was clearly visible. Deserted farm buildings lay scattered in their path where the trees ended.

The trees slipped behind, and the old farm rose in front.

At the gate of the yard stood the grey car—empty!

"Pull up! Pull up!" cried Mr. Belford.

But long before the car became stationary he had precipitated himself into the road.

Sheffield dropped heavily behind him, and grasped him by the arm.

"One moment, sir!" he said.

His voice was calm again. He was quite in his element now. A criminal had to be apprehended, and the circumstances, though difficult, were not unfamiliar. But strategy was called for; there must be no hot-headed blundering.

"Yes? What is it?" demanded the Home Secretary excitedly.

"It's this, sir: he'll give us the slip yet, if we don't go slow! Now, you take charge of the grey car. That's your post, sir. Here—have my revolver. Step out into the lane there, and see nobody rushes the car!"

"Good—I agree!" cried Mr. Belford, and took the revolver.

"You, young fellow," continued the inspector, addressing the chauffeur, "may know something of the ins and outs of this place. Do you know if there's a back door to the main building?"

"There is—yes—down behind that barn."

"Then pull out a big spanner, or anything handy, and go round there. When you reach the door, whistle. Stop there unless you hear my whistle inside or till I come through and join you. If he's not in the main building we can start on the outhouses. But his escape is cut off all the time by Mr. Belford—see?"

"Quite right, inspector! Quite right!" cried Mr. Belford. "Go ahead! I will get to the car! Go ahead!"

Off ran the agile politician to his appointed post; and the chauffeur, armed with a heavy spanner, disappeared in the shadow of the barn. Sheffield, taking from his breast-pocket an electric torch, strode up to the doorless entrance of the abandoned farm, and waited.

# CHAPTER XXVI

## GRIMSDYKE

Not a sound disturbed the silence of the deserted place, save when the slight breeze sighed through the trees of the adjoining coppice, and swayed some invisible shutter which creaked upon its rusty hinges.

An owl hooted, and the detective was on the alert in a moment. It was a well-known signal. Was the owl a feathered one or a human mimic?

No other sound followed, until the breeze came again, whispered in the coppice, and shook the shutter.

Then the chauffeur's whistle came, faintly, and with something tremulous in its note; for the adventure, though it offered little novelty to the experience of the Scotland Yard man, was dangerously unique from the mechanic's point of view. But where the Right Hon. Walter Belford led it was impolitic, if not impossible, to decline to follow. Yet, the whistle spoke of a man not over-confident. "Séverac Bablon" was a disturbing name!

Sheffield pressed the knob of the torch and stepped into the bare and dirty room beyond.

The beam of the torch swept the four walls, with faded paper peeling in strips from the damp plaster; showed a grate full of rubbish, a battered pail, and a bare floor littered with debris of all sorts, great cavities gaping between many of the planks. A cupboard was searched, and proved to contain a number of empty cans and bottles—nothing else.

Into the next room went the investigator, to meet with no better fortune. The third was a big kitchen, empty; the fourth a paved scullery, also empty—with the chauffeur at the door, holding his spanner in readiness for sudden assault.

"Upstairs!" said Sheffield shortly.

Up the creaking stairs they passed, their footsteps filling the place with ghostly echoes.

A square landing offered four doors, all closed, to their consideration.

Sheffield paused, and listened.

The owl had hooted again.

He directed the ray of the torch upon the door on the immediate right of the stairhead.

"We're short-handed for this!" he muttered; "but it has to be risked now. Stay where you are and be on the alert. Watch those other doors." He tried the handle.

The door was locked.

To the next one he passed without hesitation. It yielded to his hand, and he flashed the light about a bare room, with half of the ceiling sloping down to the window. In the corner beyond this window a second door was partly concealed by the recess. The inspector stepped across the floor and threw the door open.

Then events moved rapidly.

Someone literally shot into the room behind him, falling with a crash that shook the place like thunder. *Bang!* sounded through the house, and a key turned in a lock!

Sheffield spun round like an unwieldy top, and saw the chauffeur struggling to his feet and rubbing his head vigorously.

The detective made no outcry, nor did he waste energy by trying a door he knew to be locked. He stood, keenly alert, and listened.

Footsteps rapidly receded down the stairs.

"Who did it? How did he get behind me?" muttered the dazed chauffeur.

"Out of one of the other rooms! I told you to watch them!"

Inspector Sheffield was angry, but he had not lost his presence of mind.

"We must get out—quick! The window!"

He leapt to the low window, throwing it open.

"Too far to drop! We've got to smash the door! Perhaps they've left the key in the lock! Set to on the panel with that bit of iron of yours!"

The man began a vigorous assault upon the woodwork. It was old, but very tough, and yielded tardily to the blows of the instrument. Then a big crack appeared as the result of a stroke shrewdly planted.

"Stand away!" directed Sheffield; and leaning back upon his left foot, he dashed his right upon the broken panel, shattering it effectually.

At the moment that the chauffeur thrust his hand through the jagged aperture to seek for the key, *thud! thud! thud!* came from the lane below.

"That's the car!" cried the inspector. "My God! what have they done to Mr. Belford?"

The other paused and listened intently.

"It's the grey car," he said. "Why didn't they take the guv'nor's?"

"Open the door!" cried Sheffield impatiently. "Is the key there?"

"Yes," was the reply; "here we are!" And the door was opened.

Sheffield started down the stairs with noisy clatter, and, the chauffeur a good second, raced through the rooms below and out into the yard.

"Mr. Belford! Mr. Belford!" he cried.

But no answer came, only a whisper from the coppice, followed by the squeak of the crazy shutter.

They ran out to where they had left Belford on guard over the grey car; but no sign of him remained, nor evidence of a struggle. The hum of the retreating motor grew faint in the distance.

"Ah!" cried Sheffield, and started running towards Mr. Belford's limousine on the edge of the coppice. "Quick! don't you see? *He's kidnapped!* In you go! This just about sees me out at Scotland Yard if we don't overtake them!"

"They've gone back the way we've just come!" said the chauffeur, hurling himself on board. "I can't make out where they're going—and I can't make out why they took the worst car! It's an old crock, hired from Lewes. We can run it down inside five minutes!"

"Thank God for that!" said Sheffield, as, for the second time that night, he set out across moonlit Sussex on the front of the big car, in pursuit of the most elusive man who ever had baffled the Criminal Investigation Department.

Visions of degradation to the ranks from which he so laboriously had risen occupied his mind to the exclusion of all else; for to have allowed the notorious Séverac Bablon to kidnap the Home Secretary under his very eyes was a blunder which he knew full well could not be condoned.

Even the breathless drop into the great bowl on the Downs did not serve to dispel his gloomy dreams. Then:

"There they are! And, as I live, making straight for Womsley!" cried the chauffeur.

Sheffield stood up unsteadily on his insecure perch, and there was the mysterious grey car, which now was become a veritable nightmare, mounting the hill in front.

One minute passed, and Sheffield was straining his eyes to catch a glimpse of the occupants. But no one was visible. Two minutes passed, and the inspector began to think that his eyesight was failing, or that a worse thing portended. For, as far as he could make out, only one man occupied the car—the man who drove her!

"What does it mean?" muttered the detective, clutching at the shoulder of the chauffeur to support himself. "It must be Séverac Bablon! But— where's Mr. Belford?"

Three minutes passed, and the brilliant moonlight set at rest all doubts respecting the identity of the man who drove the car.

His silvern hair flowed out, gleaming on his shoulders, as he bent forward over the driving-wheel.

It was the Right Hon. Walter Belford!

"What in the name of murder does it mean?" cried Sheffield. "Has he gone mad? Mr. Belford! Mr. Belford! Hoy! ... *Hoy!* ... *hoy! Mr. Belford!*"

But although he must have heard the cry, Mr. Belford, immovable at the wheel, drove madly ahead!

"What shall I do?" asked the chauffeur in an awed voice.

"Do?" rapped Sheffield savagely. "Pass him and block the road! He's stark, raving mad!"

So, along that white road, under the placid moon, was enacted the strangest incident of this entirely bizarre adventure; for Mr. Belford, in the hired motor, was pursued and overtaken by his own car, which passed him, forged ahead, turned across the road, and blocked it.

For one moment the Home Secretary, racing down upon them, seemed to contemplate leaving the path for the grassland, and thus proceeding on his way; but the chauffeur ran out to meet him, holding up his arms and crying:

"Stop, sir! *Stop!*"

Mr. Belford stopped the car and fixed his eyes upon the man with a look of real amazement.

"You?" he said, and turned to Sheffield.

"Who else?" rapped the inspector irritably. "What on earth are you doing, sir? Where's the quarry—where's Séverac Bablon?"

"What!" cried the Home Secretary, from the step of the car. "You have lost him?"

"Lost him!" repeated Sheffield ironically. "I never had him!"

"But," said Mr. Belford distinctly, and in his question-answering voice, "did you not return to where I was stationed and inform me that you had them all locked in an upper room? Did I not, myself, hear their attempt to break down the door? And did you not report that, their numbers being considerable, you could not, single-handed, hope to arrest them?"

"Go on!" said Sheffield, in a tired voice. "What else did I tell you?"

"You see," resumed the politician triumphantly, "this *impasse* is due to no irregularity in my own conduct! You told me that my limousine had mysteriously been tampered with, and that the only course was for you and Jenkins to remain and endeavour to prevent the prisoners from escaping, whilst I, in their car, returned to Womsley Old Place for your men! Hearing you behind me, I naturally assumed that the prisoners had overpowered you and were in pursuit of me!"

"I see!" said Sheffield, removing his hat and scratching his head viciously.

"Finally," said Mr. Belford, with dignity, "you gave me this note for your principal assistant, Dawson"—and handed an envelope to the inspector.

The latter, with the resignation of despair, accepted it, tore it open, and took out a card. Directing the ray of his pocket-torch upon it, though in the brilliant moonlight no artificial aid really was necessary, he read the following aloud:

"Séverac Bablon begs to present his compliments to His Majesty's Principal Secretary of State for the Home Department and to thank him for according the privilege of a private interview. Whilst deprecating the subterfuge rendered necessary by the right honourable gentleman's attitude, he feels that it is justified by results, and begs respectfully to repeat his assurance that no one in whom the right honourable gentleman is interested shall be compromised, now or at any future time."

"You see," said the detective wearily, "that wasn't the real Inspector Sheffield who spoke to you. I thought you might have known him by this time, sir! That was Séverac Bablon!"

# CHAPTER XXVII

## YELLOW CIGARETTES

In our pursuit of the fantastic being, about whom so many mysteries gathered, we have somewhat neglected the affairs of Sir Richard Haredale. Thanks to Mr. Belford's elusive visitor, these now ran smoothly.

In order to learn how smoothly we have only to present ourselves at a certain important social function.

"These military weddings are so romantic," gushed Mrs. Rohscheimer.

"And so beastly stuffy," added her husband, mopping his damp brow with a silk handkerchief bearing, in gold thread, the monogram "J. R."

"Doesn't Dick look real sweet?" whispered Lady Vignoles, following with admiring eyes the soldierly figure of the bridegroom, Sir Richard Haredale.

Lord Vignoles shouldered his way through the scrum about the door.

"I say, Sheila," he called to his wife, "where's Zoe?"

"She was here a minute ago," replied Julius Rohscheimer, rolling his prominent eyes about in quest of the missing one.

"I mean to say," explained Vignoles, "her father is asking——"

"What! Has uncle turned up after all?" exclaimed Lady Vignoles, and looked quickly towards the door.

Through the crowd a big red-faced man was forging, and behind him a glimpse might be had of the shrivelled shape of John Jacob Oppner.

"Hallo," grunted Rohscheimer, "here's Inspector Sheffield, from Scotland Yard!"—and apprehensively he fingered tie-pin and watch-chain, and furtively counted the rings upon his fat fingers. "What's up?"

The shrewd but not unkindly eyes of the C. I. D. man were scanning the packed rooms, over the heads of the crowd—keenly, suspiciously. With a brief nod he passed the group, and pressed on his way. Mr. Oppner halted.

"What's the trouble, Oppner?" inquired Rohscheimer thickly. "Is there a thief here or something?"

"Worse!" drawled the other. "Séverac Bablon's here!"

"Oh, Lord!" groaned Rohscheimer, and surreptitiously slipped all his rings off and into his trousers pocket. "Let's get out before we're all held up!"

"He don't figure on a hold-up," replied Oppner; "it ain't a strong line at a matinee. A hop-parade is the time for the crystals. We don't know what he's layin' for, but it's a cinch he's here."

"How do you know?" asked a brother officer of Haredale's, who had joined the group.

Mr. Oppner took a cigarette-case from his tail-pocket and held up between finger and thumb a cigarette stump of an unusual yellow colour.

"We've got on his trail at last!" he said. "He sheds these cigs. like a moulting chicken sheds feathers. This one was in the tray inside a taxi—and the taxi dropped his fare right here!"

He returned the cigarette stump to the case, the case to his pocket, and pushed on after Sheffield. As his stooping form disappeared from view Sheard entered the room. Immediately he was claimed by Mr. Rohscheimer.

"Hallo, Sheard!" called the financier, and for the moment even the imminence of the Séverac Bablon peril was forgotten—"what's the latest? Is war declared?"

"There was nothing official up to the time I left," replied the pressman; "but we are expecting it every minute. Mr. Belford and Lord Evershed have just been summoned to Buckingham Palace. I met them going as I came in."

Rohscheimer confidently seized the lapel of the journalist's coat.

"What do you think that means, now?" he asked cunningly.

"It means," replied Sheard, "that within the hour Europe may be in arms! Haredale is on duty this evening—so there will be no honeymoon! Everything is at sixes and sevens. I have a couple of cubs watching; and if Baron Hecht, when he leaves the conference at the Palace, proceeds home, there may be no war. If he starts for Victoria Station—war is declared!"

An excited young lady wearing pince-nez, through which she peered anxiously in quest of someone, tapping her rather prominent front teeth the while with an HB pencil, sighted Sheard.

"Oh, there you are!" she cried, in evident relief. "Really, Mr. Sheard, I was despairing of finding *anyone* to tell me—but you always know everything."

Sheard bowed ironically. The lady represented one of the oldest families in Warwichshire and the Fashionable Intelligence of quite the smartest morning journal in London.

"Sir Richard's best man——" she began again.

"Didn't you know?" burst in Lord Vignoles. "Bally nuisance—I mean to say, inconsiderate of Roxborough; he could have sent some other messenger, and need not have picked Anerly."

"Oh! I know all about that!" snapped the lady impatiently; "but who was the distinguished-looking man who took Maurice's place?"

The Hon. Maurice Anerly, who should have officiated as best man, had received instructions an hour before the ceremony to proceed to the capital of the Power with whom Britain was on the verge of war. Sheard would have given a hundred pounds for a glimpse of the dispatch he carried.

"No idea," said Vignoles; "most amazing thing! Friend of Haredale's, who turned up at the last minute and vanished directly the ceremony was over. Perfect record! Don't suppose it's ever happened before."

"But he came to the house here; several people saw him here. You don't want me to believe that Dick Haredale didn't tell anybody who his best man was!"

"I was not present," said Sheard; "so I cannot help you."

"It's preposterous!" cried the lady. "I never heard of such a thing!"

"What was the gentleman like, miss?" came a quiet voice.

The eyes of all in the little group turned, together. Chief Inspector Sheffield had joined them.

The lady addressed eyed the big man apprehensively. He was outside the experience of Fashionable Intelligence, but there was a quiet authority in his voice and manner which seemed to call for a reply.

"He was the most handsome man I have ever seen!" she answered briefly.

"Thank you!" said Sheffield, with even greater brevity, and turned on his heel.

He went up to a footman, who looked more like a clean-shaven policeman—possibly because he was one.

"You are certain that Miss Oppner and the man I have described actually entered this house?"

"They were talking together in that room by the statue, sir."

"And Miss Oppner came out?"

"Yes, sir."

"But not the man?"

"No, sir."

Inspector Sheffield made his way to the little anteroom indicated. It was quite a tiny apartment, with a divan, two lounge-chairs and a Persian coffee-table. There was no one there.

A faint but very peculiar perfume hung in the air. Turkish tobacco went to the making of it, but something else too. Sheffield bent over the table.

In a little bronze ash-tray lay a cigarette end—yellow in colour.

---

At about the same moment that Chief Inspector Sheffield was trying to get used to the idea of the notorious Séverac Bablon's having actually officiated as best man at the wedding of the only daughter of the Marquess of Evershed, Mr. Thomas Sheard also had that astounding fact brought home to him.

For, in the wide publicity of Eccleston Square, the observed of many curious observers, Zoe Oppner stood shaking hands with this master of audacity.

Sheard joined them hurriedly.

"This is the height of indiscretion!" he exclaimed, glancing apprehensively about him. "You compromise others——"

Séverac Bablon checked him with a quiet smile.

"Have I ever compromised another?"

"But now you cannot avoid doing so. Sheffield is inside! What madness brings you here?"

"In the absence of the Hon. Maurice Anerly, I acted as Haredale's best man."

Sheard literally gasped.

"But you are not——"

"A Christian? My religious beliefs, Sheard, do not preclude my attendance at a wedding ceremony. Some day I may explain this to you."

"You must have been recognised!"

"Who knows Séverac Bablon?"

"At least four people now in that house!"

"Possibly. But no one of those four has seen me. No one of them was present at the ceremony; and, I assure you, I made myself scarce afterwards."

"You must hurry. You have been traced——"

"Never fear; I shall hurry. But, before I go, Sheard, take this envelope. It is the last 'scoop' that I have to offer to the *Gleaner*, but it is the biggest of all! Good-bye."

"Do I understand that you are leaving England?"

So sincere was the emotion in the pressman's voice that Séverac Bablon's own had changed when he replied:

"We may never meet again; I cannot tell."

He laid his hands upon the other's shoulders in a characteristic gesture, and to Sheard, as he met the glance of those fine eyes, this was no criminal flying from justice; rather, a ruler of peoples, an enthusiast, a fanatic perhaps, but a royal man—and his friend.

"Good-bye!" said Séverac Bablon, and clasped Sheard's hand in both his own.

He turned to Zoe Oppner, who, very pale, was glancing back at the house.

"Good-bye again!"

A cab waited, and Séverac Bablon, lighting a cigarette, leapt in and was driven away. Sheard did not hear his directions to the man; and Zoe Oppner left him abruptly and ran into the house again. Before he had time to move, to collect his thoughts, a heavy hand was laid upon his shoulder.

He started. Inspector Sheffield stood beside him.

"Who was in that cab?" he rapped.

Sheard realised that the moment to which he had long looked forward with dread was come. He had been caught red-handed. At last Séverac Bablon had dared too greatly, and he, Sheard, must pay the price of that indiscretion.

"Why do you ask—and in that tone?"

"Mr. Sheard," said the detective grimly, "I've had my eye on you for a long while, as you must be well aware. You may not be aware that but for me you'd have been arrested long ago! I'm past the time when sensational arrests appeal to me, though. I'm out to hide scandals, not to turn the limelight on 'em. You're a well-known man, and it would break you, I take it, if I hauled you up for complicity? But I've got my responsibilities, too, remember; and I warn you—I warn you solemnly—if you bandy words with me now, I'll have you in Marlborough Street inside ten minutes!"

The buttons were off, and Sheard felt the point at his throat. For there was no mistaking the grim earnestness of the man from Scotland Yard. The kindly blue eyes were grown hard as steel, and in them the pressman read that upon his next words rested his whole career. A lie could avail his friend nothing; it meant his own ruin.

"Séverac Bablon!" he said.

"I knew that!" replied Sheffield; "you did well to admit it! Where has he gone?"

"I have no idea."

"Don't take any chances, sir! I'm tired of the responsibility of shielding the fools who know him! If you give me your word on that, I'll take it."

"I give you my word. I was unable to hear his directions to the driver."

"Very good. There are other things I might ask you—but I know you'd refuse to answer, and then I'd have no alternative. So I won't. Good-day."

"Good-day, Inspector. And thank you." Sheffield nodded shortly and walked up to the driver of the next waiting cab.

"What number was the man who drove away last?"

"LH-00896, sir."

"Know where he went?"

"No, sir; but not far. He told a pal o' mine—the chauffeur of Mr. Rohscheimer's car, there, sir—that he'd be back in seven minutes."

"Good!" said Sheffield.

Matters were befalling as well as he could have hoped; for he had come out too late to have followed the cab. He glanced at his watch. Provided the man picked up no fare on his way back, he was due in three minutes. The detective strolled off towards Belgrave Road. Inside the three minutes a cab turned into the other end of the square.

Inspector Sheffield retraced his steps hurriedly.

Without a word to the man, he opened the cab door. A faint, familiar perfume reached his nostrils. He glanced at the ash-trays, but neither contained a cigarette end. He turned to the driver.

"Where did you take the gentleman you picked up here, my man?"

A newsboy came racing along the pavement, with an armful of sheets, wet from the press. The journal was the *Gleaner's* most powerful opponent.

"War de-clared, piper! War de-clared, speshul!"

His shrill cries drowned the taximan's reply. As the boy ran on crying his mendacious "news" (for the front-page article was not headed "War declared," but "Is war declared?"), Sheffield repeated his question.

"To Buckingham Palace, sir!" he was answered.

The detective stared incredulously.

"I mean a tall gentleman, clean shaven, and very dark, with quite black hair——"

"Smoked some sort of Russian smokes, sir—yellow?"

"That one—yes!"

"That's the one I mean, sir—Buckingham Palace!"

Sheffield continued to stare.

"Where did you actually drop him?"

"At the gate."

"Well? Where did he go?"

"He went in, sir!"

"Went in! He was admitted?"

"Yes, sir; I saw him pass the sentry!"

Chief Inspector Sheffield leapt into the cab with a face grimly set.

"Buckingham Palace!" he snapped.

---

Meanwhile, Detective-Sergeant Harborne, following back the clue of the yellow cigarettes, in accordance with the instructions of his superior, who had elected to follow it forward, made his way to a cab-rank at the end of Finchley Road.

To a cab-minder he showed a photograph. It was from that unique negative which the Home Secretary had shown to the pseudo-Inspector Sheffield at Womsley Old Place; moreover, it was the only copy which the right honourable gentleman had authorised to be printed.

"Does this person often take cabs from this rank, my lad?"

The man surveyed it with beer-weakened eyes.

"Mr. Sanrack it is, guv'nor! Yes, he's often here!"

Harborne, who was a believer in the straightforward British methods, and who scorned alike the unnecessary subtlety of the French school, as represented by Lemage or Duquesne, and the Fenimore-Cooper-like tactics dear to the men of the American agencies, showed his card.

"What's his address?" he snapped.

"It's farther down on this side; I can't think of the number, sir," replied the other shakily. (The proximity of a police officer always injuriously affected his heart.) "But I can show you the 'ouse."

"Come on!" ordered Harborne. "Walk behind me; and when I pass it, whistle."

Off went the detective without delay, and walked briskly along the Finchley Road. He had proceeded more than half-way, when, as he came abreast of a gate set in a high wall, from his rear quavered a moist whistle.

"70A," he muttered. "Right-oh!"

He thrilled with the joy of the chase, anticipating the triumph that awaited him. Inspector Sheffield's pursuit was more than likely to prove futile, but Séverac Bablon, he argued, was practically certain to return to his head-quarters sooner or later.

He thought of the weeks and months during which they had sought for this very house in vain; of the useless tracking of divers persons known to be acquainted with the man of mystery; of the simple means—the yellow cigarettes—by which, at last, they had come to it.

Mr. Aloys. X Alden had been very reticent of late—and Mr. Oppner knew of the cigarette clue. At that reflection the roseate horizon grew darkened by the figure of a triumphant American holding up Séverac Bablon with a neat silver-plated model by Smith and Wesson. If Alden should forestall him!

Harborne, who had been pursuing these reflections whilst, within sight of No. 70A, he stood slowly loading his pipe, paused, pouch in hand. On one memorable occasion, the super-subtlety of Sheffield (who was tainted with French heresies) had led to a fiasco which had made them the laughing-stock of Scotland Yard. Harborne felt in his breast pocket, where there reposed a copy of the warrant for the arrest of Séverac Bablon. And before he withdrew his hand his mind was made up. He was a man of indomitable pluck.

Walking briskly to the gate in the high wall, he opened it, passed around a very neat little lawn, and stood in the porch of 70A. As he glanced about for bell or knocker, and failed to find either, the door was opened quietly by a tall man in black—an Arab.

"I have important business with Mr. Sanrack," said Harborne quietly, and handed the Arab a card which simply bore the name: "Mr. Goodson."

"He is not at home, but expected," replied the man, in guttural English. "Will Mr. Goodson await?"

"Yes," said Harborne, "if Mr. Sanrack won't be long."

The Arab bowed, and conducted him to a small but cosy room, furnished simply but with great good taste—and withdrew. Harborne congratulated himself. The simple and direct, if old-fashioned, methods were, after all, the best.

It was a very silent house. That fact struck him at once. Listen intently as he would, no sound from within could he detect. What should be his next move?

He stepped to the door and looked out into the hall. This was rather narrow, and, owing to the presence of heavy Oriental drapings, very dark. It would suit his purpose admirably. Directly "Mr. Sanrack" came in he would spring upon him and get the handcuffs fast, then he could throw open the front door, if there had been time for anyone to reclose it, and summon assistance with his whistle.

He himself must effect the actual arrest—single-handed. He cared nothing who came upon the scene after that. He placed the handcuffs in a more convenient pocket, and buttoned up his double-breasted blue serge coat.

Sheffield was certain to be Superintendent before long; and it only required one other big case, such as this, to insure Harborne's succession to an Inspectorship. From thence to the office vacated by Sheffield was an easy step for a competent and ambitious man.

How silent the house was!

Harborne glanced at his watch. He had been waiting nearly five minutes. Scarce another two had elapsed—when a brisk step sounded on the gravel. The detective braced himself for a spring. Would he have the Arab to contend with too?

No. A key was slipped into the well-oiled lock. The door opened.

With something of the irresistible force of a charging bull, Detective-Sergeant Harborne hurled himself upon his man.

Human strength had been useless to oppose that attack; but by subtlety it was frustrated. The man stepped agilely aside—and Harborne reclosed the door with his head! That his skull withstood that crashing blow was miraculous; but he was of tough stock. Perhaps the ruling passion helped him, for dazed and dizzy as he was, he did the right thing when his cunning opponent leapt upon him from behind.

He threw his hands above his shoulders and grasped the man round the neck—then—slowly—shakily—his head swimming and the world a huge teetotum—he rose upon his knees. Bent well forward, he rose to his feet. The other choked, swore, struck useless blows, but hung limply, helpless, in that bear-like, awful grip.

At the exact moment—no second too soon, no second too late—down went Harborne's right hand to the wriggling, kicking, right foot of the man upon whom he had secured that dreadful hold. A bend forward—a turn of the hip—and his man fell crashing to the floor.

"That's called the Cornish grip!" panted the detective, dropping all his heaviness upon the recumbent form.

*Click! Click!*

The handcuffed man wriggled into a sitting posture.

"You goddarned son of a skunk!" he gurgled—and stopped short—sat, white-faced, manacled, looking up at his captor.

"Jumpin' Jenkins!" he whispered—"it's that plug-headed guy, Harborne!"

"Alden!" cried Harborne. "Alden! What the——!"

"Same to you!" snarled the Agency man. "Call yourself a detective! I reckon you'd make a better show as a coal-heaver!"

When conversation—if not civil conversation, at least conversation which did not wholly consist in mutual insult—became possible, the two in that silent hall compared notes.

"Where in the name of wonder did you get the key?" demanded Harborne.

"House agent!" snapped the other. "I work on the lines that I'm after a clever man, not trying to round up a herd of bullocks!"

Revolvers in readiness, they searched the house. No living thing was to be found. Only one room was unfurnished. It opened off the hall, and was on a lower level. The floor was paved and the walls plastered. An unglazed window opened on a garden, and a deep recess opposite to the door held only shadows and emptiness.

"It's a darned pie-trap!" muttered Mr. Aloys. X. Alden. "And you and me are the pies properly!"

"But d'you mean to say he's going to leave all this furniture——!"

"Hired!" snapped the American. "Hired! I knew that before I came!"

Detective-Sergeant Harborne raised a hand to his throbbing head—and sank dizzily into a cushioned hall-seat.

———————————————————

# CHAPTER XXVIII

## AT THE PALACE—AND LATER

How self-centred is man, and how darkly do his own petty interests overshadow the giant things of life. Thrones may totter and fall, monarchs pass to the limbo of memories, whilst we wrestle with an intractable collar-stud. Had another than Inspector Sheffield been driving to Buckingham Palace that day, he might have found his soul attuned to the martial tone about him; for "War! War!" glared from countless placards, and was cried aloud by countless newsboys. War was in the air. Nothing else, it seemed, was thought of, spoken of, sung of.

But Sheffield at that time was quite impervious to the subtle influences which had inspired music-hall song writers to pour forth patriotic lyrics; which had adorned the button-holes of sober citizens with miniature Union Jacks. For him the question of the hour was: "Shall I capture Séverac Bablon?"

He reviewed, in the space of a few seconds, the whole bewildering case, from the time when this incomprehensible man had robbed Park Lane to scatter wealth broadcast upon the Embankment up to the present moment when, it would appear, having acted as best man at a Society wedding, he now was within the precincts of Buckingham Palace.

It was the boast of Séverac Bablon, as Sheffield knew, that no door was closed to him. Perhaps that boast was no idle one. Who was Séverac Bablon? Inspector Sheffield, who had asked himself that question many months before, when he stood in the British Museum before the empty pedestal which once had held the world-famed head of Cæsar, asked it again now. Alas! it was a question to which he had no answer.

The cab stopped in front of Buckingham Palace.

Sheffield paid the man and walked up to the gates. He was not unknown to those who sat in high places, having been chosen to command the secret bodyguard of Royalty during one protracted foreign tour. An unassuming man, few of his acquaintances, perhaps, knew that he shared with the Lord Mayor of London the privilege of demanding audience at any hour of the day or night.

It was a privilege which hitherto he had never exercised. He exercised it now.

Some five minutes later he found himself in an antechamber, and by the murmur of voices which proceeded from that direction he knew a draped curtain alone separated him from a hastily summoned conference. A smell of cigar smoke pervaded the apartment.

Suddenly, he became quite painfully nervous. Was it intended that he should hear so much? Short of pressing his fingers to his ears, he had no alternative.

"We had all along desired that amicable relations be maintained in this matter, Baron."

That was the Marquess of Evershed. Sheffield knew his voice well.

"It has not appeared so from your attitude, Marquess!"

Whom could that be? Probably Baron Hecht.

"Your intense patriotism, your admirable love of country, Baron, has led you to misconstrue, as affronts, actions designed to promote our friendly relations."

Only one man in England possessed the suave, polished delivery of the last speaker—the Right Honourable Walter Belford.

"I have misconstrued nothing; my instructions have been explicit."

"Fortunately, no further occasion exists for you to carry them out."

Sheffield knew that voice too.

"A Foreign Service Messenger, Mr. Maurice Anerly, left for my capital this morning——"

"Captain Searles has been instructed to intercept him. His dispatch will not be delivered."

Inspector Sheffield, who had been vainly endeavouring to become temporarily deaf, started. Whose voice was that? Could he trust his ears?

There followed the sound as of the clapping of hands upon someone's shoulders.

"Baron Hecht, I hold a most sacred trust—the peace of nations. No one shall rob me of it. Believe me, your great master already is drafting a friendly letter——"

The musical voice again, with that vibrant, forceful note.

"In short, Baron" (Sheffield tried not to hear; for he knew this voice too), "there is a power above the Eagle, a power above the Lion: the power of wealth! Lacking her for ally, no nation can war with another! The king of that power has spoken—and declared for peace! I am glad of it, and so, I know, are you!"

Following a short interval, a shaking of hands, as the unwilling eavesdropper divined. Then, by some other door, a number of people withdrew, amid a hum of seemingly friendly conversation.

A gentleman pulled the curtain aside.

"Come in, Sheffield!" he said genially.

Chief Inspector Sheffield bowed very low and entered a large room, which, save for the gentleman who had admitted him, now was occupied only by the Right Hon. Walter Belford, Home Secretary.

"How do you do, Inspector?" asked Mr. Belford affably.

"Thank you, sir," replied the detective with diffidence; "I am quite well, and trust you are."

"I think I know what has brought you here," continued the Home Secretary. "You have been following——"

"Séverac Bablon! Yes, sir!"

"As I supposed. Well, it will be expedient, Inspector, religiously to keep that name out of the Press in future! Furthermore—er—any warrant that may be in existence must be cancelled! This is a matter of policy, and I am sending the necessary instructions to the Criminal Investigation Department. In short—drop the case!"

Chief Inspector Sheffield looked rather dazed.

"No doubt, this is a surprise to you," continued Mr. Belford; "but do not allow it to be a disappointment. Your tactful conduct of the case, and the delicate manner in which you have avoided compromising anyone—in which you have handicapped yourself, that others might not be implicated—has not been overlooked. Your future is assured, Inspector Sheffield."

The gentleman who had admitted Sheffield had left the apartment almost immediately afterwards. Now he returned, and fastened a pin in the detective's tie.

"By way of apology for spoiling your case, Sheffield!" he said.

What Sheffield said or did at that moment he could never afterwards remember. A faint recollection he had of muttering something about "Séverac Bablon——!"

"Ssh!" Mr. Belford had replied. "There is no such person!"

It was at the moment of his leave-taking that his eyes were drawn to an ash-tray upon the big table. A long tongue of bluish-grey smoke licked the air, coiling sinuously upward from amid cigar ends and ashes. It seemingly possessed a peculiar and pungent perfume.

And it proceeded from the smouldering fragment of a yellow cigarette.

---

When Inspector Sheffield fully recovered his habitual composure and presence of mind, he found himself proceeding along Piccadilly. War was in the breeze; War was on all the placards. Would-be warriors looked out from every club window. "Rule, Britannia" rang out from every street organ.

Then came running a hoarse newsboy, aproned with a purple contents-bill, a bundle of *Gleaners* under his arm. His stock was becoming depleted at record speed. He could scarce pass the sheets and grab the halfpence rapidly enough.

For where all else spoke of war, his bill read and his blatant voice proclaimed:

"PEACE! *Official!*"

Again the power of the Seal had been exercised in the interests of the many, although popularly it was believed, and maintained, that Britain's huge, efficient, and ever-growing air-fleet contributed not a little to this peaceful conclusion.

The *Gleaner* assured its many readers that such was indeed the case. To what extent the *Gleaner* spoke truly, and to what extent its statements were inspired, you are as well equipped to judge as I.

And unless some future day shall free my pen, I have little more to tell you of Séverac Bablon. Officially, as the Holder of the Seal, his work, at any rate for the time, in England was done. Some day, Sheard may carry his history farther, and he would probably begin where I leave off.

This, then, will be at a certain pier-head, on a summer's day, and at a time when, far out near the sky-line, grey shapes crept southward—battleships—the flying squadron which thirty-six hours earlier had proceeded to a neighbour's water-gate to demonstrate that the command of the seas had not changed hands since the days of Nelson. The squadron was returning to home waters. It was a concrete message of peace, expressed in terms of war.

Nearer to the shore, indeed at no great distance from the pier-head, lay a white yacht, under steam. A launch left her side, swung around her stern, and headed for the pier.

In a lower gallery, shut off from the public promenades, where thousands of curious holiday-makers jostled one another for a sight of the great yacht, or for a glimpse of those about to join her, a tall man leaned upon the wooden rail and looked out to sea. A girl in while drill, whose pretty face was so pale that fashionable New York might have failed to recognise Zoe Oppner, the millionaire's daughter, stood beside him.

"Though I have been wrong," he said slowly, "in much that I have done, even you will agree that I have been right in this."

He waved his hand towards the fast disappearing squadron.

"Even I?" said Zoe sharply.

"Even you. For only you have shown me my errors."

"You admit, then, that your——!"

"Robberies?"

"Not that, of course! But your——"

"Outrages?"

"I did not mean that either. The means you have adopted have often been violent, though the end always was good. But no really useful reform can be brought about in such a way, I am sure."

The man turned his face and fixed his luminous eyes upon hers.

"It may be so," he said; "but even now I see no other way."

Zoe pointed to the almost invisible battleships.

"Ah!" continued Séverac Bablon, "that was a problem of a different kind. In every civilised land there is a power above the throne. Do you think that, unaided, Prussia ever could have conquered gallant France? The people who owe allegiance to the German Emperor are a great people, but, in such an undertaking as war, without the aid of that people who owe allegiance to *me*, they are helpless as a group of children! Had I been in 1870 what I am to-day, the Prussian arms had never been carried into Paris!"

"You mean that a nation, to carry on a war, requires an enormous sum of money?"

"Which can only be obtained from certain sources."

"From the Jews?"

"In part, at least. The finance of Europe is controlled by a group of Jewish houses."

"But they are not all——"

"Amenable to my orders? True. But the outrages with which you reproach me have served to show that when my orders are disobeyed I have power to enforce them! Where I am not respected I am feared. I refused my consent to the loan by aid of which Great Britain's enemies had designed to prosecute a war against her. None of those theatrical displays with which sometimes I have impressed the errant vulgar were necessary. The greatest name in European finance was refused to the transaction—and the Great War died in the hour of its birth!"

His eyes gleamed with almost fanatic ardour.

"For this will be forgotten all my errors, and forgiven all my sins!"

"I am sure of that," said Zoe earnestly. "But—whatever you came to do——"

"I have not done—you would say? Only in part. Where I made my home in London, you have seen a curtained recess. It held the Emblem of my temporal power."

He moved his hand, and the sunlight struck green beams from the bezel of the strange ring upon his finger. Zoe glanced at it with something that was almost like fear.

"This," he said, replying, as was his uncanny custom to an unspoken question, "is but the sign whereby I may be known for the holder of that other Emblem. My house is empty now; the Emblem returns to the land where it was fashioned."

"You are abandoning your projects—your mission? Why?"

"Perhaps because the sword is too heavy for the wielder. Perhaps because I am only a man—and lonely."

The launch touched the pier, below them.

"You are the most loyal friend I have made in England—in Europe—in the world," said Séverac Bablon. "Good-bye."

Zoe was very pale.

"Do you mean—for—always?"

"When you have said 'Good-bye' to me I have nothing else to stay for."

Zoe glanced at him once and looked away. Her charming face suddenly flushed rosily, and a breeze from the sea curtained the bright eyes with intractable curls.

"But if I *won't* say 'Good-bye'?" she whispered.

Milton Keynes UK
Ingram Content Group UK Ltd.
UKHW031046120324
439302UK00006B/545